THE RAINS
OF WAR

The Rains of War

M. H. Mayfield

The Rains of War
2nd Edition
Copyright © 2011, 2013 by M. H. Mayfield

Cover Art by Lisa Mayfield
Cover design by Lisa Mayfield
Interior text design by Lisa Mayfield
Interior artwork by Scotaidh MacIonmhuinn
Editing by Lisa Mayfield

Published by Wandering Bard Press (wanderingbardpress.com)

ISBN: 978-0-6155-3046-8

Acknowledgements

My first thanks must go to God for blessing me with this wonderful story. I would also like to thank the following people:

Lisa Mayfield for all of your hard work and support in getting this published. You helped me to realize my life-long dream, *mo sonas*. (ML)

John Mayfield for many great ideas regarding water pumps, car engines, and the many hours studying maps.

My sons, Joshua and Daniel, who combined to create the delightful, albeit aggravating character of Jamie.

Richard Mark Green for answering numerous questions regarding Scottish dialect, Yorkshire pudding, and introducing me to Leeds United.

Scotaidh MacIonmhuinn for Gaelic translations, Celtic knotwork, and being a proud Scotsman. *A' charaid chòir, cha b'urrain dhomh a dhèanamh as d'aonais!*

Everyone at the CompuServe Writers Forum: Barbara Rogan, Regina Vincent, Amarilis, Steven Lopata, Kylie, Karen Watson, Jo, Janet, Piper, Hall(not 'Hal') and many, many other wonderful and creative people so willing to help and share.

The knowledgeable and helpful Science Forum members, such as Don Cooper, for answering questions regarding such things as Electromagnetic Pulse and Global Warming.

Cass of the Military Forum, as well as the rough men standing ready in the night to visit violence on those who would do us harm. Thank you for all you do, the very least of which was answering questions about disarming landmines. You know who you are.

The Sniper Club: Denis Murphy, Fintan Farrelly, Todd Lee, Jeff Koren, and Gerry Ginnane for copious amounts of Guinness and inspiration. To our target, Mark Bell, "Play WHISKY IN THE JAR, ye bastard!"

Shelly Threas Keck, my very first "fan", but more importantly, my friend of many years. Thank you for the generous use of your name.

My sista, Jane Denice Fritz for sharing a wonderful journey with me, as well as Nat Alea Hile and Jessie Egli (otherwise known as "Spider-woman"). Here's to Strongbow, firehouses, and Monday nights.

SFC Kenneth Rogers, SFC Lawrence Lehr, and SFC Rafael Figueroa, because Combat Medic is just another way of saying hero. You will always be "top shelf".

Last, but certainly not least, I owe a special thanks to Diana Gabaldon for inspiring me to also write a book that no one would ever see. There is a small tribute to you embedded in these pages, but you'll just have to read the book to find it. <bg>

DEDICATIONS

For my sister Kathryn,
SGT Steven Clark,
and the man who won World War II,
1SG Ransom Lafayette Mayfield.

PROLOGUE

Nicholas gazed through his study window at the storm clouds draped across the sky.

Steam billowed from his morning tea as he watched the painful stir of Edinburgh below, a torrential downpour battering the city without remorse. The threat of flash floods was too great to ignore when commuting on horseback, even within urban boundaries.

The rains of the Third Season had not been the worst the Alban Region had ever endured. Most of the damage as of yet had been limited to the southern coast. After years of abuse, the old levees in London finally surrendered to one of the recent hurricanes, leaving the roads more like canals. No great loss there, he thought.

Nicholas blew into his cup before taking a sip. His Minister of Resources was due in less than an hour to sort a few things before their meeting with the Ambassador of Trade for the European Union. If they were finished by half two,

1

he could spend some time with Morgan before the St. Andrew's Day celebration later in the evening. As the ambassador had been instructed to accept whatever Nicholas offered, their negotiations shouldn't take long.

A sharp rap on the door caused him to start, a drop of tea escaping onto his fresh trousers. His cup clacked hard against the glass-topped table when he set it down before jerking his jacket from the back of his chair and shoving his arms into it.

Silk tie in place, he called out, "Come!"

A young blonde in a dress blue uniform came round to stand beside him, holding out a small slip of paper. "Prime Minister Payne, this just arrived."

He perused the familiar handwriting, careful to keep the smile from his lips as he read. "Where are they being taken?"

"To the Cauldron, sir."

She reached to take the message. He kept a firm grip and locked eyes with her. "Instruct Lachlan to begin the interrogations."

"Yes, sir," she nodded. Her footsteps echoed quietly as she saw herself out.

Rain torpedoed the window as if nature itself were attempting to reach through the glass, then all at once subsided. Dark clouds pulled back to reveal a dull, grayish-blue hidden behind them. After a moment of relative calm, the faint tattoo of raindrops started up again.

He picked up his cup from the table and cradled it in his hands. Providence had ordained him the liberator of humanity; the Prometheus of mankind. With such a task before him, Nicholas knew the end would more than justify the means. It would define them.

He blew into his cup and took a sip, then looked out over Edinburgh and smiled.

PART ONE

OH MICHAEL FAIR, RECEIVE MY DEPARTURE

CHAPTER ONE

YEAR 573, NEW WORLD
MONTH ONE, FIRST SEASON
MARCH

I was beginning to worry about Miyanna.

Dirt and moisture matted her straight, black hair. A faint redness encircled her almond-shaped eyes. The chill in the air hung about us like a cloak, making her deep, chesty cough a concern.

The pace we had been forced to keep was agony for Miyanna's weak joints. I'd expected more complaints, but all she'd really done was to fiddle with the sleeves of Papa's old canvas jacket hanging down past her hands, when she wasn't scratching at her jeans. I knew she was uncomfortable from so many hours in the saddle, but I thought it best to ride a bit further before stopping for supper. The route I'd mapped out was far more protracted, but better roads weren't worth the risk. At least we'd not run into any flooding from the previous season.

Eros pulled to a stop, setting a hoof on a chunk of rock before choosing another spot. Rays of evening sun cut through the gloomy foreboding of clouds like shards of stained glass. I scanned the thick parapet of trees on each side as we trudged through mud left from last night's drizzle, the sweet mixture of rain and sap prominent in the cold March air.

Finding a dry place to bed down and make a fire would prove difficult. Hopefully Miyanna would be able to make it to the Campbell Hills before needing to stop. The dry seclusion of one of their overhangs might also offer a fair amount of security.

Night would come all too soon.

Warmth floated around us as we nestled inside our makeshift burrow, bellies stuffed full from the brown hare I'd bagged. Our horses rested in silence near the mouth of the cave, just inside the dark blanket I'd hung to trap most of the heat and light from the fire, even though the night was fairly well lit with stars and a half moon. The rhythmic tribal dances of shadows born of the small blaze soothed me.

Miyanna had stayed inside, occupied with her wee bag of polished rocks while I had gone out hunting. I was apprehensive about leaving her, but we'd nearly depleted what we'd brought with us, the need to travel light notwithstanding.

The floor, as it were, pressed against my back, but wasn't altogether uncomfortable, at least compared to some of the places I'd slept before. Miyanna seemed to be doing fair enough with my sleeping pad stacked on hers for extra comfort.

We stretched out a bit more than arm's length apart, yet stayed within range of the fire's heat. I had just begun to doze off when Miyanna's soft voice drew me back.

"Kyrie," her voice was barely a whisper. "Am I different?"

My eyelids rebelled against the laborious task of opening, but finally complied. She was staring out into nowhere, deep in thought. "Why do you ask that?"

The corner of her mouth pulled back a bit. "Everything is hard for me."

She looked over at me, so I smiled at her. "You are good at lots of things. Some things you're even better at than I am."

Her voice rasped when she giggled, a slight rattling in her chest. "Like singing?"

I stuck my tongue out and crossed my eyes. She laughed out loud, but then quickly sobered. "Sometimes I wish I could be with Mama and Papa. In Heaven."

My chest tightened. "I'm glad you aren't."

"At least they're together now." Her hazel eyes flashed sparks of emerald in the firelight. For a brief moment it was as if the veil lifted.

I scooted my sleeping bag next to hers. "It's getting colder, and the fire will die out soon."

Her head popped up off her pillow. "It's 18 degrees Celsius. I checked my thermometer whilst you were out, but didn't bother your soldier maps."

She'd been vigilant in monitoring the temperature since we set out, determined to contribute. "Thank you for remembering to check. Did you put your vitamins away after supper?"

"Yes. I heard Mama say that hundreds of years ago there was a medicine that would make DownSyn go all away." Her sentence was punctuated with a cough.

I yawned, my eyes tearing. "What do you reckon?"

It was a moment or two before she answered. "I think I'm fine the way God made me."

Her back felt warm and soft pressed against mine, snuggling as we did when we were children, the scent of Mama's peppermint lotion strong on her skin.

"Mi?" I reached behind me, resting an elbow on top of her arm. "Do you remember the song Papa used to sing?"

She nodded, clearing her throat. A higher, huskier version of our father's clear and perfect pitch echoed off the stone walls.

Hush-a-bye, baby,
The night winds are sighing,
Go to sleep, baby
The crickets are crying;
Sleep 'til the dew
On the green grass is winking,
Sleep 'til the morning sun,
Wakens you winking…

As she sang, I closed my eyes and found myself back home with Papa sitting by our beds, pipe in hand, his rich baritone guiding us to our dreams after one of his stories.

Warm in their wooly folds,

10

Lambskins are resting,
Soft in their swaying beds,
Birdies are nesting;
All through the night,
In your cradle lie dreaming,
'Til the bright sun
Through the window comes streaming...

When she finished, the sweetest words I'd heard in a very long time reached out to me. "Good night, Kyrie. I love you."

"Wake up," I shook Miyanna's shoulder until she stirred. "It's time to get up."

She wiped a hand across her eyes, coughed, and then rolled back over on her stomach.

"Already? Can't I sleep a wee bit more?" Her voice sounded cracked and raspy.

"No, *mo sonas*. We have to go." I left her with a final pat and rose to see to the horses. Eros snorted when he saw me lift his saddle, scratching his front hoof on the stone floor.

Miyanna sat up, pouting and picking at a string on her sleeping bag. "This isn't fun anymore. It's taking too long."

She stood and walked over to me, in spite of my request the night before not to walk in her socks. I sighed. "We don't have much further to go."

She covered her mouth and succumbed to another coughing fit. When it subsided, she cupped her hand around her throat, wincing a bit as she spoke. "When can we go back home?"

The look on her round face made me wish that asking a question over and over could somehow bring you closer to the answer. "I've no idea, but as soon as we can, we will."

She perked up suddenly. "Will Madoc help me polish rocks?"

I chuckled. "Has he ever not?"

Gear packed and tracks covered, I waited for Miyanna to eat breakfast and get dressed, then helped her onto her mare. Getting as far as we did by nightfall had gained us much. Even so, I knew I couldn't push her two days in a row.

Eros danced a bit when I mounted him. I tightened my grip on the reins. Miyanna was busy fiddling with her jacket sleeve, a slight frown creasing her brow, her lips pursed in concentration. Crushing down the urge to dismount and hug her, I nudged Eros into motion.

Negotiating the old farm roads was hard going for her, and it wasn't long before she asked to rest. I'd hoped to be further past Bellsbank and on a faster road towards Gass before having to stop. As it was, making the ferry at Turnberry by nightfall no longer seemed realistic. It would have been different if we could have used another ferry, but as it was, Turnberry was the only one that could get us where we needed to go.

Miyanna had just pulled her canteen out for a quick drink when I caught sight of a dark shape down the road, heading our direction.

"Mi, remember what we talked about?" I kept my voice calm, but my tone firm. "Can you get your horse into that the clump of trees over there?"

She rubbed her eyes, then put her canteen away. "Yes. How long shall I go for?"

"Until I come and get you. Scoot!" I scanned the road and trees, but didn't see any signs of others.

The rider's head and face were hidden beneath a hood, but they were most likely male, judging from their size. It was hard to say which was more ragged-looking; the navy blue Macintosh he wore or the horse he rode. The poor bastard labored down the path as if it might collapse in midstep. A good indication he wasn't a bounty hunter, but I still couldn't take the chance.

I slid a hand under my riding coat to grip the hilt of my father's *sgian dhu* and smiled, ignoring the cool mist of rain tickling my eyelashes. "Now then."

The rider reigned up alongside me and just sat there for a moment or two. My hand tightened on the hilt, easing the blade out of its sheath as I watched for any movement.

Using my knee, I nudged Eros closer, ready to grab the front of his jacket and pull him towards me. "Sorry to bother you, but I'm a wee lost."

The stranger eased his hood back. I froze for a moment, then exhaled sharply.

"Uncle Rowan!" The *sgian dhu* went silently back in the sheath as I searched his face.

His dark, wavy hair was cropped close. Blue eyes beamed at me, red-rimmed and swollen. "Kyrie, I thought you... I was trying t'get Miyanna..."

I squeezed his arm. "Wait here while I go fetch her."

Not being able to remember the last bit of contact I'd had with Uncle Rowan roused a small pang of guilt. Perhaps that was why it had never occurred to me that he would try to reach Miyanna, and why he had no way to let me know that he was. Even so, she was my sister. I still would have gone myself.

After moments of searching, the relief at seeing my uncle drained away like the last bit of water in a sink. My heart pounded as if it would crack my ribs as I worked my way back to the road.

Uncle Rowan had dismounted and was adjusting the cinch strap on his saddle. He looked over at me, the smile dropping from his face when he saw I was alone. The affirming knot that formed in my abdomen almost took my breath.

Jerking the reins, I headed back into the trees, both swearing and praying.

CHAPTER TWO

Morning at Làidir Academy had flown by. The classroom was now empty save for the ghost of giggling and chattering, owing to the usual Monday morning fidgets.

Madoc frowned over a writing journal belonging to one of his first year students. He'd hoped for more improvement by now, but progress was hard-earned and slow to come when dealing with autism, even in less severe cases. After jotting down a few quick notes, he flipped it shut and went on to the next one until the entire stack was done.

He laced his fingers behind his head and arched his back, then pulled out his diary to review his afternoon schedule.

The requisition forms he'd collected needed to be submitted to Supply. The maintenance report on the drainage pumps and levees, as well as the damage report for last season's storms, needed to be reviewed and signed-off on. Later he would need to make his rounds through the physical and occupational therapy sections, and then close the day with the end-of-month staff call.

His eyes burned a bit as he tried to blink away the last two hours of marking papers. He pulled out the small mirror he kept in his desk, wiping the loose lash from his eye.

Blond hair nearly brushed the tops of his ears, reminding him to try to squeeze a haircut into his schedule.

He dropped the mirror back in the drawer and slammed it shut, not quite ready to get back at it. Perhaps some fresh air would help him shake the stuffiness of the classroom.

Before he could push his chair back to stand, the door nearly burst from its hinges.

"Mr. Monss! M-m-m-m-miss Kyrie and Mr. Rowan are here and they n-n-n-n-need you right away!" Jared Hamilton's gangly frame skidded to a stop in front of the desk. He began taking slow, deep breaths in and out.

Madoc stared a moment, realizing what Jared had said. "Is Miyanna with them?"

Jared shook his head. "No, sir."

"Dammit," Madoc mumbled as he snatched his tweed jacket from the back of his chair, ignoring the slight widening of Jared's eyes.

Kyrie and Rowan were engaged in a shouting match just inside the front gate, which was to say Kyrie was shouting, and Rowan was listening. The black leather riding coat she wore outlined the sleekness of her body like a second skin; the lavishness of it made her seem a stranger.

Her thunderous tirade halted when Madoc called to her. She rushed over, her words tumbling out over one another. "Maddy, she's gone. I told her to hide when I saw Rowan coming towards us on the road, and when I went to fetch her, she was gone. She's gone and… I don't know…"

A small tear ran the course of a short, thin scar on her left cheek. Madoc pulled her into his arms and pressed a kiss on her forehead.

"We'll find her," he reassured her. "Tarrick and some of his best men are on the way to the ferry right now. They won't rest until she is safe."

He tucked a curl behind her ear, thinking how little she'd aged since he saw her last and how much she still looked like her mother. Dark, chestnut hair showed no sign of gray, and warm brown eyes had settled into an interesting rum color.

She stared up at him a moment longer, then pulled from his embrace and turned to go to her horse.

Rowan seized her arm. "Where are you going? You've been up for days. You need…"

Kyrie jerked her arm free, her leather-clad back stiff with determination. Rowan hung his head a moment before following her over to the horses. Hearing her mother in her voice, Madoc knew there would be no changing her mind.

"I'm coming with you."

Jared gnawed at his thumbnail, his eyes darting between Kyrie and Rowan.

Madoc squeezed Jared's shoulder. "You'd best get back to the stables, or else you'll be late for work."

Madoc watched Jared walk away, then looked over at Kyrie. She sat rigid in the saddle, staring hard out in front of her. He sighed and went to go change.

Kyrie could barely hold herself in the saddle when they arrived back at Brodick Castle six days later. It took Madoc's word that the search for Miyanna would continue before she would agree to come back to Làidir, if only for a brief respite and to see if Tarrick had returned or sent any word.

The private apartments at the castle were spacious, comfortable, and most importantly, quiet. After seeing her to bed, Madoc went to a neighboring guest room, a slight twinge gripping his lower back as he lay down. It seemed he'd only just drifted off when he was awakened by shouts coming from Kyrie's room.

He shoved his legs in his pajama bottoms, pulling his shirt on as he tore down the hall. Rowan barreled towards him from the opposite direction. Madoc threw the door open and charged in, Rowan hot on his heels.

Kyrie sat in the middle of the bed, hands stretched out in front of her, the moonlight from the window not quite reaching her.

"Kyrie?" Madoc gave her a firm shake. When she didn't respond, he leaned into her line of sight. "Kyrianna! Look at me!"

Rowan fumbled for matches to light the candle on the nightstand. The glow shone like a lighthouse at sea, allowing full view of Kyrie's face, which was twisted in the painful embrace of a nightmare. After a moment, her breathing slowed and her features smoothed.

She opened her eyes. "Dark. So dark."

Rowan laid a hand on her shoulder. "It's alright now. I lit a candle."

Kyrie shook her head hard. "No… it's dark there, and she's afraid."

"Wee Bonnie, it was only a dream," Madoc sat down on the bed and pulled her into his arms, pressing his cheek in the mass of curls brushing against it. "We'll find her."

Madoc looked up at Rowan. "I think I'll stay for a bit."

He brushed his thumb across her check and waited until Rowan had shut the door, then blew out the candle and leaned back against the headboard, holding his arms open in invitation. He cradled Kyrie against his chest, stroking the hair from her face and continuing the prayer that had been his constant companion for the last few days.

Madoc squinted in the morning sun as he eased out from under the blankets, arching his back to stretch out the tightness. He'd fallen asleep sitting up, waking only once during the night to scoot down by Kyrie.

The side of her face not buried in the pillow was completely relaxed; lips parted slightly, blankets drawn up under her chin. Faint lines branching from the side of her eye gave him the urge to run his thumb over them. Instead, he eased off the bed, took some clothes from his wardrobe, and left her to rest.

The guestroom lavatory was cold. He shivered as he brushed his teeth, then inspected his reflection in the mirror, rubbing a hand over a bristly cheek. The translucent gray of his eyes looked hard and dull next to the swollen, red rims of his eyelids. His normally tan complexion seemed a bit washed-out from too many nights with too little sleep. Rather than shave, he splashed water on his face, then pulled his jumper over his head and set out to find Rowan.

The staircase was hushed and shadowed. For the first time since he was a wee boy, he could feel the noble stare of the stags' heads follow him down to the entrance hall, the skin on his back tingling. As was his custom when leaving the castle, he looked up at the great wooden crest carved with the school motto resting above the chimney piece. *Is urrain dhomh.* I am able.

After a few moments of searching, he found Rowan seated on one of the wooden benches in the walled garden, a clear tea cup in one hand, the other shoved into the pocket of his Macintosh.

"Now then. Sleep well?" Rowan asked, his eyes red and puffy.

"About as well as you did, from the looks of you," Madoc set his watch by the sun dial, then swung his arm back and forth in an arc to recharge the battery. "Kyrie was a wee restless, but no more nightmares. Anything?"

Rowan shook his head, moving over to give Madoc room to sit down. "Nothing. Not even a trace. You know that could mean…"

Madoc held up a hand. "That's not something I'm willing to consider."

Rowan sighed. "It's something we need to consider."

A slight pressure began to build behind Madoc's eyes. "Are you trying to be negative?"

"I'm trying to be realistic," Rowan blew into his cup and took a sip. "It could explain why we've not found a body."

Madoc shot to his feet. He took a moment to calm himself, then met Rowan's cobalt stare. "If the eyes really are the window to the soul, it makes me shudder to look in yours."

Rowan tossed the rest of his tea on the ground and rose,

brushing past Madoc. "You should try looking out them."

The morning seemed chaotic, either from Madoc's exhaustion or by virtue of it being Monday. The frenzy eventually relaxed into an afternoon lull, so he decided to go sit in the garden for a few minutes to decompress. He checked his watch and took a seat on a bench, his body feeling unhinged now that it had finally stopped moving.

After the conversation with Rowan, Madoc made his rounds, finding out what had transpired during his absence over the last few days. Thankfully, no major crises had arisen.

He breathed deep, and then exhaled slowly. It was so easy to pretend the outside world didn't exist. Was all they were trying to accomplish, had accomplished, soon to be for nothing? At times life seemed so senseless, but in such times God often revealed a higher purpose. It was what he'd always believed. It was what Kyrie's mother had taught him.

Threas Maclaren had been more than the district coordinator for Làidir. She had been his inspiration as a teacher, and while she'd never tried to act as surrogate mother, she filled the void from having not known his own.

Someone calling his name caused him to start. Madoc rose to see Jared coming towards him at almost a dead run, his face flushed to nearly the same glowing shade of red as his hair.

Madoc threw up his hands to shield himself. "Jared…?"

"Sir," Jared forced out while gulping in air. "W-w-wwhen I was in the stable this mornin', I noticed Miss Kyrie's horse gone. I didn't say anything because I thought perhaps she was out for a ride. When I checked back I noticed aww... all her gear was gone. I asked one of the groomsmen if anyone had s-s-s-s-seen her come back."

As the next few seconds passed, it became evident Jared was concentrating on the rhythm of his breathing.

"Well?" Madoc prodded.

Jared swallowed hard. "No one has seen her since last night."

A dull pain just under Madoc's ear and along his jaw reminded him to unclench his teeth as he charged to the stables with Jared in tow. It was now late afternoon, and there was no telling how far she'd made it to wherever she was headed nor which ferry she'd taken. Common sense would say the one out of Brodick as it was closest.

Madoc caught sight of his security officer emerging from the stable doors. "Any news?"

Tarrick rubbed a hand over his bald head. The capillaries in his eyes appeared as lines on a map, his olive complexion a bit sallow. "The same as before. We weren't able to find out anything else."

Madoc frowned. "Before?"

"We sent a message as soon as we got information," Tarrick paused a moment. "Miyanna's been taken to the Cauldron."

Madoc felt his stomach turn upside down. "What message?"

"Fletcher! Tell Ryan get his arse out here now. Move!" Tarrick bellowed to a nearby stablehand.

Word was a bounty hunter had caught site of Kyrie and

Miyanna on an old farm road just past Bellsbank and began to track them. He noticed her go off into the woods on her own and made his move. Sometime after, Miyanna had been spotted in the back of a wagon with about ten others.

"She looked tired, but other than that, unharmed." Tarrick looked towards the stable door.

It wasn't likely to stay that way long, Madoc thought, assuming she was even still... he flinched, a faint metallic taste flowing through his mouth from where he bit too hard into the lip.

"Some food, fresh horses..." Tarrick began.

Madoc laid a hand on Tarrick's thick shoulder. "No, I need you here. Maybe I..."

His words were cut off by the appearance of Ryan, the lad's small frame rigid in an attempt at bravado. "Sir?"

"What the hell did I tell you, boy? Why didn't Mr. Monss get the message you were instructed to give him?" Tarrick thundered.

Ryan shrank an inch or two in the hurricane-force of Tarrick's questioning. "Sir, I met a woman here in the stables when I arrived. She said for me to get some chow, and she'd see Mr. Monss got word."

Madoc looked from Tarrick to Jared, and then headed back to the castle to find Rowan.

Chapter Three

The sun was just peeking over the tree line as I stopped at the edge of the horseshoe-shaped clearing. A dense fog rested on the ground, bringing to life the pungent smell of birch and pine. Patches of ivy blanketed the earth beneath them, making plush beds for fallen needles.

I pulled the letter from the hidden pocket in my waist-coat, a tinge of brown faded onto the worn edges. With care I peeled it from the small family picture I'd carried with me ever since I'd left home. The sight of his familiar scrawl comforted me. After a moment, I folded the letter away and tapped a heel against Eros' side.

A good-sized two story residence topped with a metal roof and dormer windows sat center of the far back edge of the clearing. Rain gutters stretched out to an above-ground water tank. A barn and byre with a nearby hand pump and water trough were on the opposite side.

I dismounted, and led Eros over to the hitching post, my hands shaking as I tethered the reins.

The smell of chimney smoke and fresh flat bread wafted about. Plump bushes with dark leaves and some sort of blooms formed a wall nearly as tall as the porch. Two mid-size terra-cotta pots filled with potting soil were perched along the rail; the word "aloe" slanted across one and "rosemary" on the other. Beside them, colander-like copper bowls for a rain chain were stacked one in the other, gleaming a rich blue-green from years of use.

I raised a hand to knock, but my eyes were drawn upwards to a small, pewter plate crowning the door. Etched in the center was a pictish boar, encircled by Celtic knotwork. A mere ornament to most, those lines rendered a much more significant meaning to anyone familiar with the owner. He was a *Gàidheal*; a Highlander.

My throat closed and tears stung my eyes at the sound of the faint, familiar whistling coming from inside. I drew a deep breath and knocked.

The door creaked open. He stared a moment, then swept me up into his arms, my feet dangling several inches above the wooden porch. Just when I thought my lungs would collapse, he put me down. My stomach uncoiled for the first time in days as I looked up into the gentle face of Elias Buchanan.

He towered over me a good twenty centimeters. Wide shoulders tapered down to the trim waistline of the navy denims he wore. His muscular chest pressed against a matching fleece shirt; sleeves rolled up to his elbows revealed chiseled forearms. Hands that could have squeezed my brains out my ears cradled my arms like a newborn.

His hair was the same smartly trimmed dark auburn, except for the slight tapering of gray from his temples. A thin, faded scar snaked down from his right ear to just above his jaw. The bridge of his nose was just a wee thick where it had been broken once upon a time. Blue eyes narrowed as he searched my face, then took on a familiar gleam.

The way he looked at me caused my throat to ache again. I swallowed hard. "I need your help."

Without a word, he ushered me inside and led me to the kitchen. Large double windows lined the walls, each one blazing with morning light. Two sizable Zeer pots marked "fresh veggies" were stowed away in a small mudroom leading out to the back door.

Pots and pans hung over an oak worktable positioned a safe distance from a wide wood-burning stove, which at the moment had a huge soup pot simmering in silence on top.

He set a bowl of fried potatoes with egg and a glass of milk on a long, thick table flanked by two matching benches, and then motioned for me to sit down.

"The others will be back soon. They've been awa' since yesterday," he took a seat across from me. "I wasna expecting ye until after you finished Staff Course."

My stomach rumbled. I fought the urge to shovel food in my mouth, reaching for my drink instead. "My sister's been taken to the Cauldron."

Something flashed in his eyes. "How long ago?"

I drained my glass, then wiped away the milk clinging to my upper lip. "Word is around four days."

"Sweet Christ," he breathed.

I took a small bite of potatoes. "We can ride hard and be there in as little as two."

He looked at me a moment. "Mind, it will only be the five of us."

"Three Commandos..." I pointed a thumb towards my chest, "... a troop commander trained in EOD..." I motioned towards him, "... and a Combat Medical Technician.

What more do we need?"

The corner of his mouth lifted. "How aboot the rest of the Fighting 59th?"

Elias had gone out to the storehouse to gather supplies and pack the horses while I ate for the first time since lunch the day before.

Meal done and dishes washed, I headed out to the front porch, nicking a piece of flat bread on the way, sucking the overflow of fig jam from my index finger. A constant drizzle almost too fine to see was coming down, deepening the sharp bite of late morning air.

The fresh supply of salt-cured pork would bask unattended in the new smokehouse, but the milk cow and three piglets would have to go to the nearest neighbor, some thirty kilometers south until… whenever.

Popping the last bite in my mouth, I headed down the steps to go help Elias.

"Mac!"

Elias's younger brother, Seth, met me halfway across the yard. He scooped me up into a quick, but firm cuddle, then leaned back. "Ye cut yer hair."

He'd filled out a good bit since I'd last seen him. The close cut of his dark denim jacket and matching jeans hugged his frame. Dark work boots added to his already towering height.

Reaching behind him I playfully tugged at the neat queue a shade or two darker than his older sibling. "And you didn't, Corporal. I can just hear your brother now."

Seth grinned. "I made Sergeant, thank you, and he antles on incessantly. Ye would think he was my da' instead of me *brither*."

Elias was a full fourteen years older than Seth's twenty-six years, though he didn't look it, and had always been more like a father than a brother; a fact that didn't bother Seth as much as he often pretended.

I shoved my hands in my pockets. "Are Seamas and Donny…?"

Seth motioned towards Seamas and Donnacha O'Murchu just as they rounded the side of the house. From a distance the two were almost impossible to tell apart, sharing the same height, stocky build, and blonde hair.

What started out the welcoming embrace of comrades somehow turned into a hearty rugby scrum. After a few good-natured shoves and grunts, I released my grip on Seamas and twisted Donny into a headlock.

Seamas laughed, pulling his tan canvas jacket back in place. "Careful, Mac. To us dat's considered foreplay."

The kernel of hope I was beginning to feel made it hard to keep myself together. Though we had always honored the officer/enlisted boundaries, we had served together in combat. That made us more than mere comrades. More than friends. In some ways, even more than family. We were soldiers.

I cleared my throat. "I was surprised you were here. I reckoned maybe you'd gone back home after your discharge. Back to Dublin."

A look passed between the two of them. Seamas reached in his pocket to pull out rolling papers and tobacco.

Noticing the quick death of that topic, I pressed no further. Instead, I nodded towards Donny's leg. "How's the knee?"

He clapped his hands together and rubbed them back and forth. "*Ceart go leor, mo chara.* Busted knee is a hell of a twenty-eighth birthday pressie, yeah?"

Seamas blew out a stream of smoke. After a quick exchange with his cousin in their native *Gaeilge*, he turned to Seth. "We'd best go help da' aul man."

I watched them walk away, thinking it a good thing "da' aul man" was out of earshot when referred to as such, then turned to Donny. "Did Elias tell you…?"

Donny laid a hand on my shoulder. "*Quo Fas et Gloria Ducunt*, Captain."

Whither duty and glory lead.

Predawn pinkness streaked the sky above Edinburgh, an exhilarating crispness filling the air.

Morgan combed the fingers of one hand through the long, brown waves of her wig, holding the reins of her stallion loosely in the other. The collar of Fiona's leather riding jacket felt like a yoke, rubbing against the borrowed turtleneck jumper.

Early morning rides disguised as Fiona helped keep Morgan centered. It was the only time she felt she could relax her guard. Any semblance of sanity or personal identity would have escaped her were it not for the creative genius of her personal assistant, spiritual advisor, and dearest friend.

Once she was riding back up the hill from town and passed Nicholas's coach as it pulled through the main gate of the castle. The breath felt trapped in her chest as her husband drove by without so much as a wave or glance in her direction. Nicholas never addressed Fiona without a specific reason or purpose and, thankfully, had neither that day.

Morgan reined up in front of the old Witches' Well to pay homage to the lost souls held within the fountain, her ritual before heading off. What had they done to be damned to the stake, she wondered? For all the times she asked that question, this time something seemed to answer.

An intense heat seared through her clothes and raged against skin. Flesh felt as if it were melting from bone, agony crawling up calves, thighs, all the way through her fingertips. Hot tears scalded her eyes when she squeezed them shut to block out the barrage of faces, forever frozen in death, assaulting her one after the other. She drew a few deep breaths until the vision subsided.

When her hands stopped shaking enough to grip the reins, she left the castle grounds and had just cleared the Esplanade when her stallion bellowed, tossing his head from side to side, curling his lip back.

A rider on an ancient-looking mare approached, not close enough yet to make out a face. She straightened her wig, then let her hand drift down to the hilt of the dirk resting in the leather sheath attached to her saddle.

The stranger drew nearer, then stopped and pulled back the hood of his worn Macintosh.

Chapter Four

The ride from Lochearnhead to New Carronbridge had been hard and fast, with few stops along the way.

New Carronbridge seemed the most logical place to base out of for more than one reason; its proximity to the Cauldron and a good mate of ours who'd served with us during the Rising lived there, as well.

Haytham Worthington had been the logistics officer for the Fighting 59th and was someone we thought would be sympathetic. He didn't disappoint, offering a warm welcome and a hot meal when we rocked up at his door unannounced.

Light from the candle chandelier fired the blues and reds of the mid-size Saltire draped against the dining room wall. Haytham stepped into the kitchen to brew another round of Turkish coffee, tidying up as he went.

Seth and Donny had managed to gather a good bit of intel from a few hours in the local pub. Not all the staff of the Cauldron was loyal or of upstanding moral fiber. Our bellies full of stew, we sat round the table and listened to Seamas comment on the sketches he'd been studying, small shapes reflected in his glasses.

In years past, the Cauldron had served as a maximum

security prison for crimes ranging from murder to treason. Surrounding fortifications were fashioned of the same sheer stone as the prison itself. The entrance was a large steel gate controlled only by the front guards. Various offices and an infirmary comprised the ground floor of the main building, as well as staff living quarters. The entire upstairs was the private apartment of the senior administrator, who served as the senior research analyst, as well. Underneath the ground floor were observation cells for up to sixty subjects and what were formerly known as the torture rooms, now referred to as surgeries. Those waiting to be moved to the observation cells were kept in two outer barracks, each with a seventy-five person capacity. A large, stone structure at the back of the compound housed a gas chamber and three massive incinerators used to burn the dead, or the dead enough.

Seamas' finger traced a line snaking from an emergency exit in the boiler room of the main building to a passageway which led to a cave in the outlying mountains to the south.

"We can go in t'rough here, and get out wit'out being seen."

Donny rested an arm on the mantel above the small, stone fireplace. "Guarded?"

"Not according to our source." Seamas drummed his fingers on the table, making a dull tapping sound through the paper.

"Are you certain your 'source' won't be a problem?" Haytham gathered up empty cups and placed them on a serving tray.

"Aye," Seth tapped the blackwood handle of the *sgian*

dhu hidden beneath his trouser leg. "Quite sure."

Haytham nodded, then went back into the kitchen. I didn't doubt he could be trusted, but the less he knew the better.

Donny finished off his coffee. "Seth and I can go recon the route there and back."

Seamas folded the drawing and laid it on the table before following Seth and Donny outside, rolling papers in hand. Elias waited until they'd shut the door behind them, then set his cup on the table.

"You should rest whilst ye can. Ye've not had more than a wee kip here and there since we left."

"Are you staying here?" I asked.

He laid his arm on the back of my chair. "Why, d'ye want me to?"

When I nodded, he held my gaze a moment, then smiled and did the same. My eyes began to tear up, so I pretended to yawn.

"I'll be in the guestroom."

The sky was well-lit enough we could see to cross the river without the risk of using a torch. As of yet, the night had been quiet and uneventful.

Everyone had directions to Làidir. In the event anything should happen to me, they would be able to get Miyanna somewhere safe, then back to Maddy. He would take her in, regardless how angry he was with me. I hoped to have the chance to explain, but now was not the time to worry about his bruised feelings.

With a clean sweep of determination, I cleared my mind to focus on the matter at hand.

The passageway was roughly a kilometer into the cave, an earthy smell strengthening the deeper we got. A huge iron door filled the end of the tunnel.

Seth pulled out a small torch and shook it back and forth to charge the battery. He held it in his mouth as he worked to pick the lock. At the sound of a small click, he turned off the light, and then shoved it back in his pocket. We eased the door open, weapons at the ready.

Lingering heat from a colossal furnace suffocated us. Seth moved back to the mouth of the cave with the horses to stand guard. A quick glance inside the rooms flanking the wall told us we were passing the torture cells.

I motioned for Donny and Seamas to make a sweep, then nodded to Elias that he was with me.

The hallway was dark, except for a lantern on each wall, still burning, but turned down low. The rhythmic sound of dripping water echoed from somewhere nearby. The putrid stench of urine, feces, and infection grew stronger as we drew closer to the observation cells. I had witnessed many horrific scenes on the battlefield; remnants of entrails and partial limbs of men, women, and even children scattered about so only patches of ground were visible. Even so, I was still sickened as we walked through the bowels of the Cauldron.

Each observation cell was about four square meters, a small cot shoved in the back left corner. A small, metal toilet crusted with filth in the opposite corner accounted for some of the smell. Residual fecal matter and vomit smattered the surrounding floor. Most were vacant, but a handful of them were occupied by those whose ages appeared to span from mid-twenties to elderly, however the youngest couldn't have been more than five or six years old.

"Are you new workers?"

The voice came from a woman sitting next to the wall of her cell. The state of her made her age hard to guess. Her forearms were covered with small, circular burns. A large bruise covered each knee, the toes on one foot completely smashed; the others were red and enlarged with the nails missing.

"Are you new workers?" she repeated, barely managing a whisper.

I shook my head. "No. I'm here for my sister."

Elias and I exchanged a look; he was going to search for a key. I sheathed my weapon.

The woman frowned. "What does she look like?"

"She has dark hair and hazel eyes," I held up my hand, "She is about this tall with a somewhat thick build. She has DownSyn. She was brought here about…"

"I can't tell one day from the next," her eyes darkened for a moment. "I can tell you she was brought down here as soon as she arrived."

I grabbed the bars. "Where is she?"

A look skimmed her features. "Taken."

"Taken where?" I looked down the hall. What the hell was taking Elias so long?

"To the chamber," she whispered. Her eyes brimmed with tears. "The Senior Administrator ordered it personally and what he orders…"

The bars dug into my palms, the only thing that kept

me standing. "When?"

She leaned her head back against the wall as if she couldn't hold it up any longer.

"Yesterday morning. That's why the cells are mostly empty. They took most of us yesterday."

"Maybe you're wrong. Maybe it wasn't my sister..." I looked around at the other cells.

"Is your name Kyrie?" She asked.

My throat tightened. No words could pass, so I nodded.

She struggled to her feet, keeping a hand on the wall for balance as she limped over to stand face-to-face with me. A smudged and scrawny arm passed through the bars, her fingers unfolding. Nestled in the palm of her hand were four small polished rocks.

"Mama, why does Miyanna have to be that way?" Arms crossed squarely across my chest.

"Kyrianna Threas Maclaren, if God made us all the same, the world would be such a boring place," Mama replied.

"But she won't play right! All she wants to do is play with her dumb rocks Papa polished for her," I answered with a bit of stomp.

The slight tilt of Mama's chin was a well-recognized warning signal. "Then maybe you should play with the rocks with her."

From somewhere far away I felt someone grasp my shoulder to gently move me aside, then heard the jingle of keys. My eyes came into focus just as the woman laid her hand on Elias's arm.

"You'd never get us away before they came after you."

Elias looked at her for a long moment. "We can't just leave ye here."

She lifted a bony finger. "The child in the cell over there. He's my son. Take him with you."

His gaze narrowed, looking her up and down in a clinical fashion. "Why are you in here? Are ye afflicted in some way?"

Her smile didn't quite reach her eyes. "Not in the way you think."

My voice sounded strange to my own ears. "Do you have any family?"

"We have no one. You have to take him from here," She pleaded.

"Of course we will." I turned to Elias. Our eyes locked in agreement.

"Here. It's this one," she pulled a key from the bunch, then looked over towards her son. "His name is William Jameson Shaw. I call him Jamesie, but most just call him Jamie."

I helped her over to the cell that held her son and let her lean against me while Elias unlocked the door. The boy looked even smaller cradled against Elias's chest.

She stroked the boy's hair with a trembling hand, seeming to try and convince herself to stop touching him. Tears rolled from her face into his hair as she kissed him.

"Down the hall on the left you would have passed a medicine closet. The key is also on that ring." She looked up at Elias. "We can all just... go to sleep."

When we didn't respond, muted pleas from some of the others called out to us. The ones unable to speak were dragging themselves over to the bars. A girl about the age of fifteen simply sat and stared.

"We're scheduled for the Chamber in the morning. A few hours won't make much difference." She looked at me, then back to Elias. "If you don't want to help, at least give me the keys."

Now that she was closer, I noticed the front of her shift hung flat, whether from the lack of proper nourishment or something worse.

Elias looked at the woman for a long moment, then over his shoulder toward the cells, and then finally down at the woman's son. Without a word, he left to go find the others.

Elias met Donny and Seamas coming out of one of the torture cells and handed the boy to Seamas. As the three turned to go, he caught Donny by the arm.

"Kyrie's sister is…"

"We know," Donny answered. "We were just coming ta' find ya."

The two of them looked at one another. Finally, Donny rubbed a hand on the back of his neck. "We found… come wit' me."

Seamas left with the bairn as Donny opened the door and stepped to the side.

The reek of preserving chemical assaulted Elias the moment he crossed the threshold. An examination table took up most of the undersized room; a bone tray stood next to it, complete with holding forceps and cutters, sterilized and ready for use.

Shelves lined the back wall, each filled with an assortment of glass jars. Hands, feet, or some other organ soaked in what smelled like formaldehyde, pieces of a macabre puzzle, polished and put on display like someone's fine china.

Donny pointed at one of the larger jars which contained a shaved head.

"Dear God." Elias spun round to head for the door. Before he'd managed a step, he was pulled up short at the sight of Kyrie standing in the doorway.

He caught her gaze, but it was as if she weren't really there anymore; as if she were empty.

She turned and walked to the medicine closet, opened the door, then stepped to the side. Elias scanned the contents until he found vials of morphine and an injection needle.

As Kyrie moved everyone into a single cell, he gave them each an injection, beginning with the woman who'd helped them. Time being a factor, he gave them each double the dose it would take for someone his size, feeling sure that would get the job done.

He stood and looked from one face to the other. With a silent prayer, he shut the cell door behind him and dropped the used needle into the sharps container on the outside wall.

Kyrie stood like a statue, arms crossed over her chest. If she'd torn the place apart, he wouldn't be as worried, but as it was she'd still not spoken a word.

He laid a hand on her shoulder. Kyrie stared through

the bars. He followed her gaze. The peaceful look on the mother's tear-stained face indicated she was already gone.

"You and Seamas take the boy to Haytham's." Kyrie dug into her pocket and pulled out the bundle of keys, searching for one in particular. "Donny and Seth are with me."

He caught her arm as she brushed past, holding on until she looked up at him. After a moment, he let go, then watched her walk down the hall until the darkness swallowed her.

Namon finished his pipe and stepped in out of the chill, closing the balcony doors behind him. He walked over to the cannonball style bed and took off his robe, glancing first at the intricate design carved deep in the headboard, then up at the antique Asian tapestry emblazoned with a bold red dragon.

He normally wasn't even allowed on the Senior Administrator's floor, much less in the private apartment, but whilst the cat was away, the mouse could enjoy its amenities.

Namon's own room felt entirely beneath him, and he loathed every moment he was forced to endure it. At least that dreadful maintenance person from the neighboring room with his awful snoring was away. It had been about four days since the man had gone to New Carronbridge, and he'd yet to return, for any number of reasons Namon didn't give a piss about.

Reaching to pull the covers back, he stopped in mid-thought as he caught sight of a woman standing over by the foot of the bed.

She was tall, his height if not taller. Her curly brown hair barely brushed her shoulders, making it a little short for his taste, but the face and body more than compensated. The dark leather she wore hugged every line and curve of her lean frame. She didn't seem at all impressed by the fact he was stark naked.

Something flickered in her eyes. "Who are you?"

"Shouldn't that be my question to you, darlin'?" he grinned. "Were you sent by Malcolm? I have my favorite, but perhaps she had business elsewhere tonight."

He sat down and lounged back against the massive headboard, letting his legs fall apart in what he envisioned to be a seductive posture.

She walked over next to him and rested a knee on the side of the bed, seeming not to notice his display. "You work here?"

"My dear, I am the head of this facility. Nothing happens here without my knowledge and approval," he lied, placing his hands behind his head. Women loved important men.

She reached down and took him into a gloved hand. He stretched his arms out to each side, pressing his palms against the mattress, instantly aroused at the smooth feel of her glove.

The next thing he knew he was on the floor, feeling as if his groin had been ripped apart. He balled up on his side. For the first time, he noticed a big bloke standing behind her.

She took the amputation knife he handed her, then

walked over to stand beside Namon as her companion checked the bathroom. The blade curved as if it were reaching for him, awakening the realization it would now be pointless to admit he lied.

Tears streamed down Namon's cheeks unchecked as he attempted the only defense he could muster. "The punishment... for my death will be swift and harsh!"

His head felt as though clamped in a vise as the man pried open Namon's mouth, allowing the woman to grip his tongue with the forceps. Bitter-tasting stomach acid burned his throat; the sudden urge to vomit gagged him.

"Your death? I think you know..." she smiled, stroking his cheek with the blade of the knife, "... it's going to be so much worse than that."

Chapter Five

"It is Friday, Madoc David Monss. You should not be working so late," Angelina admonished with a delicate hand resting on the doorknob, brow furrowed in jest.

Her dark head and petite shoulders looked mounted to the doorjamb as she peered in the classroom. In the two years she'd been at Làidir, he'd not wearied of the twist of her Russian accent.

Madoc moved the batch of papers he'd just finished to the side of his desk. "I shan't be much longer. Are you taking the ferry to the mainland?"

She answered his cocked brow with a good-natured eye roll. "It wouldn't be much of a vacation if I stayed on the island, now would it? I'll be careful."

He smiled. "Bring me something."

She blew him a kiss, her entire countenance shining like a beacon. "Would you prefer the door open or shut?"

"Shut." He scanned his diary, scratching down quick notes here and there.

Blurry vision and an aching neck prompted him to turn and look out the window for a moment, the squeak of his chair amplified by the stillness of the room. Dust particles floated along the rays of light cutting in through the glass.

It had been days since Kyrie had left Làidir, and there was still no word. In one respect he wished Rowan were back, but part of him was thankful for not having to deal with his devout pessimism.

In the years she'd been away, Madoc had devoured the rare letters about where she was and how she was doing. During her summer visits before joining the forces, they would talk for hours, sometimes well into the next morning. Often they would just sit down by the water or atop Goatfell, not a word passing their lips.

Maybe he'd assumed too much. She had sent word to say she was bringing Miyanna here, but not much else. Maybe coming back to Làidir hadn't meant what he thought.

He slammed his diary shut, the room all at once like a coffin. A walk in the garden seemed in order, his mind too tangled with other thoughts to concentrate on what he was doing. Perhaps the fresh air would clear his head a bit.

Dark clouds sagged across the sky like poorly hung curtains. He sat down on a nearby bench and looked out over the ocean waves tossing to and fro, arms hugged around his torso.

The infirmary greenhouse needed a visit later in the afternoon to inspect the repairs to some louvers damaged during last storm season. Hopefully they'd not lost too much. There were one or two small suppliers on the island, but outsourcing beyond them would be too risky.

He pulled out the small polished rock he carried in his shirt pocket, smooth except for the letter "M" carved into one side, then closed his fingers around it. Tears stung his eyes as he clutched his fist to his chest. He shoved it back in his pocket and cleared his throat.

Someone called to him. He rose to see Tarrick coming into the garden accompanied by two men, neither of whom Madoc recognized. He crushed down the urge to run the other direction and began walking towards them.

Rowan straightened his tie, trying to smooth the wrinkles from his suit, the tweed pants and jacket making a noble attempt at smart.

Since his arrival at Stirling Castle, he wondered if he was doing the right thing. Closing his eyes, he thought of Threas, feeling comforted. Miyanna, feeling reassured.

He rose to look at one of the elaborate portraits lining the Outer Hall, smiling. It had been done some years before, judging by the age of the little girl with her father. Even at no older than ten years or so, she had the same determined tilt of her fair head. Light bluish eyes with the hint of purple when caught in the sun burned with the same ferocity.

The soft click of footsteps caught his attention. He turned to see an older version of the face he had just been admiring. Morgan looked at Rowan with the satisfaction of one who'd just won an argument.

"Father will see you now."

She led him into a private study. The room was spacious with a fireplace and bookshelves lining one wall. An ornate ceiling of nearly a hundred carved-oak roundels, the Stirling Heads, stared down. Newer ones had been added with scenes depicting some of the key battles from the Rising. The room held an air of superiority, of station. Just as he remembered.

Standing before the heavy oak desk, prepared to do the very thing he swore he never would, he met the crystal gaze of the man who sat behind it.

Chapter Six

Lachlan pulled a boot from his stirrup to stretch out the cramp in his calf, his long legs rebelling against so many hours in the saddle.

The afternoon wind was high, adding bite to the fine mist of rain, bits of his hair not saturated with humidity happily whipping him in the face. Now past Peebles and into Borters, it would only be another hour or so to home.

Nicolas had seemed pleased with the quarterly report, as he well should be. The Cauldron had remained the fore-runner in implementation of the Euthanasia & Eugenics Directive. It was the largest, most efficient research facility in the region, charging towards the end goal by any means necessary.

Personally, Lachlan thought his time was much better spent working rather than giving sodding reports. Several projects had been put on hold for him to make this trip. That thought made him dig his heels into his horse's sides.

Evening was just beginning to wake when the entrance of the Cauldron came into view. The gate guards lowered the massive barrier at his wave, every muscle in his body relaxing at the resonant thump of it shutting behind him.

Seeing the sterile plainness of the grounds made him

realize how much he'd missed it; neither flower nor tree adorned the well-manicured lawn. The hushed peacefulness told him the outer cells had been cleared as he instructed.

Dismounting, he pushed his reins into the hands of the waiting groom and bounded up the steps of the main building with renewed energy.

The door opened before he reached it. His executive assistant walked out on the porch. "Sir, I'm afraid we've a problem."

Lachlan wanted to wash the ride off before writing in his journal. "What is it, Owain?"

"Your private apartment." Owain sounded breathless from the effort to keep up with Lachlan's long strides. "I left everything as it was so you could see for yourself."

Lachlan took the stairs two at time up to his apartment, and then threw open the door. He followed the familiar scent of formaldehyde into his bedroom, then felt something he hadn't in a very long time - shock.

A row of jars, each filled with the various anatomy of Namon, were dress-right-dress at the foot of the bed, not a drop of blood or fluid on carpet or sheet. He picked up the one with Namon's tongue and testicles before looking back at Owain, torn between crashing the jar into the wall and laughing.

"When did this happen?"

"Shortly after you left for Edinburgh. I dispatched soldiers to town for questioning, as well as tightening security here. I would have called you back straightaway, but…"

Lachlan waved a hand. Even with their history, the Prime Minister would not have looked kindly on rescheduling their meeting.

He held the jar out to Owain, who laid his hands on it, but didn't take it. Lachlan raised a brow.

"Sir, there's more." Owain set the jar on the floor. "I need you to come below."

Madoc walked through the horseshoe shaped clearing and stepped up onto the porch while Seth and Seamus tended to the horses.

Elias introduced himself, speaking whilst ushering Madoc inside to a narrow staircase. "She's been in Seth's room since we returned from the Cauldron. Her only sustenance has been whisky and more whisky."

As glad as Madoc was Elias sent for him, he was unsure of what Kyrie might think. Surely she would have sent for him herself if she'd wanted him there. "Does she know you sent for me?"

"No." Elias laid his arm over the banister. "Did Seth tell you aboot what happened?"

"He told me you were too late. That Miyanna was…" Madoc still couldn't say the words. He cleared his throat. "Was there something else?"

Elias looked up the stairs, then shook his head. "It's the room on the left."

Madoc nodded and took a deep breath, crushing down the urge to run up the stairs, or out the front door for that matter.

The landing was shadowed and hushed, excepting a

creak or two as he walked. He listened for a moment, but heard not a sound coming from Seth's room. His hand hovered a moment before he finally forced himself to knock.

"Sod off!" Her voice was slurred and hoarse, lacking its usual resonance.

"Kyrie, it's me..."

A loud bang against the door accompanied the sound of breaking glass, causing him to jump back. He stood there a moment, then tried the knob on the off chance it would be unlocked. It wasn't.

"Please, Bonnie, let me in."

When no further response was offered, he turned to go back down the hall, then stopped, all at once charged with every ounce of frustration, hurt, and helplessness he'd felt over the last few weeks. He stepped back and planted a kick right next to the doorknob. The door smacked the wall with a resounding slap before it rebounded. He shoved the remnant out of his way, then advanced into the room, glass crunching underfoot.

Heavy curtains blocked out every bit of light, a candle burned down to a stub was the sole illumination in the room. Beeswax spilled onto the small nightstand next to an empty bottle identical to the one broken on the floor and the full one in her hand.

Madoc squared his shoulders. "I've something to say and, by God, you will listen."

She sat on the bed with a bottle half way to her lips, looking like death warmed over and gone cold again. Her hair covered her head like a matted helmet. The white linen shirt, already a size too large, draped her scrawny frame, indicating she'd not eaten in days. She would have looked like a small girl playing dress up were it not for the fact she was blatantly drunk.

She leaned back against the headboard and crossed her bare feet at the ankles, flicking the cork over on the floor, not caring in the slightest that half a bare buttock flashed at him when she did so.

He sat down beside her. "What are you trying to do to yourself?"

She rolled her eyes before taking a long drink.

A slight pressure began to build behind his eyes as compassion clicked another notch towards irritation. "So you're just going to give up?"

She ignored him and took another swig.

"This is not who you are." He started to lay a hand on her arm, and then decided against it.

The temperature of the room seemed to drop as she met his gaze. "You have no idea who I am."

"I know I don't care. Your mother. Miyanna. I can't lose you, too." He laid a hand on her arm. "I still love…"

In one motion she slid off the bed and let the bottle fly across the room, shattering against the wall. "Get out!"

"Kyrianna, please." Madoc threw his legs across the mattress, rising to stand before her, grasping her arm.

Her fist struck his chin like a hammer. The air in the room froze in place. Blood trickled down his lip, catching in the corner of his mouth.

In one motion, he wiped his nose on his sleeve, and then slung her over his shoulder. Ignoring the fists pounding his back and curses he'd never even heard before, he strode down the stairs and out the front door.

He marched over to the watering trough and unceremoniously dumped her in it. She sat up sputtering, but only had a moment to catch her breath before he grabbed a handful of hair and shoved her under the water. After a few seconds, he pulled her back up.

"You mother fuc…" she sputtered.

Without letting her finish, he pushed her down again, this time holding her under a bit longer before relenting. She was barely out of the water before she leaned over the side and vomited.

He waited a moment, prepared at any moment to defend his life or, just as importantly, his manhood. "Are you ready to listen, or would you prefer to finish the bath you so desperately need?"

She rested her head on the side of the trough, then sat up and wiped her mouth.

He laid his hands along the edge. "You are going to pull yourself together, because I need you."

A singled tear hung in her already wet lashes. She offered no response whatsoever, but appeared at least to be listening.

"There's a time to lay down the sword," Madoc stood and looked down at her, "and a time to pick it up."

Not wishing to press his luck, he left her to stew in the trough and headed back to the house.

Elias sat on the front porch steps talking to his brother. Seth's fresh khaki pants and shirt made Madoc's own clothes feel even more sullied. They each had a cup in hand, a small black leather case resting in between them.

Elias noticed Madoc looking at it and grinned. "First Aid kit."

They both gave Madoc the once over. Seth leaned a bit

towards Elias. "Donny, Shay, you, me. That makes four of us and only one of her."

The raised brows and concerned looks made Madoc want to laugh, in spite of everything. "I think I can hold my own well enough."

"Aye, but she won't stay bare-arsed and drunk all the time." Seth raised his cup to take a drink, pausing to flash a wicked grin. "No matter how much ye ask her to."

Madoc sat on the porch steps, drained, but feeling better than he had in weeks, scratching his neck under his wool shirt while indulging in a yawn.

Kyrie had just gone to bed after a bath and three bowls of Elias's Scotch broth.

The ride was starting to catch up to him; his bones ached with weariness, yet he couldn't bring himself to turn in, instead sitting on the porch enjoying the crisp, fresh air.

He buttoned his denim jacket, then stuffed his hands in the pockets, wondering if he should have kept his Macintosh on.

"Somethin' warm, and ye out in the chill." Elias sat down next to him, handing him a stoneware cup, steam drifting up past the rim.

Madoc's mouth relished the soothing sting on his tongue, keeping both hands wrapped around the cup, reveling as it crept through his limbs. "Earl Grey. Milk, no sugar."

Elias blew into his mug, seemingly oblivious to the

evening chill, wearing nothing more than a fleece pullover and jeans.

"Kyrie said ye were partial. I prefer mine a wee more stoot." This was punctuated by the waggle of neat, ruddy brows, almost black in the moonlight.

The subsequent lull was comfortable and pleasant, so much so Madoc barely noticed when Elias spoke. "Beg pardon?"

Elias rolled his cup between his hands. "I asked if ye kent wha' started all this. Wi' Kyrie and her wee sister."

Madoc took a deep breath. "About six months ago, Prime Minister Payne initiated the Euthanasia & Eugenics Directive. Local politicians were summoned to Edinburgh in order to schedule 'clearances', beginning with schools, hospitals, and assisted living facilities."

All handicapped, seriously infirmed, or past the age of seventy-five were evaluated, and then taken to so-called research facilities, such as the Cauldron. Assisted suicide had been a legal, accepted practice for hundreds of years, but the EED was the first attempt at government regulation, the justification being limited resources for healthcare. Most went along out of fear, but there were those who refused. Kyrie's mother was one. She knew the cost of her defiance and that the schools she officiated would be cleared anyway, but she was at least able to protect the location of Làidir.

In the beginning, Làidir had been a private school, but only for children without special needs. Children that did have them were relegated to specialized schools on the mainland. After Miyanna was born, Threas began experimenting with an inclusive program, feeling the exposure would be beneficial for both groups of children. One could model necessary life skills, while the other learned toler-ance. Threas had been gathering data, but didn't feel she had enough yet to support her theories. That secrecy had turned out to be the very thing to save Làidir.

"Through various connections, we've managed to smuggle in a handful of children in the last few months," Madoc shrugged, staring into his cup. "We had to do some-thing."

Elias's eyes closed, then snapped open, as if he'd seen something he'd rather not.

Madoc gave Elias's shoulder a firm squeeze, then rose to go inside, feeling as if his bones would slide right out of his body.

"Sleep well." Elias called over his shoulder.

With a hand on the knob, Madoc turned to shut the door behind him and was caught by the humbling sight of a large man sitting there, dark head tilted towards the heav-ens.

A whisper took flight in the eerie stillness of moon and darkness. The voice husky with heartfelt sentiment spoke low, but with confident assurance.

"By this soul on Thine arm, O Christ,
Thou King of the City of Heaven.
Amen
Since Thou, O Christ, it was who bought'st
this soul,
Be its peace on Thine own keeping.
Amen..."

Madoc eased the door shut, blinking hard to banish the

hot sting of tears from his eyes. After a moment, the same mysterious energy holding him from sleep pulled him up the stairs, at last willing to let him rest.

Chapter Seven

Soft light fell in the square of The Lion's Den, the air filled with a palpable dampness Rowan could almost taste. His belly ballooned in protest at the mere thought of any physical activity other than languishing in the courtyard of Stirling Castle and savoring his after-supper pipe.

The click of heels on the stones behind him signaled Morgan's approach. "You look like a fat cat with feathers stuck to its lips."

She squeezed his shoulder and took a seat on the small stone bench next to his, shivering delicately before drawing herself deeper into her cloak. The gray fur lining made her eyes look like amethysts in silver satin as she stared at the sky, steam from her cup disappearing into the light breeze.

"Well, Sinclair and I are both still breathing. I only expected that for one of us," Rowan chuckled, then sobered. "By the way, thank you for trying t' help."

"I just wish I'd found out in time where she was." She tilted her head the other way as if changing the subject with her movement. "Tell me what happened to my mother."

He'd been leaning down to pick up a piece of tobacco wrapper from the ground and nearly lost his seat. How to answer that question, he wondered. Surely her father had…

"He's never told me anything." Her voice was little better than a whisper.

A chill scurried up and down his spine. "That's a wee bit unnerving."

Morgan grinned, then blew into her cup. "You aren't the first to tell me that."

Rowan toyed with the wrapper, folding and unfolding it before finally slipping it in his pocket.

Stars speckled the sky like glitter spilt over black velvet; the moon burned like a fiery opal. He watched a shooting star streak overhead, then looked over at Morgan.

She cocked a brow to say 'I'm waiting', something he was sure she wasn't accustomed to.

Feigning preoccupation with the bitter taste of smoke rolling over his tongue bought him a moment, but only just. He wished now he'd gone straight to bed.

"The first time I saw her after... after her and Garret..." Nearly thirty-five years later, Rowan still couldn't say the words. "She was six months' pregnant."

The only thing more painful than seeing her pregnant with another man's child was the thought of her being alone and pregnant with another man's child. So, he chose to stay.

Three months later, Sonia gave birth to twins. The girl, Morgan Elizabeth, had the gemstone eyes of their mother, while the boy, Madoc David, had the translucent gaze of their father. With every day that passed, Rowan forgot a little more that Garret Sinclair was their father. Every day they felt more and more like his.

For the next year, he and Sonia kept to themselves, not yet willing to share their little family with anyone; however, they'd decided it was time to take the twins to meet Symin and Threas.

Sonia shared the saddle with Morgan, her tiny hands on top of Sonia's to help guide the reins. Madoc, skinny neck sticking from the top of his wee denim jacket, sat tall and quiet in front of Rowan. Tears welled in Rowan's eyes. A sudden fear that he would not be able to keep them safe overwhelmed him; in the space of his next breath, that fear was realized.

Masked riders dressed in black burst through the trees from either side, one of them holding a white flag bearing a red cross.

In unison, he and Sonia dug their heels in, clutching the children, hearts matching the pounding hooves. Not more than a kilometer or two, they pulled up short at the sight of more riders.

A bit up the road, he recognized Threas in the center of some fifteen men. To her right Tarrick. To her left Symin. Travel in the south had become quite dodgy due to mounting political tension. Symin and Threas had insisted on meeting them with some sort of escort, thankfully ignoring his protests.

With a firm hold on Madoc, Rowan looked from his sister to the masked pursuers, able to now tell for sure there were four of them.

Time hung in the air as a decision was made. Jerking their reins, the anonymous riders turned and escaped into the darkness.

Threas and Symin rode forward, reaching out for Morgan to introduce themselves to their niece. Rowan nudged his horse with his knees to move up alongside Sonia, then leaned towards her, their lips a hair's breadth apart.

The muted whoosh! followed by meaty thunk! didn't register at first. Sonia's face froze before she slumped over. Rowan saw a bolt protruding from each side of her neck just before she fell from her horse.

Threas grabbed Madoc with her free arm as Rowan reached for Sonia while jumping to the ground to kneel beside her. Tarrick and Symin thundered past with half the soldiers hot on their heels; the rest took up defensive positions.

Rowan tore off his gloves, and then clamped a hand on each side of her neck, the bolt sticking out between his middle and ring fingers. Blood pumped up between his fingers, soaking his skin and sleeves, no matter how hard he pressed. Tears flowed just as freely as he watched her gurgling, trying to breathe, trying to speak. Her fingertips trailed his jaw like a feather before her hand dropped, eyes closing to mere slits.

The hollow call of an owl banished the vision of Sonia's countenance, bringing into focus the mirror image of her daughter.

The barrel of his pipe felt warm in his hand as he tapped it on the bottom of his boot. The muscles of his body suddenly joined together in a chorus of exhaustion, so he rose to go inside.

"Why only me?" Morgan whispered. "Why didn't Father want both of us?"

Rowan sighed. A warm, salty wetness tickled his lips as he brushed a kiss on her cheek. "I have no idea."

Aromas of sausage and homemade bread still wafted around the private dining area as Rowan shoved his shaving kit into his satchel, anxious for more than one reason to be on his way. Another telegram had arrived over the Net from Madoc to say where he was staying.

Morgan had insisted on Rowan using one of the rooms in the palace rather than one of the new guestrooms in the King's old building. It was a bit too close to her father for Rowan's taste, but they had successfully avoided each other since their meeting the day before.

He'd risen early enough before breakfast for a walk atop the Wall to have a look at the valley, hills, and craigs below. As much as he'd dreaded coming here, the scenery surrounding Stirling Castle was as breathtaking as he'd remembered.

He headed out the door and down the stairs. With the exception of Threas, Madoc was the strongest person he'd ever known. Something he appreciated much more now that Madoc was older, Rowan thought with a smile. He'd known from the time Madoc was a small child that there was something unique and powerful about him.

Madoc had just turned five years old. They had spent the day helping the new grooms with some of the horses, in particular a young mare that had come into season for the first time and was to be serviced by a two-year-old colt. In an instant, Rowan was slammed into the teaser, his shoulder absorbing most of the force from the unforgiving board.

At first it wasn't so noticeable, but by evening the pain made it impossible to sleep. He eased himself up to a sitting position, thinking he should go find the nurse to get more primrose paste when he noticed Madoc standing in the door.

Without a word, Madoc walked over, laid a tiny hand right where the pain was. A momentary burning sensation pulsed through his shoulder, and then went away, along with the pain he'd been feeling just moments before.

Madoc ambled toward the door, tiny shoulders melting Rowan's heart, making him wonder how anyone could help but love this child.

Rowan opened his mouth to speak when Madoc looked back over his shoulder and smiled. "Something woke me up and told me to come."

The pungent scent of hay and horse droppings chased away his recollections. Rowan walked through the stable door and was headed for his horse's stall when stopped by a familiar male voice coming from behind.

"I see we're not too late."

Rowan turned to face Morgan and her father, both dressed to the nines in posh, charcoal-colored leather riding gear.

He sighed, running a hand over a mended spot on his Mackintosh. "Going somewhere, are you?"

"We're in a stable dressed in riding clothes. What do you reckon?" Garret leaned towards Morgan and added, "He always was a bit slow to grasp the obvious."

The smile punctuating Garret's words caused Rowan to consider voicing a multiplicity of obscenities, all of which were highly inappropriate in front of a lady, even if said lady was likely better versed in things obscene than he was.

Rowan took a deep breath, reminding himself to unclench his jaw. "Where are you going, and why should I care?"

Garret stepped just past Rowan and bellowed for the stable hand before turning back, grinning whilst using hand gestures to compliment his words. "Since we are here... with you... and leaving... with you, then we must be going... with you."

Rowan heard Morgan's silky voice behind him, as he stood watching Garret mount his horse. "Oh, won't this be fun."

I woke early the next morning, throwing off the quilts which shielded me from the chill, bare skin tingling from gooseflesh scurrying up and down my body. I pulled on Elias's robe and made my way downstairs, lifting the hem so I wouldn't trip.

Little creaks on one or two of the steps were the only sounds in the house. Through the window I could see Maddy on the front porch drinking his morning tea, already dressed in his riding clothes, the black denim adding height to his already tall frame.

His hair had always been cropped short, but now brushed the top of his collar. Dark blonde stubble on his chin gave him more the look of pirate than teacher.

He turned when he heard the door and smiled. "Now then. You're up early." He wrapped his arms around me, a hand vigorously rubbing my back.

"I got cold." I clasped my hands in between us in front

of my chest. "This is a peaceful place, isn't it?"

"It is. It reminds me of Làidir." A shadow darkened the silver spark of his eyes.

"Were you serious about what you said yesterday?" I felt certain what the answer would be, but had to hear him say the words.

"Life today for them is no life at all. It's no more than living death." His smile was sweet, if a bit sad. "Someone has to do something."

Sunrise fired the blueness of morning. I wondered if there were any words that would make him understand. Tucked away at Làidir during the Rising, he'd never seen war from the same side I had. For all I'd witnessed, even on the brightest of days, the world seemed a shade or two darker.

Madoc's fingertips teased the silver cross he always wore, a gift from Rowan for his sixteenth birthday. He looked down at me a moment, then pressed a kiss against my forehead. "Get packed. I have somewhere I want to take you."

Chapter Eight

"Just sit in the chair." Lachlan kept his voice calm and smooth.

An older subject who'd been diagnosed with Alzheimer's had been brought in to the Cauldron by his daughter. There was a slight shaking of the right hand, but as of yet, the mind was still functioning.

Lachlan knew it was only a matter of time before the dementia began. It was understandable why the man chose to turn himself in, rather than wait for a mandatory referral. Once the EED was fully implemented, the man's daughter would have been legally bound regardless. As it was, Lachlan was required to notify her physician to flag her medical record and monitor her for any symptoms of the same condition.

"I changed my mind. I don't want to be here." Bushy brows of gray raised in appeal to his daughter. "Let's be off home now."

"Papa…" She looked back at Lachlan before turning to face her father.

"As I said, the procedure is painless." He'd hoped the straps wouldn't be necessary, but it seemed he would have no choice. He motioned for the two assistants standing behind the chair.

The daughter stepped forward to speak, but Lachlan stopped her. "Perhaps we should step into the hall until he's settled."

Her voice was thick. Her eyes kept darting between Lachlan and her father. "I don't want to leave him... alone..."

"Amy? Where are you going?" Despite his age, his arm muscles were as taut as the straps holding them in place, his legs now taking up the fight. "I'll do better. Just... please... I want to go home." His voice rose the closer she got to the door.

Lachlan nodded to one of the assistants standing by, then shut the door.

She squared up to look him in the eye. "I'm taking my father home."

"Your father seems a proud man. He knows what is to come and doesn't want to be remembered that way." Lachlan laid a hand against the small of her back. "He has that right."

Her voice was firm, each syllable steeled with determination. "I am taking... my father... home."

Lachlan stepped aside and let her open the door, stopping just inside as if she'd hit a wall. The man sat motionless in the chair, eyelids drooping halfway shut. She was beside him in two strides.

"Papa? Are you ready to go?" Her voice trembled as she took his hand.

"Yes. I am." A dreamy smile fluttered across his face as he closed his eyes.

Owain had escorted the man's daughter from the premises. She had been hysterical after her father expired, forcing Lachlan to give her something to calm her before donning his surgical gown and shutting himself in his private lab.

Picking up a fresh loofah sponge from the back of the utility sink, he scrubbed his hands and nails to redness before being satisfied enough to put his gloves on. Eyes closed, a slow neck rotation and a few deep breaths faded the visions of the last few hours; he was ready to get to work.

The hair was thin enough it could be removed with scissors before lathering the scalp and finishing the job with a straight razor. Rubbing a gloved hand over the smoothness, he reached with the other to pick up a scalpel.

He made an incision across the top of the skull, from ear to ear, then laid the scalpel back on the tray in order to peel away the face to expose bare skull. After a quick assessment, he chose the handsaw he wanted to use and began incising the bone across the forehead just above the eyes, taking care not to cut too deep and damage the frontal lobe.

Removal of the brain would be easy due to the apparent shrinkage, having pulled away from the walls of the skull. With crisp movements, he picked up two instruments that to a layman would have looked like oversized metal shoehorns and eased them in on each side between skull and brain until he was able to get a good finger hold.

Once it was free of the spinal cord, he squirted distilled

water between the folds and curves to rinse away the residual cerebrospinal fluid, and then placed it on a small tray covered with wax paper, making note of structural changes to the cerebral cortex and possible states of the hippocampus.

Turning it in his hand like a gem of some sort, he was a little surprised at the sound of his stomach growling. Had he been working that long?

He rolled the tray with the brain next to one just like it that had a plate resting perfectly in the center. After discarding his gloves, he washed his hands, then sat down and uncovered his plate.

Raising his egg sandwich in mock salute, he ate in silence, his eyes never leaving the brain.

Lachlan climbed the stairs, rubbing the back of his neck, his vision a bit blurred. The accomplishment he'd felt after the brain extraction was soon tinged with frustration after viewing the results of an attempted hand straightening for a young girl with Palsy.

What would it take to transplant a viable appendage successfully, he wondered? Would the donor need to be alive? Would the donor need to be the same age or sex?

In spite of the nature of his previous work, the pain the subjects sometimes felt gave him no pleasure. Still, he felt confident the culmination of his research would someday be the recompense for it all.

He shut the door to the lower level and turned to see

Owain headed down the hall.

"Sir, you've a visitor in your office." Owain stepped to the side out of the way.

Lachlan groaned as he walked past. "Who is it? I have charts I have to finish documenting."

"A woman who claims to have information regarding the incident with Namon," Owain informed him.

Lachlan rested his hand on the doorknob. "Have the maintenance crew disinfect the observation cells. I'd also like the name of the supervisor on duty whilst I was away."

"Sir, the crew just finished…" Owain's voice trailed off at Lachlan's raised brow, then he cleared his throat. "Yes, sir."

A small-framed woman rose as Lachlan entered the room, her head titled slightly back. She was fairly pretty in spite of her mousy hair and slight over bite. An insolent look lay in her eyes that irked him like something small and sharp in the bottom of a sock.

He viewed her with increased interest, giving a slight bow. "My name is Lachlan. I am the head of this facility. And you are…?"

"My name is Ishbel." She crossed her arms over her chest, looking like a child. "I've information for ya, but it won't be cheap." This was punctuated with a flop down into her chair.

If he'd had to venture a guess, the southern accent would have put her from down around the coastal region. London, perhaps?

"I'm sure we can come to some sort of arrangement." The leather of his chair squeaked a bit when he sat down. He pressed his fingertips together. "You were saying?"

"It were the night I's to come to Namon. I's runnin' a bit

late. Didn't get here 'till round two in the mornin'." She examined her nails as she spoke. "I was passin' down the hall when I saw his door open and a woman and two men come out. I ducked into a vacant room before they could see me."

Her words pulled him forward in his chair. "Did you see what the woman looked like?"

"Course I did. Be stupid to come here if I hadn't." She rolled her eyes with a slight shake of her head.

"Quite." Lachlan's eyes narrowed. "Go on."

"That weren't the first time I saw her. Saw her in town, as well." She pulled a string from her skirt.

Perfect. He was beginning to feel the profit of the day even more when his thoughts were interrupted by Ishbel.

"As I said, it won't be cheap. Nothin' I do is free." She finished with a smug look of setting him straight.

Lachlan stared at her moment, and then leaned back in his chair. He crossed his arms over his chest and smiled.

"I couldn't help but notice... you have very lovely hands."

The evening sky wore its usual depressed look. We had taken most of the day, with only brief stops along the way for meals, to reach our destination.

It had been years since I'd been home. Not even when I came for Miyanna. Our family had been quite independent living here, making trips to Craigdarroch for what we couldn't grow, kill, or churn.

My heart quickened as we rode up the hill. I had a full

view of the house as we made our way down the other side.

A starburst shaped hole marred the bay window of the dining area. The rocking chairs Papa had made to flank either side of it were gone. Steel flood gates still surrounded the porch, a smaller one sitting beside the front door.

I looked to the window of my room, the screen drooping at one corner. At times I felt so invaded by the little sister always tottering about in my space, always wanting to sleep with me. But other times the small, warm lump pressed between my shoulder blades smelling of Mama's peppermint lotion and the sound of the rain tapping on the metal roof converged to form a soothing presence after one of my nightmares.

Passing between the house and the shop, I could still hear the faint clinking emanating from inside. Archaic motorbike engines had fascinated Papa. Finding a buried part of some sort was like striking pure gold for him. He would lay out the rusty bits and stare at old drawings, imagining how it would have sounded, how it would have felt to ride, how the petrol would have smelled.

It seemed some wild fairytale to hear him talk of life during the Petroleum Age, when motors were more than just relics. Mama would say he'd gone daft, but I would have climbed up right behind him, ready to race the wind.

Dark clouds hung thick overhead and kept what little sun left in the day hidden, the breeze making me shrink a bit deeper into my coat. I dismounted Eros, leaving him to graze. Maddy caught my eye, holding my gaze for a moment, then handed me a small wooden box.

It was a short walk to the mud-drenched graveyard at the end of the path. Two lone graves, one giant headstone bearing the Maclaren coat of arms centered in between two smaller ones: Symin Jameson. Elizabeth Threas.

Hot tears blurred my vision at the sight of them side by side. Papa would have wanted Mama next to him. The Thomas family must have commissioned her stone when Miyanna was with them, waiting for me.

The box nearly became too heavy to bear as I stared at my mother's grave, which soon faded into warm light glowing through the window of our house as I packed my father's saddle bags.

It was near to the end of the Second Season and the air was heavy with the promise of coming storms. We'd just buried Papa a few months before. A huge weight pressed down upon me and I told myself it was the long ride to Làidir, and then training that lay before me.

Ready to ride, I'd stepped up on the front porch to tell Miyanna goodbye. She sat in Mama's rocker, eyes brimming with tears, not saying a word as I turned to go.

Before I reached the steps Mama put her arms around me and whispered in my ear, "You don't have to do this." Hugging her, I whispered back, "Yes, I do."

Maddy squeezed my shoulder before kneeling between the two graves. The entrenching tool squeaked in protest as he flipped it open, the ground making soft sucking sounds with each turn.

I hugged the box containing a small bag of polished rocks to my heart, feeling the round hardness of the one I'd placed in my pocket dig into my skin.

The beautiful etching in the wood reflected the words in my heart. "*Mo milis Sonas.*" My sweet sister.

Haytham stretched the cramp from between his shoulder blades, a rumbling stomach and sinking sun announcing it was near to supper time.

He'd fed the horse and now needed to have a look at the back door to see what he might need for repairs. Perhaps when he went to the supply store, Ishbel would shut her yattering long enough for his order to not be balls up.

Spreading hay for the last two hours had his back in quite a state. He stabbed the pitchfork into a nearby pile and drank from his canteen, wiping the stray drops from the front of his flannel shirt.

Seth was due in soon, just to see if anything had stirred up since they left. It made his heart ache to think of Kyrie when they'd returned from the Cauldron and what had happened to her dear sister.

Haytham turned towards the door, then stumbled back as if he'd been struck. Nausea churned in his stomach. He swallowed hard.

Five men spread across the stable door. With the exception of the tall one in the center, he didn't recognize their faces; only their uniforms.

An unnatural looking smile on the familiar, thin face caused nausea to be replaced by something else; an intense and all encompassing fear.

PART TWO

TO SEEK YOU AND SEARCH FOR YOU

CHAPTER NINE

Madoc closed his eyes and drew a deep breath, the redolence of the loch refreshing after spending the last few hours trapped inside with Rowan, Morgan, and Garret.

It had been a shock to find them at Elias's, to say the least. Garret offered to reach a few contacts that might be sympathetic, but made it plain it was only in response to Morgan's threat to do it herself if he didn't. Garret would never allow her to take such a risk, something Morgan was most likely aware of.

Madoc picked up a small stone and rubbed his thumb over the smooth surface. The only reason he'd even come back to Elias's after leaving Miyanna's graveside was to have more time with Kyrie before returning to Làidir. Her leave would soon be up and he had no idea when he would see or hear from her again once she returned to her post, assuming she didn't resign her commission altogether. She'd not yet expressed her intentions, and he wasn't willing to ask questions she might not be ready to answer.

Stars dotted the sky well enough he was able to see without a torch. The loch was still and peaceful, like a watery blanket stretched out from shore.

"There you are."

Madoc turned to see Kyrie walking towards him, his heart thudding a tattoo in his ears. She lowered herself down next to him. Her hair was swept up, exposing just a bit of neck above the collar of her leather jacket.

"Elias is about to open a bottle of scotch," Kyrie smiled and nudged him with her elbow. "Want to come back up?"

Madoc shook his head. "I think I'll pass."

She nodded, then rested her arms on her knees and laced her fingers. "There seems to be some bad blood between Uncle Rowan and Sinclair. I wonder why."

"About a year after Rowan and my mother married, she gave birth to a son." Madoc saw Kyrie's eyes widen. Rowan had never spoken of it, but in recent years Threas had told Madoc what had happened.

The stone whizzed from Madoc's hand, making a plopping sound when it hit the water. "He was only a month old when he died of crib death. Rowan disappeared without a word for months, until one day he turned up at Stirling."

Rowan had not been ready to face Sonia yet, nor did he want to see Threas. Instead he turned to his closest friend; Garret. When he arrived, Rowan found Sonia and Garret together.

Around the time Rowan and Sonia's baby died, Garret's wife had committed suicide. She had been desperately trying for years to have a child, only to find out that she would never be able to conceive.

Garret left her one morning for an all day business trip to Edinburgh. They had breakfast before he left, she kissed him goodbye, and told him she would see him when he got home. When he returned that evening, Garret found her in the tub, her wrists slashed, holding a doll she'd bought when they'd begun trying to have children.

Rowan had been at Làidir for months before Threas convinced him to go see Sonia. When he went to her, it was then he found out she was pregnant and Garret was the father.

Madoc looked at Kyrie, feeling a release at having finally told her what he'd never spoken of before. "I can only believe what happened between Garret and my mother resulted from the need to feel alive in the midst of so much death."

"People are often surprised to learn what they're truly capable of. It's when you stop being surprised that you know something is wrong." She seemed to slip inside herself for a moment, then stood and tugged at his sleeve for him to join her.

The world shifted out of focus as she wrapped her arms around him, her lips cool against his cheek. It wasn't long before he felt a familiar pressure begin to build. His hands trembled as he stroked her back, her lips teasing his jaw line.

He sucked in his breath when she kissed the corner of his mouth. "Kyrie..."

With the all the delicacy of a lightning strike, the spell was broken. A desperate voice called their names as someone burst from the trees.

Maddy sat beside me on the settee, drawing small circles on the back of my hand with his thumb. Donny had come to fetch us, and then went to Elias and Seth, all three still outside.

Garret stood in front of the bay window looking intently into the darkness, his face unreadable. Morgan sat in the chair next to Rowan watching her father out of the corner of her eye, each of them in their own little world.

Rowan stirred, clearing his throat. "It's safe to assume that this Lachlan knows who was at the Cauldron. If your mate gave up anything..."

Morgan's voice was hoarse, a crease between her perfectly arched brows. "It's not a matter of 'if'. It's how much."

Garret moved over near Morgan. "If Lachlan does know anything, you can bet soldiers are already underway."

"We don't know how much time we have." Rowan took his Macintosh from the back of his chair and draped it over his arm.

"I don't think Haytham knew exactly where this place is, but we can't assume that to be the case." I patted Maddy's leg and stood. "I need to speak with Elias."

"Where will you all go?" Morgan pulled on her gloves as Garret held her cloak out for her.

I noticed everyone looking towards the door and turned to see Elias standing next to Seth, with Donny and Seamas right behind them.

Madoc looked at Elias for a moment, then took my hand and smiled. "To Làidir. Let's go home."

CHAPTER TEN

The glare of morning light shone through the cathedral-style windows of the main library of Brodick Castle, most likely the closest thing to sunshine we would see all day.

After leaving Elias's, Seth escorted Morgan to Stirling, while Seamas took Garret via an alternate route. The two of them had arrived back at Làidir in the wee hours of morning, and I'd been too wound up to go back to sleep. I'd come down to the library to read for a while, but so far I was having a hard time concentrating.

Tucking my legs underneath me, I settled in to read the same page for a third time.

In the early years of the New Millennium, a group of scientists known as the Global Regime began working to develop technology that would offset the severe weather and climate changes. Geoengineering was one of many achievements to usher in what would become known as the Computer Age. Cars no longer required petrol. Books no longer required paper.

Less than a decade later, firearms and heavy artillery became obsolete, replaced by computerized stunners and Star Wars, a technology begun in the late 20th Century. The World Treaty for Nuclear Disarmament soon followed, ushering in a time of un-

precedented peace, though it would not last for long.

In what historians speculate to be the year 2335, a large-scale terrorist organization targeted the world's tele-communications systems, power grids, financial and banking systems, and transportation systems using High Power Microwave Weapons (HPM) and Ultra Wide Band Weapons (UWB).

Defenses such as electromagnetic hardening and failover systems proved futile. Computer systems from satellites to cell phones were rendered irrevocably useless; information stores were permanently destroyed.

No longer held at bay by the advancements of science and engineering, the forces of nature unleashed an unholy revenge, giving quarter to none. The southwestern part of the United States burned to a wasteland by fires caused by massive drought, while Alaska and Canada endured devastating floods.

Four seasons in many regions, such as Western Europe, were shortened to three; winter rains, summer droughts, and fall flooding. A vast percentage of the world's population succumbed to starvation due to damaged agricultural systems and diseases brought to life by warmer temperatures. Societies were transformed by civil war. Cities became countries. Countries formed regions.

It was a time of change the world had never known before. One it hopes never to see again.

The words on the page began to blend together again as I grew more and more restless. It seemed half a life time since I'd ridden the coast around the island, one of my favorite things to do when I used to visit.

I slammed the book shut and dropped it into the chair, then headed up to my room, taking the stairs two at a time.

My fingertips were ineffective at massaging the nagging pain from my temples.

Eros had thrown a shoe and I'd decided to take him on into Corrie rather than back to Làidir so that I could hike up Goatfell. If I was to be on foot, I might as well make the most of it.

My small canteen, first aid kit, and the block of cheese I'd bought in one of the shops to carry me over to supper fit quite nicely in the small satchel I'd kept in my saddlebag.

The footpath along Corrie Burn was just beginning to gain height as I left the woodland. It wasn't the tallest of mountains at just under a kilometer, but the views were breathtaking nonetheless. I'd thought of jogging up the parts that weren't too steep, but decided against it when I began to see spots in my right eye.

Though I enjoyed hiking, or most any outdoor activity, riding was still my favorite. Even more so when I rode Eros. He'd been trained at the French Calvary School, excelling in the Military Versatility Test, his long legs perfect for cross-country or jumping.

How many people can say they won a Cleveland Bay-Thoroughbred mix in a card game with one of the officers of the Cadre Noir? As a general rule, I believed in being honest and straightforward, but I had never been one to shy away from an opportunity, either.

The view over the Firth of Clyde was as good a place as any to stop for a drink, the blue haze of sky and water a beautiful contrast to the green grass on the rocks.

I'd no interest in the gardens or rhododendron forest, appreciating the rocky dirt trails flanked with grass, heather, and boulders much more as I finished up my ascent at the narrow ledge of rock that was the highest point on the entire island.

The cool spray of mist tickled my face, the only sound the wind in the long grass. Behind me I could just make out the Paps of Jura; Glen Sannox to the north; Brodick Bay to the south.

I continued on, first to North Goatfell and then on to *Mullach Buidhe*. Green grass looked smeared here and there on the rocks. Only a few houses of High Corrie were visible through the trees, but I could see the footpath leading down, Corrie Burn flowing next to it.

My gazed lifted to the horizon, blazing golden as the setting sun tried to show itself from behind dark clouds, a glimpse of moon visible, as if it were waiting to take its post. I hiked along looking out over Glen Rosa and Kyntire. Looking at the dark threat of the sky I thought I'd better head for South Sannox and then back into Corrie.

I turned to take a step and saw a sudden flash of light, just before everything went dark. I stumbled a few steps, my hands grasping at nothing but air as my foot caught the edge of a rock.

All at once, my body felt weightless as the world went black around me.

A sharp pain in my arm woke me. I squinted hard to see in the dark. How long had I lain here?

I wiggled my fingers and toes, then tentatively tried my arms and legs. Nothing seemed to be broken. There was a buzzing in my ears as I tried to sit up, rocks stabbing into my hips and palms as I did. A warm, slow seeping from my forearm had soaked my sleeve. I peeled it back to take a look at the wound. At least there's enough moonlight to...

My heart pounded against my ribs. The roar of the wind magnified in my ears. The darkness seemed suffocating. My hands trembled, feeling my eyes, the thick lashes lining them.

They were wide open.

A familiar voice called my name. "Kyrie! Are ye all right?"

I shook my head. "I'm not sure."

"Yer going tae have tae climb down a wee bit."

"I can't see. It's too dark," I choked out.

"Ye have tae. Just mind wha' I tell ye." The sureness of the voice gave me the courage I needed.

I crawled more than climbed down to meet the voice, grabbing where it told me to. "How will I find my way?"

The voice sounded right in front of me now, as a hand reached to gently help me the rest of the way. Tears streamed down my face as I realized who it was.

"Easy, *leanabh*. I'll see ye home."

The fireplace in the piano room radiated warmth, succeeding against the room's chilliness, but hardly a match for the cold sense of dread Madoc felt inside.

He paced in front of it, arms clasped tightly across his chest, a faint metallic taste in his mouth from the raw place he'd chewed on his lip.

There'd been no word from the doctor as of yet. He gripped the mantle and bowed his head to use the only power he possessed at the moment, only to be interrupted by Elias rushing in, followed by Rowan.

"What happened?" Rowan shrugged out of his Macintosh and dropped it across an arm chair.

Madoc drew breath to answer when one of their nurses strode in, a severe look creasing the smooth, fullness of her face. All three of them started towards her at once, causing her to take a step back.

They looked at each other a moment, then Madoc took a half-step towards her. "I'm sorry. We're just anxious to hear how she is."

She waved his apology away. "The cuts on her face and lip were minor. The gash on her arm required some stitches, but nothing too serious."

She paused for a moment, looking at each of them. "The doctor has determined that the retinas in both eyes have detached, most likely due to hemorrhaging of the blood vessels in the eye."

"So what does all that mean?" Rowan asked in a clipped tone, shaking his head.

Elias answered before the nurse could. "It means she's blind."

Madoc stood frozen in place, giving the words time to reach him. The urge to laugh was overwhelming. A small chuckle bubbled free, the slight taste of salt in the corner of his mouth when he licked his lips. Everyone stared for a moment.

Madoc brushed the wetness from his cheeks. "I should go to her."

The nurse touched his arm. "I need some information for our records. I know you two have always been close, so I thought it best to ask you." She glanced at the others before turning her back to them, her voice hushed. "The doctor performed a pelvic exam to determine if there'd been any tearing or other injuries. She discovered some scarring."

She paused a moment, then continued when it became obvious Madoc was waiting for her to finish. "How long ago was the abortion?"

Madoc's vision blurred. He saw her lips moving, but nothing the nurse was saying penetrated the fullness in his ears. Elias's words, however, did.

"I can answer that." Elias took the nurse by the arm and ushered her a few steps away.

Madoc felt a slight pressure begin to build behind his eyes as he stared at Elias, barely aware of the gentle squeeze on his shoulder.

"I can go up first. Will you be alright here?"

Madoc tore his eyes from Elias, looking at Rowan for a

moment before dropping his head just enough to pass for a nod, not raising his gaze until he heard the quiet thud of the door shutting.

The room seemed hollow now that they were alone. Elias motioned towards the settees by the fireplace. Madoc sank into the cushions, feeling as if his soul had drained from his body, leaving behind a numb shell.

Elias looked into the fire, red-rimmed eyes reflecting tiny sparkles from the blaze. "I had been assigned tae the training Squadron in Surrey as OIC of the medical clinic."

Most of the troops were away on a four day pass, so he'd decided to spend the evening in his quarters after pulling a double-shift. He'd not even gotten his boots off when there was a knock at his door. After a quick debate with himself, he decided to answer it.

A young female trainee staggered in, nearly doubled over with abdominal pain. She had been looking for a mate of hers from the clinic, but had found his room by mistake. It took the threat of notifying her chain of command before she finally broke down and told him what was going on.

Without offering any details, she told him that she'd recently discovered she was pregnant. During the pass, she'd found a place that performed abortions; mostly for prostitutes under the legal age of sixteen or women wishing to avoid the bureaucracy of the more reputable clinics. She chose it because she knew no questions would be asked, which meant no one would know that she was a soldier, much less a trainee.

Looking back, he still didn't know why he agreed to help her, but help her he did, on the condition that she let him take her to the clinic. For whatever reason, she trusted him to keep his word. The official report read food poison-ing; she recovered and returned to training. A follow-up exam revealed that she'd suffered a uterine perforation, as well as intrauterine adhesions, resultant of the D&C. In her case, the scarring was extensive enough to cause infertility.

"The mate she'd been looking for was the one who had performed the test for her, on the sly." Elias leaned forward into Madoc's line of sight. "Kyrie wasna far enough along when she arrived for it to show during her initial physical. It was weeks after she left Làidir that she found out."

The lull after Elias finished speaking seemed palpable; the crackle of the fire was the only sounds in the room, which gave Madoc time to digest what he'd just heard.

A thought struck Madoc, something he'd not stopped to consider until just then. "In the time since we met, did you ever consider telling me? That I had a right to know?"

Elias met Madoc's gaze without the slightest hesitation. "Not even once."

Madoc snapped to his feet, feeling as if he were suffo-cating and filled with the urge to escape the lifetime that had been the last hour.

The brass doorknob felt frigid in his hand, then warmed the few seconds he stood holding it. "Everyone keeps saying I know her so well." He jerked the door open. "I'm beginning to think I don't know her at all."

Madoc hugged his arms around his chest as he rushed into the garden, no longer able to hold his tears. He ran a hand over his face, fighting the urge to vomit.

No light shone from the castle, save for one or two windows blazing through the dark. Everywhere he looked, he saw evidence of life, but had never felt more alone, more isolated. So much pain muddled together, he couldn't tell what began where.

He drew a deep breath, still trying to process all that he'd taken in. A part of him had lived and died, and he'd not even known. A son? A daughter? Perhaps both. He closed his eyes, the past ten years falling away, bringing him back to the last summer Kyrie visited before leaving for training.

Flowers outlining the loch were still full of color, while the mixed perfume of bogbeans and bluebells floated delicately in the air.

Leaving his robe on the bank, he dove off the flat rock that stuck out over the edge of the water. He surfaced to see Kyrie sitting on the rock.

Her thin robe left little to the imagination as it formed to every line and curve. Curly hair piled on top of her head in such a way it made him want to taste the skin of her neck.

"A little late for a swim, isn't it?" Her dark eyes sparkled with a mischievous glint.

"I couldn't sleep." He waded closer, the water only chest deep. "How did you know where to find me?"

"I just know you that well." She gazed up at the sky. "It's beautiful out."

Not as beautiful as you, he thought. "Another

dream?"

She smiled a bit sheepishly. "Is it that obvious?"

"I just know you that well." He smiled.

She looked at him. "I went to your room. When I didn't find you there, I knew to come here."

"I'm sorry. Did you want someone to talk to?"

"Not someone. You. And who said I wanted to talk?"

She rose and let her robe drop to her feet, meeting his gaze without the hint of shyness or reserve. Soft, round lines of a young girl had been replaced by the sleek leanness of a woman fully-formed.

She stepped down into the water. He heard a quick intake of breath and realized it had come from him as she wrapped her arms around his neck.

Knowing full well she'd never been with anyone before caused him to hesitate, but only until he felt her lips feather slow kisses along his jaw. In a moment of decision, he drew her tightly against him and lowered his mouth to hers.

She was not his first, nor had she been the last. But, it was never the same as it was with her. Until now he had thought she'd felt the same way.

He wiped his sleeve across his face and walked back to the castle. With no one in sight, it seemed as gutted as he felt inside. The hallway was dark and empty as he walked past Kyrie's room and down to his, shutting the door behind him.

Fingertips stroked the side of my face, slight calluses tickling my cheek. With no small effort, I pulled myself through the fog of my dreams.

Every inch of my body felt battered to the bone. My bottom lip felt gummy from some sort of salve. I opened my eyes.

I sucked in as hard and deep as I could, desperate to draw a breath, straining to see through the white, smoky fog filling every inch of my vision. Someone grasped my left arm. I cried out before I could stop myself.

"It's alright, Petal."

I recognized my uncle's voice, felt his hand on my face, turning me towards him. "It's alright. I'm here."

Bile churned into my throat. "My eyes won't open. I c-can't breathe… can't breathe."

"Just take it slow." He pressed against my shoulders to keep me still.

Sharp pains shot through my arm as he checked the bandage on my right arm, the wound stinging as the gauze pulled free from broken skin.

He eased it back into place, brushing my hair off my forehead. "I'll just go get…"

"No! Please, don't go." I reached out, opening and closing my fingers until I found his arm. "He'll come back soon. Just stay with me until then."

I laid my head on my pillow, still clutching his sleeve. Yes, he'll be here soon.

Rowan brushed a thumb over Kyrie's wet cheek. He hadn't the heart to tell her it had been close to three days since the accident. He and Elias had been alternating shifts so she wouldn't wake up alone. Madoc hadn't even darkened the door.

"Shhhh… there you are." Before the last syllable left his lips, she had drifted back to sleep.

After a moment, something seemed to startle her awake, then she turned her face towards his hand. He reached over to turn down the bedside lantern and stopped, realizing there was no need, feeling as if he'd just been punched in the gut.

Her breathing evened, but her grip on his sleeve remained tight. He watched her for a moment or two. Laying a hand on hers, he slid off the side of the bed and leaned back against it, closing his eyes.

Chapter Eleven

Rowan shoved his hands in his jeans pocket, the early morning chill seeping through both wool shirt and under-shirt as he headed for the stables. The air was still, and the sky displayed the faint colors of predawn.

He'd left Kyrie a little before two in the morning. Afraid of sleeping too late, he tossed and turned most of the time he laid there, only to rise before the sun came up with his shoulder in bits.

The stable was quiet, though not for much longer, as the horses were beginning to neigh for their morning meal.

Madoc was saddling up Butterscotch, her yellow/brown coat warm in the low light. Rowan looked across her back and waited, noticing the sharp movements of Madoc's hands, the tightness around his lips.

The fact that Madoc had yet to speak was a signal that conversation of any sort was not welcome. Normally Rowan would have respected that, but this time would have to be an exception.

"Headed out for a ride?" Rowan asked, pretending to check one of the cinches.

Madoc nodded without looking up.

"Haven't seen much of you lately. Kyrie..." Rowan noticed Madoc tightening the leather straps of the saddlebags with just a bit more force than necessary, "… was wondering when you were coming up?"

Madoc met Rowan's gaze, his eyes clear and unreadable save for the dark circles under them, then gathered the reins in his hand and headed for the stable door.

"You have t'go see her." Rowan caught the bridle, and then walked round to stand in front of Madoc. "She is waiting for you."

Madoc's eyes narrowed, a strange and dangerous calm in their silvery depths.

"Maybe she shouldn't." He clucked his tongue and tugged the reins.

Rowan stepped out of the way, running his hand through his hair. "She has been a bit preoccupied since she came back."

Madoc stopped just inside the door of the stable, the dark outline of his body contrasting with the morning light that seemed almost afraid to enter the door. Rowan decided to press on.

"I know what it's like to feel betrayed by the one you love the most in the world. I know what it's like to lose a child, as well."

Rowan walked up behind Madoc and put a hand on his shoulder. "For both your sakes, go talk to her."

Without a word, Madoc passed the reins back and walked out the door.

Rowan stroked Butterscotch's neck, feeling the tears begin as the icy fingers of the past clasped his heart. Bowing his head, he gave himself over to the grief and regret that had haunted him for so long.

I was maneuvering my pillows to prop-up a bit when I heard the door creak open. "I said I'm not hungry."

The presence filling the room alerted me to the identity of my visitor. His scent caused every hair on my body to stand at attention. I could hear the deep rhythm of his breathing from across the room. My eyes watered at the near over-stimulation of my senses. I turned towards the door, squinting to try and make out some sort of shape through the milky haze.

The sound of his voice prickled along my eardrums. "I've received a message from Garret, asking me to come to Stirling."

"Oh." My chest tightened. "How long will you be…?"

Again I heard the creak, this time much faster, and my words were cut-off by the door slamming shut.

I leaned my head back and closed my eyes. "Gone."

Morgan lounged on a velvet reading settee in her father's private study, sipping her sherry and listening to the voices coming closer to the door.

Nic was touring a potential site, affording the opportunity to come home to Stirling with little explanation. Fiona would be sure to send word when he was on his way back to Edinburgh.

Morgan heard voices nearing the door. Hugh La'Tier

followed her father into the room, eyes widening at the sight of her. He crossed the room at once, a broad smile on his thick face.

"Morgan! I wasn't expecting you here." he kissed her hand, then turned back to Garret, wiping the slight sheen from his bald head. "I've a gob like an Arab's flip-flop."

After ensuring both their glasses were suitably full, Garret sat down in a fireplace chair and waited patiently as Hugh attempted to cross his stout legs, then gave up.

"So, you wanted to see me regarding the Anglanders. Have you heard of something stirring?" Hugh took a generous sip.

Morgan caught the look her father shot her out of the corner of his eye. He swirled the amber liquid in his glass, then looked at Hugh. "As a matter of fact, I have."

"Right this way, sir."

The senior member of the house staff led Madoc down the first floor of the King's Old Building and into what was without a doubt the most elaborate room he'd ever seen.

A king size rice-cut four poster bed carved from solid mahogany with matching armoire and secretary were tastefully complimented by silver framed paintings hanging on the walls. Crown molding ran along the ceiling, the dark ridges and lines contrasting with light gray paisley wallpaper.

He'd felt a bit strange letting someone carry his bag for him, especially as the gray and black suit with satin trim and matching velvet gloves the old gent sported was finer than anything he himself had ever owned.

"Supper will be at six. Should I sort something for you in the meantime?"

Madoc crossed his arms over his denim clad chest for lack of anything else to do with his hands. "Perhaps something to drink."

"Yes, sir." The butler nodded, shutting the door on his way out.

Madoc stowed his bag under the bench chair at the foot of the bed, feeling a nervous excitement at his new surroundings, wondering if all the guestrooms here were this posh.

"You made it, I see."

He spun around to face his sister, admiring the glow the pale lavender of her velvet dress gave her, the faint aroma of rosewater following her into the room.

"Morgan. I wasn't expecting…" Madoc began.

"Me to be here?" She finished for him, smiling. "I just came round to see if you were settled."

A quick familiarity lay between them as she led him over to the carved double back loveseat by the window. He was beginning to not feel so out of place.

The door opened again and a small woman in a black dress and white apron toddled in, slender arms and legs not quite matching the roundness of her body. She placed a tray with a crystal decanter set on the table in front of them, curtsied, and left at Morgan's nod.

She offered him a glass. "Here you are."

The pungent smokiness rising from the snifter burned his nose slightly. His traitorous features twisted into a protesting grimace as painful warmth crawled down his throat.

"Don't drink much, do you?" She chuckled, swirling the liquid in her glass before taking a sip.

He shook his head, not trusting his singed vocal cords to function properly without causing a coughing fit.

She cocked a brow at him, a slight smile covering her delicate features. "Bowmore is an acquired taste."

He rose, setting his glass on the tray. "Perhaps we can finish this later. I haven't seen Garret or Hugh since I've arrived and I'm certain they're waiting."

"Oh, I'm certain they aren't. They don't even know you are here." She poured them each another drink. "The message Hugh received was from Father. The message you received was from me."

The sun filtered its last tired rays through the window-pane, bouncing off the near to empty bottle.

Madoc noticed Morgan's hair seemed to be catching and playing with the light in an almost angelic way. Rowan had told him his mother had unusual eyes, and he'd always wondered what they looked like. Now he knew.

"How long has Hugh been here?" Madoc asked.

"He arrived yesterday evening," Morgan answered. "When the 61st Earl of Mar summons a person, even if said person is the Assistant to the Minister of Security, it's best to make an appearance."

Madoc looked over at Morgan's glass, then swirled his

drink, hypnotized by the glowing amber liquid.

"Especially when this particular Earl's son-in-law is the Prime Minister of Alba." He looked up at her. "I was... delayed, but I'm here now."

He sat his glass down hard, feeling a bit odd from the whisky. Odd, as well as annoyed.

He rose to offer a hand to his sister. "Are you hungry?"

With a sly smile, she took his hand. "Absolutely famished."

They stood just outside the door of the private dining room, peeking in. Garret sat at the end of the table with his back to the door. A tall, well-dressed man placed two full snifters of brandy on the table and stepped back.

"... So, there was nothing left for me to do but offer my most humble apologies for her dress," Hugh choked out with a laugh.

Garret laughed, a foreign sound to Madoc, as he couldn't remember ever hearing it before.

"Let's join them, shall we?" Raising her voice, she spoke to Hugh and Garret. "Now then, gentlemen."

"Well, any longer and I..." Garret trailed off looking almost as if his bollocks were on the receiving end of a good, swift kick.

"Monss!" Hugh rose halfway out of his chair. "Christ, man. I've not seen you since University."

"Sit down, La'Tier. I see you are wearing your hair much shorter these days," Madoc teased, slapping him soundly on his thick back.

"Ha. Ha." Hugh shook his head, rolling his eyes. "You always were the funny one, weren't you?"

"No, I was the one who liked women," Madoc parried with a wink at Morgan.

The server turned to Garret. "Sir, will the gentleman be staying for dinner?"

As Garret drew a breath to answer, Madoc piped in. "Yes, the gentleman will."

He plopped down into a chair next to Hugh and flipped his napkin across his lap, then looked at Garret and smiled. "So, what's for dinner... Papa?"

Garret looked as if something very small and painful had just struck him in the eye.

The bedroom door almost banged the wall before Madoc caught it, the long curtains sucking in and then resting again when he shut it behind them, moonlight peeking in the crack.

Morgan's voice was hoarse from laughing. "I thought he was going to have a seizure when you called him 'Papa.'"

"Almost as good as the time I put honey in Rowan's hand while he was asleep. Until he woke up, that is." He reached around and rubbed himself on the rear before sitting down on the loveseat with his back to the window. Sighing, he laced his fingers behind his head and stretched his legs out in front of him.

"So I remember."

The voice behind him sounded soft and familiar. He

turned as if moving would cause some treasure to disap-
pear right from his very hand. This one, however, didn't.
Light years away, he heard Morgan's voice.

"Hello, Threas. It's good to see you."

CHApCER CWELVE

Elias followed Rowan across the pitch.

Smatterings of dark clouds contrasted against the brilliant azure background, as June opened the door for the scorching months of the coming Second Season. Classes had been cancelled for the day in lieu of the annual Special Olympics.

"I'll introduce you t'Aaron, then I'll go after Kyrie. She and Miyanna loved the games." Rowan's eyes wilted a moment, then he cleared his throat. "Here he is."

A small-framed child around the age of six sat in a pushchair quietly soaking in the entire bustle swirling around him, hardly noticing the young lass waiting with him until properly relieved. Catching sight of Rowan's nod, she jogged off into the swarm.

Rowan leaned down next to Aaron. "Aaron, this is Elias. He's going t'be your partner for the day."

In a burst of excitement, Aaron clapped the palm of one hand on the back of the other, both of which were slightly bowed at the wrist.

Rowan stood up and gestured towards the crowd. "You can tell what year the students are by the number on the back of their shirts."

Just as Rowan finished speaking, Aaron parroted every word and syllable, matching his accent perfectly.

Rowan smiled and mussed Aaron's hair a bit, inspiring another clapping fit. "I'll leave you to it."

Rowan strode across the game field, turning to look here and there. Not only had he volunteered to help organize today's event and tomorrow's banquet, he'd also been putting his civil engineering experience to good use, working on an improved design of the school greenhouses. The more Elias got to know him, the more apparent it became as to why Kyrie held him in such high regard.

Aaron's exuberance bubbled up again in the form of giggles intermingled with sporadic hand clapping. Rowan had said Aaron was unable to walk due to Palsy, but could support his body weight for a few seconds when assisted with balancing.

His thin fingers were of minimal use, but he could target his touch with a fair amount of accuracy. The characteristic which drew the most attention was the boy's eyes. The cheerfulness in their observant brown depths would have rivaled the sun on its brightest day.

Elias squatted in front of Aaron, resting his hands on the arms of the chair. "Are ye ready?"

Aaron went very still, the smile dropping and an open curiosity taking its place, the iris of his left eye drifting a millimeter or two towards the outside corner. In the time it takes a molecule to travel, Aaron began to giggle again, repeating Elias's question with every roll and inflection.

Elias smiled and tried again. "How about the ball toss first?" But, before the last word past his lips, Aaron exploded into another fit of giggles.

"How about the ball toss first?" Aaron rolled out an impressive sounding burr, clapping his hands at Elias's laugh.

"Aye, laddie. Dinna min' if I do." Elias used an exaggerated intonation to the extreme delight of his young companion.

Grasping the handles of Aaron's chair, they headed for the first event of the day.

The sun had been blistering all morning. After the ball toss, bowling, and the Touch game, Aaron let it be known he was hungry, a baffling state after watching what his cup-sized stomach had held during lunch.

Elias parked Aaron under the tent at the end of the table closest to the snack stand, keeping him in sight while securing two massive popcorn balls for desert.

Elias sat down and broke one in half. "Here ye are, ane gustie gree tae line yer wame."

At the moment, Aaron seemed more interested in rubbing his left eye than entertaining dialect or snacks. Elias leaned in a bit for a closer look. "What ails ye, mannie?"

Aaron then abandoned rubbing his eye, resorting instead to backhanding himself in the offending area. Elias reach out and held him by the forearm. Aaron responded by groaning and grunting, straining in an unsuccessful attempt at breaking free.

"Here now. That willna help, but make it worse, and ye keep on like that." He laid the half a popcorn ball back on the wrapper and then used a thumb to gentle raise Aaron's eyelid a bit.

Small red particles were smattered on the iris and surrounding white of Aaron's eye, most likely from the large feather in the Touch Game. After the blindfold was removed, Aaron rubbed the plume hard across his face enjoying the tickle of it.

Elias called over his shoulder. "Could someone be sae kind as tae fetch… SHITE!"

The explicative pealed through the tent like the ringing of a bell, muting every bit of the surrounding noise. A small ring of bright red teeth marks shone on the meaty part of Elias's hand just below his thumb.

He shook his head. "Ye wee diel."

Aaron leaned back, his eyes drooping half-shut, his voice barely above a whisper. "Aye."

Aaron displayed only mild frustration at being tended to, growling and grimacing once or twice.

"There." Elias dabbed away the final drops of Clary solution. "Better, aye?"

Aaron answered by roughly wiping his nose, leaving behind a prize boogie perched on the back of his hand.

"Och! Ye willna be needin' that." Elias wiped it off with a towel, handing that along with the first aid kit off to the school nurse.

It was nearing early evening; the sun was low, but the heat had yet to concede. Most of the events were beginning to shut down, with only a handful still open.

Elias had noticed how Aaron would lift his legs in his chair, straining against the strap that kept him from kicking out during muscle spasms.

He looked out over the field and saw one of the remaining events was the 20-meter Fun Run. Elias cocked a brow at Aaron. "How about it, mannie?"

Over by the starting line, Elias un-strapped Aaron and held him facing outward, one arm around his tiny waist and the other curved under his bottom.

Aaron giggled and squirmed as he looked down at the other students lined up beside them.

"I think he wants you to put him down," a second grader advised, whilst wiry legs the color of ebony visible below her skirt wriggled with pent up energy.

Elias nodded towards her. "Ye seem a fair runner."

She shrugged her lanky shoulders in a modest gesture, smoothing a stray hair back into the neat bun on top of her head.

A classmate standing next to her smacked her on the arm, his smile reminding Elias of a jack-o-lantern.

"She's slow as a snail. She never wins a race." He rolled his eyes, shaking his head. "I'll be waitin' for ya' at the finish line, Turtle!"

Her face took on a look of disbelief, dark eyes wide, head turning slowly from side to side. "Who does he think he is?" She laid her hand against her chest. "He will never beat me."

A whistle blast drew everyone's attention to the official standing offside. She raised a hand. "Runners! On your mark! Get set! Go!"

Elias took off at a slow jog with Aaron, watching the

look on the boy's face turn from shocked surprise to the re-alization of freedom. Too busy watching Aaron, he'd failed to notice the other runners until that moment.

Each of them had run to the finish line, but hadn't crossed it, instead turning to face Aaron and call shouts of encouragement, sending Aaron into a near epileptic fit of enthusiasm. If there had been any doubt before, the feel of strength in Aaron's leg muscles argued successfully against it.

Elias stopped a couple of meters short of the red ribbon and stood Aaron on the ground, supporting most of his weight for him. Aaron was moving almost as soon as his feet touched the ground, his steps laborious to say the least. Several times, Elias had to reach forward and untangle Aaron's feet and legs, wishing he'd thought to take off the huge shoes Aaron was wearing.

"I'm doing it! I'm doing it!" Aaron squealed, his right palm clapping madly on the back of his left hand.

The children were now jumping up and down, chanting Aaron's name.

Just as they reached the finish line, the children turned back around, took a step back, and stood there, letting Aaron break the ribbon in triumph.

Elias lifted Aaron high into the air, while the children danced circles around them, shouting victory chants with Aaron's name. The girl from the starting line tugged at Elias's belt.

"Here's his ribbon!" she screeched in a voice that could have cracked glass.

Taking the ribbon from her, Elias held it close enough to let Aaron grasp it, rubbing it against his face as he looked up at Elias.

"I'm a winner!" Aaron laid his head against Elias's chest and spoke in a much more subdued tone. "I'm a winner."

The rest of the children had begun milling over to their teachers, the moment of exhilaration fading into quiet.

Elias rested his chin on top of Aaron's head, a single tear slipping into the lad's thick, wavy hair. "Aye. You're a winner."

I sat in the garden, feeling much like a three-year-old forced to sit through a church service.

Uncle Rowan had hounded me all day to go to the Special Olympics, but finally settled for me coming outside for a bit. It had only been about ten minutes and I already wanted to pack it in.

My cheeks felt sunburned, my back ached, and I wanted to lie down; my first real walk, save for trips to the loo, left me dizzy and nauseous. My acquiescence was on the condition of him coming to collect me within the hour.

Engrossed in showering myself with the pity from which I was denied by others, I almost didn't notice the footsteps rushing closer. Before I could even ask who was there, the frantic voice of a young child reached me.

"You have to come!"

The boy sounded no more than six or seven. When he was close enough to grab me, I was able to make out the barest hint of shape and movement. He urged me to my feet.

"What's wrong?" I felt myself being towed along, legs stiff with the fear of stumbling.

"Jamie and me went down the loch 'cuz we wanted to go fishin' and he fell off that big rock!" he cried, tugging me harder with every step.

The sweet scent of flowers along the path was almost sickening. I listened for splashing, but didn't hear any. As the smell of the water grew stronger, the boy cried out.

"Jamie!"

"What is it?" My heart was pounding, and I was winded from the short walk down the path.

"He's gone! He's gone!" he bellowed and moaned.

All conscious thought stopped. I slipped out of my shoes and ran towards the water, ignoring the stones pricking the soles of my feet, my breath sucking in sharply when it splashed around my thighs.

"Go find help!" Drawing as deep a breath as I could, I dove in.

All sound died down to an eerie stillness as the cold water enveloped me. I squinted to try and see in the darkness, feeling it would somehow help. I knew the rock was to the right from the path facing the loch, so I swam in that direction.

I made great sweeping motions with my arms, praying I might brush an arm or leg. When my lungs felt near to bursting, I turned to kick up towards the surface for air when I thought I heard someone call out to me.

"Over there! Under the rock!"

The voice sounded faint, but clear and it barely skimmed my consciousness it shouldn't be. I dove down and kicked hard towards the rock. Reaching my hands out in front of me, I could feel its smooth surface and pushed my way down until I could feel along the bottom edge.

My fingertips brushed something more forgiving than stone. I wrapped my hand around a leg and pulled. I clasped the small body against my own and kicked hard for the surface.

The breath I'd been holding exploded from my lungs to make room for fresh air. Feeling my feet leave the water, I knelt to stretch Jamie out in front of me, rain starting to patter my back with fruitless effort, wet as I already was.

Jamie wasn't coughing nor was his chest moving. I felt his neck, praying for a pulse. The faint thump against my fingers drummed in answer. I found his mouth, leaned down, and began breathing my air into his lungs. Please breathe, please breathe.

A vibration in his chest began before he actually started to cough. A loud gagging followed as Jamie forced the water out.

Footsteps thundered down the path towards us. I could hear Jared speaking to Jamie as strong arms lifted me up against the massive hardness of a chest.

Elias growled low as he exhaled, his voice tinged with exasperation and relief. "Christ, Mac. If ye wanted tae go for a swim, all ye had tae do was ask."

"Now, then. All done." The nurse placed the used syringe in the waste receptacle before washing her hands and reaching for the sweets. Jamie didn't return the smile she offered, but reached through the opening of the blanket wrapped around him to snatch the treat from her and pop it in his mouth.

Elias took a tissue and held it in front of Jamie's mouth, contemplating shaking the little prick by the ankles when he swallowed it whole instead of spitting it out.

Jamie had been scheduled for his vaccinations the following week, but between the chill and any bacteria squiggling about in the water, Elias thought it best to bring him into the clinic.

Oral Polio, as well as mumps, measles, and rubella, was a standard vaccination for a child. Typhoid, cholera, and influenza were routinely given to soldiers, as well as civilians with the means for proper medical care. The small vial with a red slash across the label was a complete surprise. WNV-40 was one, as far as he knew, limited for military use. He noticed the nurse smiling at him.

"Don't be too shocked. It's not full strength. We still push the use of insect repellent during mosquito season." She motioned to the small, brown mole on Jamie's neck. "Have you been keeping an eye on that?"

"Aye." Elias scrutinized the perfect roundness of it. "He's had it as long as I've known him. It might be best tae hae it removed, nonetheless."

Once everything was tidied up, she moved to the door, her hips rocking side to side causing her arse cheeks to jiggle underneath her white uniform. "You know, skin growths are not to be taken lightly. Perhaps you need a thorough going over, as well."

Elias flashed a grin. "Och, I'm always willing tae take the matter tae hand. Sometimes even twice in one day."

He could still hear her cackling as she walked down the hall.

Elias eased Jamie's bedroom door shut. Jamie had finished off his broth, falling asleep with the mug still in hand.

Nearing Kyrie's room, Elias could hear curses virtually striking the door like knives. Rowan had mentioned that she had, in a less than gracious manner, expressed her desire to have supper on her own.

After a quick rap on the door, he walked in without invitation, finding her sitting up in bed with a tray of food across her lap.

"Dammit, I said…" her head snapped up, "… oh, it's you."

"Well done." He shut the door behind him, then walked over to stand by the bed. "How could ye tell?

"I can make out enough of your shape to judge your size. You are the biggest fucker around here." She turned her attention back to her meal. "And besides, I can tell by the way you smell."

"Och, yer sae kind," he chuckled. "So, how's it goin'?"

A small river of spilt cider ran around the tray, a pool of it nesting in the center of her mashed tatties like homemade bree. Only the very edge of the brisket she was sawing at remained on the plate.

He watched her struggle and knock things about for a moment or two before going to fetch a small hand towel from the cludgie. He lowered the toilet lid and sat down, clutching the towel in both hands, closing his eyes.

After a few deep breaths, he nodded to himself and went back in, taking a seat beside her. Dabbing the cider from the tray with one hand, he laid the other one on hers to keep them out of the way.

Her brow furrowed. "I can…"

"You can fuckin' listen is what ye can do. Jackass." Dropping the sodden towel to the floor, he took her knife and fork, using them to pull the meat back onto her plate. "Yer meat is at yer six o'clock. Yer tatties at three. Yer bread tae yer nine. Now, gi' me yer hands."

She stared straight ahead, her face unreadable. Slowly, she raised her hands, palms upward.

"Yer fork is in yer left; the knife in yer right. Go easy, and listen for the sound o' knife on the plate."

After she'd managed a few bites, he took her mug and rose. "How about a wee bit o' cider tae wash it down?"

"So, you're coming back, then?"

He'd taken no more than a step or two when the slight tremor of her voice stopped him. Her brows were lifted, a delicate crease dead center of dark amber brows.

"Aye. I'm coming back," he answered.

Knife and fork were poised above her meat. "I'll just wait for you, then. I'm a bit thirsty."

Elias smiled, knowing that was as close to admitting the need for help as she was likely to come. "I'll be right back."

He'd just stepped into the hallway when he heard her call to him.

"By the way… I like the gravy."

I woke to a supernatural stillness which never visits during the day.

My throat had a raspy dryness that made me feel like I was swallowing pins, my nightshirt clinging to the sweat on my back. I felt for the edge of the nightstand and inched my hand over to the glass of water, stopping when I felt the coolness on my fingertips. Careful not to spill, I raised it to my lips, the contents bathing my throat in relief.

I folded the covers back to air my sheets a bit as I visualized the layout of the room, and then counted my steps to the window, feeling down the frame to find the lock. The whistle of the wind in the trees, an owl hooting in the distance, and other sounds of night all seemed to ease the feeling of disappearing.

My knees touched the chair three steps from the window, so I sat down and began to think of Jamie. I thanked God I'd been able to help him, and then began to wonder if he hadn't helped me just as much. To say I felt some sort of control again would be a gross understatement. It was more than that. I was beginning to feel like me.

Tomorrow promised to be a full day. Since I seemed to be getting on well in sensory and visualization training, Elias claimed my promise to start an exercise program. Tarrick had asked if I'd much experience with something like Judo. During training we'd been taught hand-to-hand, which I found enjoyable except for the first few days after the...

I leaned my head back and closed my eyes, a damp

breeze reaching in the window to caress my skin. There should have been some word from Maddy by now. There had not. If Rowan had heard anything, he wasn't telling me.

The mist began to thicken into rain. I heaved a deep sigh and closed the window before going back to bed and the chaos of my dreams.

Chapter Thirteen

Month One, Second Season
July

"Dinna go onto the rock!" Elias watched Jamie back off the rock, then ease closer to the edge of the water.

Morning sun just skimmed the tops of the pines and made the loch glisten like gemstones. Light dappled through branches onto the blanket where he and Kyrie sat watching Jamie fish.

Elias wiped the sheen of sweat hanging on his forehead with the heel of his hand. The water level hadn't begun to shrink from shore yet, a steady flow pouring over the spillway. Perhaps he'd get a chance before they headed back to see if that was indeed maidenhair fern growing in the shade on the opposite embankment.

Kyrie had said that Rowan designed the loch when she was just a wee thing. If looking at his work now hadn't been a testament to his engineering skill, years ago he'd also been the lead designer for the remodeling of Ramsey Gardens.

Jamie frowned down at his fishing pole, having managed to hook the hem of his shirt for the second time. It would be much easier if Jamie would throw right-handed and not left, though it was just as well. Unless Jamie managed a lusty *sluagh-gairn* so as to rouse the fish from the water, his angling skills would be a moot point.

Kyrie adjusted her sunglasses after wiping more sunscreen on her face. He was amazed at how she'd handled everything over the last few months. Amazed, but not surprised.

"Are you still taking Jamie to Corrie with you?" She laid back and stretched her arms above her head, linking her fingers and bending her knees. "I have to meet Tarrick this afternoon for a workout. Jamie's going to be so surprised tomorrow."

He brushed a curl from her face and traced the fine line of her nose, warm against the tip of his finger. "Aye and aye, he will be. D'ye want me to go by yer wee cheese shop for anythin'?"

The gift of a fast metabolism kept most of what she ate from showing, her body having a natural leanness. The hem of her tank top just barely brushed the waistband of the short jeans she liked to wear, but he could never remember the name of. The cuffed hem drew his attention from her flat stomach to shapely calf muscles, rippling under tanned skin as she curled and stretched her toes.

"Surprise me." She rubbed the back of her hand across her forehead. "I'll like anything you bring back, I'm sure."

He laid his arm next to hers, marveling at how much darker she was than him, not surprising considering her lineage. Her father's side was all Alban; however, her mother's side had a somewhat interesting history.

Kyrie's great-grandfather was a Spanish missionary

from Palma who had been sent to serve in Tunisia. He'd spent his first few months in country reaching out to several of the small, remote villages. One of the families he worked with had a daughter around the same age he was. Elias wasn't sure of the whole story, but did know that Kyrie's great-grandfather helped her leave Tunisia and brought her to Spain. The two married a short time later, Kyrie's grandmother being born not long after the ceremony. No one really knows why, but they immigrated to Yorkshire when their daughter was only two years old.

Elias began thinking how different things would be if they had never decided to leave Spain, but was interrupted by a squeal coming from the water's edge, followed by a loud splash. His peripheral vision caught a flash of Kyrie sitting bolt upright in the second before he ran over to Jamie.

Fishing line looped around one small leg and the pole was cast to the side. A large catfish was secured under an arm in what could best be described as a headlock. The front of Jamie's blonde hair matted against his forehead; he was grinning so hard he risked a strained muscle.

"Looks like I caught a fish!" Jamie screeched, keeping a death-grip on his single spoil.

Elias laughed as he freed Jamie's leg. "Aye, *a bhalaich*, ye certainly did."

Elias and a dried Jamie tied their horse to the rail and stepped up on the porch of the shop.

Having seen the day's catch properly attended, they rode into Corrie and made their way to a shop Rowan had told him about.

Seth, Donny, and Seamas had gone to see what the pub scene was like and would meet up them in an hour or two.

The wind made a whooshing sound mixed with the jingling of a bell as the door shut behind them. The shop was small, but well organized and inviting, the polished oak floor reflecting light and shapes.

Sharp scents of fresh spices filled the room along with those of various candles. Displays of dried flowers and grasses adorned the walls. A wide variety of staples sat on the shelves lining the outside of the room. Smaller shelves with giftware, such as porcelain and crystal imported from neighboring regions, filled the middle of the room.

Elias gave Jamie a warning look. "Dinna touch a thing. This shouldna take long."

Jamie rolled his eyes, yanking his sagging pants back into place, then just stood scratching his side through his shirt.

Footsteps approached the drape hanging over the door behind the counter, and then the panel flipped aside to reveal a smallish old fellow, smiling as he passed through.

Had they been side by side, Elias could have easily rested his arm on the crown of the man's head. His age was impossible to guess, as he couldn't have been as long in the horn as he looked and still be vertical.

Networks of lines crisscrossed his face and forearms visible below rolled up sleeves. Cordial greeting and handshake done, the shopkeeper rested slender hands lightly on the built-in cutting board.

"Whit it like?" A crumpled eyelid drooped further into a quick wink in Jamie's direction.

Elias grinned at the familiar intonation, pulling a slip of paper from his pocket. "I hae somethin' I'm wantin' tae cook and am in need of certain ingredients."

"Och, a fine recipe, that one," the frown of concentration the old one wore was lost in the folds of his brow. A withered finger trembled above an item on the list. "I've all, but this. Ah'll hae a keek in back tae be sure."

No sooner had the curtain come to rest than Elias heard a suspicious clink. Whipping around, he saw Jamie attempting to lift a crystal rose from one of the shelves.

Elias glared, keeping his voice hushed. "Min' yersel!"

Jamie answered with a mind-your-own-business look before picking up the flower in a shaky hand, eyeing it with a defiant tilt to his chin.

In two steps, Elias crossed over to snatch it away and place it back on the shelf, then grab Jamie by the chin. "Touch that again and I'll skelp ye proper."

The rising voice of the shopkeeper preceded the flip of the curtain. "I dinna hae that one, and ye try this it should work."

With a last threatening look at Jamie, Elias walked over to the counter and took the small jar, nodding his thanks. He drew breath to speak, but was interrupted by a loud crash behind him. Surrounding Jamie on the floor were the crystal shards of the forbidden flower.

Elias managed to crush the urge to wrap his hands around Jamie's neck long enough to apologize and insist on paying for the damaged merchandise, as well as his goods.

No sooner had they cleared the door than Elias knelt

and spun Jamie around to face him. "I told you not tae touch that flower."

"I didn't touch that flower," Jamie brushed Elias's hand aside in a grand show of distaste. "It was a different flower."

Not quitting while he was ahead, Jamie turned with an air of dismissal. Elias snatched up Jamie by the collar and ushered him into the alley next to the shop.

Finding a place to sit, Elias placed the package on the ground and unceremoniously draped Jamie over his lap, raising his voice over the remonstrations of his captive.

"This is goin' tae hurt you more than it will me." Lifting a hand in preparation, he added, "Trust me."

Elias knocked, then opened Kyrie's door, the evening sun glaring through the window.

Tarrick had said the workout went well for Kyrie, something that had surprised her a lot more than it did Elias. After they were done, Jared accompanied her to her room to wash up before the banquet, which had been a good two hours ago.

"Come on in!" She called out from the cludgie.

He followed the trail of dirty clothes to the door, and pushed it open.

"Mac, it's almost time… oh, pardon me." Elias turned to go back out when he saw her sitting in the tub.

She chuckled. "It's alright. Not like I've grown anything new since you saw me last."

He stood with his hand on the doorknob, wondering if

she could somehow know where he was looking.

"Come wash my back." She held out a bath sponge to him.

The water was a bit cloudy from some sort of bath oil, but he could still make out the roundness of her hips, flattened as they met the bottom of the tub. He took the sponge in his left hand so he could face away from her and began scrubbing with quick strokes.

"Slow down!" she laughed. "I'll need that top layer of skin, you know."

He started out doing as she'd asked. It wasn't until he noticed the smoothness of her skin that he realized he'd been rubbing her back with his bare hand. He also noticed she wasn't stopping him. He laid a hand on her shoulder, intending to make a joke of some sort and leave.

She turned and placed a kiss on the back his hand, then guided it down between her breasts, grazing her belly, and finally into the water.

He told himself he should stop as his traitorous arm circled her shoulders, pressing the softness of her cheek against his.

A small groan slipped from her throat when he ventured deeper, his mouth watering as he imagined the taste of what he touched. A tell-tale swelling foretold what was fast approaching even before the rest of her body did.

She grabbed his wet sleeve; her back curved like a bow. She squeezed his arm with a strangled cry as her body rocked back and forth, a single tear rolling from the corner of her eye.

It was a moment before she eased her grip on his arm. Her voice was husky when she finally spoke. "There's room enough for two."

He eased his hand out of the water, laying his palm against her face, her skin cool to the touch. Pulling her towards him a bit, he pressed a gentle kiss to her forehead.

She was quiet when he took her arm and helped her out of the tub. He folded a bath sheet around her and led her back into the bedroom, then pulled her into his arms and held her.

His shirt dampened where her check pressed against it, her voice strained. "Doc, I'm so sorry..."

"Shhh." He brushed his thumb across her check, catching a tear on the tip.

The kiss only lasted a moment, but it was long enough he could feel how warm and soft her lips were, just a hint damp from the humidity of her bath.

He pressed another one against her forehead. "The banquet starts in about an hour."

Not looking back, he shut the door behind him, muffled sounds of crying tearing at him. Before he could change his mind, he turned and walked down the hall.

Shouts of laughter reverberated off the walls of the Great Hall, the banquet in honor of yesterday's Special Olympics well under way. The gentle glow of chandeliers floated down, relaxing the entire room. Aromas of freshly grilled meats wafted around like banshees, tempting and teasing.

Rowan pushed his plate away feeling as if he'd just ingested an entire Aberdeen Angus. After a quick look around, he unbuttoned his pants, then peered over towards where the long metal tables were set up, decorated with gold and silver foil garlands. Large platters with a variety of meats, to include three large roast pigs, were strategically placed on one of the long tables, a neighboring table filled with various vegetable dishes, and yet another with his personal favorite, desserts.

Kyrie sat back and gingerly rubbed the tiny bulge in her flat belly. "I don't know if I can fit anything else in here."

He cut another glance at the sweets, wondering if he should take his chances and wait or stake his claim now. "They have strawberry cheesecake."

She pushed her sunglasses back up her nose, then eased her hand across the table until her fingertips touched the bottom of her pint glass. "Oh, really?"

An earsplitting wail generating from nearby the dessert table shattered his thoughts. A small crowd was looking down at the floor with much concern. One of the school nurses ran over and crouched down where Rowan couldn't see.

A wave of relief seemed to wash over the onlookers as a girl in her early teens rose shakily to her feet. The nurse helped her over to the nearest bench as the small gathering returned to the business of eating and socializing.

A tug on his sleeve drew his attention from the fray. Jamie gave him a look that was a little too innocent. He put his arm around Jamie. "What have you been up to, boy?"

One shoulder raised in answer as Jamie started pulling away. Rowan looked towards where the crowd had been standing and saw Elias speaking with a friend of the girl who'd been the center of attention. She raised a hand and pointed in Jamie's direction.

Elias began his charge as soon as he caught sight of Jamie. Rowan tightened his arm to no avail as the little rascal slipped from his grip like a skilled escape artist.

Rowan watched as Jamie skillfully predicted his pursuer's approach. As Elias rounded the end of the table, Jamie maneuvered to the opposite end, all the while looking over his shoulder. Elias changed direction, only to be countered by Jamie changing his line of retreat. Their intense, albeit amusing dance lasted only a few seconds before they wound up opposite each other, eyes boring, standing their ground on each side of the table. Which-ever way Elias seemed to shift, Jamie was ready to dart the other. A brilliant shade of red began to radiate from Elias's collar, much to Jamie's delight. Jamie placed a thumb on each temple and fanned his little fingers out.

"Ha! Can't catch me!" He punctuated this statement by thrusting his tongue out, the tip stretching almost down to his chin.

Elias slammed his foot into an empty chair and catapulted himself over the table. Jamie was too shocked to move at first, but as soon as the sole of Elias's boot touched the floor, Jamie's instinct for survival kicked in. Unfortunately, it did so a hair too late.

In one powerful motion, Elias grabbed Jamie by the collar and lifted him from the ground, holding him like some sort of rabid animal. Ignoring Jamie's colorful albeit inept curses, Elias marched towards the large double doors leading out of the Great Hall.

Rowan looked over at Kyrie. Not a word passed her lips

for a full moment or two, and then she turned her face towards him and cocked her head to the side.

"Soooo... cheesecake?"

Rowan buttoned up his sweater, then leaned back in his chair. Empty dishes had been cleared and fires lit in the huge stone fireplaces in preparation for the upcoming entertainment.

Kyrie set her glass down. "Want to move closer?"

He looked round to see where the musicians were setting up. "Yeah, let's."

Rowan took her hand and placed it just above his elbow, then picked up their glasses one at a time. He maneuvered to the table where Elias was sitting, right next to the small dance floor in front of the stage. The rest of the lads were at a nearby table, busy chatting up a couple of birds.

Their position afforded excellent view of the band. Strings twanged in protest at being forced into tune, but finally submitted. Turning to the rest of the group, the lead musician, a little fellow with a neatly trimmed beard and bald head, raised a brow and was answered by strummed chords and drumbeats. They began with two guitars, one *bodhran*, a mandolin, and last, but not least, a set of pipes. After greeting the crowd, they tore into "Trippin' up the Stairs", "The Hay in the Kiln", and "My Darlin' Asleep".

One by one, memories assailed him of Sonia listening to this style of music and the mood it often put her in.

Before the last notes completely died down, applause

erupted around the room. In the subsequent pause, Rowan was surprised to hear Kyrie shout to the band.

"Where's the fiddler!?" She smiled, cutting her eyes in the general direction of Elias, who choked on the brandy he'd been in mid-swig of.

The singer made a grand show of cupping his ear with a hand and looking out at the crowd.

After a moment, Kyrie shouted again, her voice mingling with a few others scattered around in the crowd. "I said, where's the fiddler!?"

He grinned to the crowd before setting his guitar in its stand and walking behind them to where an assortment of instruments lay in wait. Taking up a fiddle, he turned round and held it before the crowd like the head of a fallen foe, then looked straight at Elias. The whoops and cheers made his grin spread wider across his robust face.

"So? What are you waiting for, Doc?" Kyrie turned her face a little more towards Elias, ignoring the rest of the crowd who'd now joined in the cajoling, drumming rhythmically on their tables and chanting the word "fiddler".

Elias rose to a thundering ovation, making his way to the makeshift stage, baring his teeth to the crowd in an exaggerated smile.

Seamas shouted above the quiet murmur of the waiting audience. "Play 'Whiskey in the Jar', ye bastard!"

A fusion of laughter and the sharp intake of breath exploded all round. Donny leaned in to give his cousin a sharp clap on the arm whilst Seth, sitting with his arms across his chest, hung his head and smiled.

"Stop swearin', ye feckin' eejit!" Donny chided.

Seamas touched his mouth with his fingertips, causing

some sitting near him to squeal with laughter, others to frown and shake their heads.

Elias answered with an impressive replication of Donny's twang. "Ah'll get ya's later."

He then hugged the fiddle to his shoulder, the hum of the strings soon joined by the rest of the band and blended into the fluidness of "Bonnie Dundee" followed by "Cock of the North", drawing quite a few dancers to the floor.

The wave of shouts for more kept Elias trapped on stage, but he now seemed to be enjoying himself.

After looking out at Kyrie, Elias turned to the band. They nodded their approval and plucked their strings to make sure they were still in tune. Elias turned back round and closed his eyes as he began the solo notes of "The Rowan Tree". Rowan looked at his niece in surprise, but she looked as taken aback as he was.

"I should have known he would remember," she whispered as she held out her hand.

Rowan scooted his chair over next to her, resting his cheek on the top of her head as she lay against his shoulder.

With magic all its own, the music faded the crowd into a vision of Sonia playing that very song on Rowan's thirtieth birthday.

A four-year-old Kyrie cuddled up in his lap as he rested his chin on the top of her unruly curls. Madoc sat down by Rowan's feet, chin on his skinny little knees, hypnotized with each slide of the bow. Symin stood over by the fire smoking his pipe, Threas pulled in close beside him.

Rowan didn't notice at first when the one song ended and melted into another called "The Battle's O'er". God, I wish it were, he thought to himself. His heart then turned inside itself to find its way back to a little house filled with the song of love and laughter.

Chapter Fourteen

"No! Open mine first!"

Jamie pulled the party hat back on his head for the hundredth time, refusing to let anyone hold it as he opened his presents.

All Jamie could recollect of his birthday was it was sometime in July. To solve the problem, Kyrie had rolled a die which had landed on two, thereby making July 2nd Jamie's official day of celebration.

Rowan subdued the bits of torn wrapping paper and stuffed them into the bin next to the table. Elias kept an eye on the smoke billowing from the large iron barbeque pits whilst affecting exaggerated surprise as Jamie tore away the wrappings to reveal the treasures inside.

One of the girls from Jamie's class passed them to Jamie in such a way Aaron could brush a hand against each and every one, as Jamie refused to accept anything without Aaron's blessing.

"Uncle Rowan! Is mine up there as well?" Kyrie called out to him.

She was at present in a lawn chair not far from the grills, whether to chat with Elias as he cooked or to increase her chances of getting a plate first, who knew.

Rowan looked at each of the packages wrapped in different colored coarse paper until he came across the one signed with a "K". Once the proper ritual had been observed Jamie shredded the wrapping to reveal a blue ball cap with the words "Gone Fishing" neatly stitched on the front. Jamie slapped it on his head, thrilled at the burst of laughter when everyone read it. The last present was a tiny crystal flower which made Rowan wonder at Elias's choice of gift.

Elias lifted his cap and rubbed the heel of his hand across his forehead. "The food is no' quite ready. Ye've time for a game or two."

Jamie's classmate grabbed him by the arm. "How about Hangman?"

When he jerked away, Rowan quickly ushered everyone under the neighboring picnic canopy, feeling immediate relief once they were in the shade. Enlisting the aid of an idle parent, Rowan managed to get the children seated in a horseshoe in front of the portable chalkboard they'd brought to use for games. Jamie didn't want to go first and instead chose someone else to. One by one, each of the children went to the board, marking off five or six spaces for letters at most.

It was nearing time to eat, so Rowan handed Jamie the chalk. "Why not have a go?"

Jamie took the chalk, squared his shoulders, and walked over to the easel, ambitiously marking off ten spaces. Starting on his left, Jamie let each classmate have a guess, filling in only two spaces after at least three passes.

With over half a figure drawn and still only two letters, Rowan's curiosity got the best of him. "That's a long word. I can't wait t'see what it is."

Jamie's eyes widened, a streak of chalk smearing his forehead. "I know! Me either!"

Rowan massaged his lower back, wiping his neck with his bandana and then shoved it back in the pocket of his shorts.

They'd all pitched in to mop up the remnants of the party; refuse had been sorted and Jared was off to take the used paper to Supply for recycling.

Looking at his watch, Rowan reckoned he could make the telegraph office in town just before closing to see if anything had come in from Madoc over the Net. He'd checked every day, and as of yet, had received nothing.

His eye stung suddenly from a mixture of sun block and sweat rolling down his nose. He pulled his sleeve up to the corner of his eye, wiping at it and blinking rapidly to clear his vision.

From the path he could see a handful of solar panels and skylights in the buildings below soaking up the last rays of light, wind mills sitting idle. The sun was low enough in the sky to offer a bit of relief from the heat. As miserable as it got, at least the high temperatures squashed the insect population until the rainy season.

By the time he'd made it to the telegraph office and back to the castle for supper, sweat was coursing between his shoulder blades and hanging in the crack of his arse. He popped up to his room for a dry shirt and to wash-up, then headed back down to the private dining room.

Wood paneling looked the color of warm caramel in the luminosity of the lanterns spaced about the room. Kyrie, Elias, Jared, and Jamie were already attending to plates full of leftover barbeque.

"I'm sorry, Uncle Rowan." Kyrie laid a polished rib bone back in her plate, sucking barbeque sauce from her thumb. "We weren't sure what time you'd be back."

"No worries." Rowan poured himself some water, while Jared filled a plate for him with ribs, potato salad, and beans.

Kyrie and Elias both looked as if they were waiting for him to say something. He shook his head. "Nothing yet."

The sweet spiciness of Elias's sauce practically danced on Rowan's tongue. He'd had barbeque before, but nothing compared to this. It could have been that after not much lunch and his walk to town, he was well after joining the Gray Lady in her haunting of the castle. Either way, it was delicious.

By the time he'd made his way round his plate, Kyrie and Elias were well into their second pint of cider. Jamie was sitting on the floor looking impressed as Jared performed various card tricks.

Kyrie stifled a yawn. "How much longer are you going to wait for word from Maddy?"

Rowan felt knackered himself, ready for a nice bath and his pipe. "I don't know. If nothing comes soon, perhaps I will head to Stirling."

Kyrie and Elias both chuckled at the sackless enthusiasm with which he'd spoken. If it came to it he'd go, but Madoc was likely to be subject to a prolonged ear bashing as a result. He wondered if Kyrie would want to go as well, thinking it best to ask when they were alone.

Elias drained his pint, then leaned back in his chair. "Now that he's had some time, d'ye suppose he's changed his mind?"

"Not likely." Rowan cocked a brow. "We are talking about Madoc."

Elias rubbed the empty glass between his palms. "Aye, but we're also talking about another Rising."

Rowan had not been involved with the Rising a few years back, other than to offer up prayers for Kyrie, along with those of Threas and Madoc. They had all stayed here on the island during the whole conflict, safe and forgotten. He understood Elias's point, but still.

"Just because a person isn't afraid of something doesn't necessarily mean they are anxious for it." Rowan waved a hand. "I'm sure Madoc knows what he's getting into."

"How could he?" Elias snorted. "*Bidh dùil ri fear-feachda, ach cha bhi ri fear-lice.*"

Rowan looked from one to the other, not having the slightest idea what that meant.

Kyrie turned towards Elias, her expression a reflection of his. "The man of war may return, but not the buried man."

Rowan felt as if he were intruding, both respectful and a bit annoyed at the closeness between the two of them.

Kyrie rose, gathering up her dishes. "I think I'm going to stretch my legs a bit."

"I c-c-can get those, Miss Kyrie." Jared gathered up the cards, holding up an index finger to Jamie. "One more, then you help m-m-me clear the table, o-k-kay?"

Jamie nodded and rubbed his eye. "O-k-kay."

Kyrie leaned down and kissed Rowan on the check on her way out, Elias right behind her. Rowan hadn't even noticed how quiet the room had become after their departure, drifting off to nowhere in particular. His attention was pulled back by a gentle tug on the leg of his shorts. He glanced over to see the cards unattended, Jared and Jamie nowhere in sight. There was another tug, this time a bit more insistent.

Rowan grinned. "Who's there?"

A muffled voice answered, the owner sounding ready to pop with excitement at any moment. "Guess who? Is it me or is it Jared?"

"Time for bed!" Elias bellowed while fluffing the covers.

Jamie had been in the cludgie since Jared had dropped him by on his way to bed. Finally, the door creaked open.

Jamie emerged, but made no move towards the bed. "It's still hard for me to poop."

"Is it? We'll see aboot that tomorrow." Elias pulled the covers back, jiggling them in invitation.

Jamie looked as if some cloth monster had swallowed him feet first and stopped just at the neck. His hair was damp, which made the cowlick on the back of his head stand at attention.

"Are you tucking me in tonight?" Jamie whispered, his head drooping like a wilted flower. The big toe on his left foot wiggled like a worm on a hook.

"Aye. Kyrie went to bed already." Elias waved a hand toward the bed, but Jamie made no move towards it.

"She'll be mad if I don't tell her goodnight." Jamie hugged his arms around himself and shook his head. "Can I sleep in front of the window? On the floor so I can see the sky?"

Elias hardened his tone just a tad. "Not tonight. Come tae bed and I'll tuck ye in."

The mattress squeaked when he sat down, trying to recall the story of "The Two Shepherds" before finally deciding on "Tam Lin" instead. There was a bump at his knees, and then small hands fumbling at the front of his pajama pants.

He grabbed Jamie's hands and held them in front of him, keeping his voice calm. "Jamie, what are ye doin'?"

"You said you wanted to tuck me in," Jamie said despondently.

It seemed a puzzle had just been poured from the box, but the pieces were starting to form a picture. Elias lifted the covers for Jamie to climb into bed, making no move to touch him.

Jamie squeezed his eyelids in an effort to seal in the tears before they fell, escaping down his contorted little face as soon as he opened eyes. "When my mama worked in the big place there was a man we used to eat dinner with sometimes. When she would work at night, I would stay with him."

Jamie clenched the covers tighter under his chin. "He would say, 'It's time for me to tuck you in.'"

Elias's heart shattered. For all he'd seen in his life, he'd never once doubted the existence of God, but there were plenty of times that he questioned His reasoning. This was one of those occasions.

"It sometimes still hurts… back there… when I use the bathroom…" Jamie stared straight ahead, his voice the barest of whispers. "After the first time, he took me downstairs and showed me a room that had lots of jars filled with specisms. He said he would make my mama one if I ever told."

Jamie stopped to take a few hiccupping sighs before he could finish. "One time she came home early and walked in when he was still back there. She got mad and hit him over and over and… then he turned her into one."

Jamie trembled from the inside out, spittle teasing the corner of his mouth. He sat up, eyes red-rimmed and swollen, hazel now a gleaming shade of jade. "I know what happened to Mama is my fault."

"It is not your fault. None of it." He held up his sleeve for Jamie to wipe his nose. "Yer mam loved ye sae much and was only doin' right by ye."

Jamie's eyes widened. "You kent my mama?"

He brushed Jamie's hair back. "I met her the night I found ye. She loved ye and wouldna want ye believin' such jibber about it bein' yer fault."

Jamie rose to his knees, looping his arms around Elias's neck. "Would you sing that song about the lady whackin' her feet?"

Elias chuckled, then carried Jamie over to the large wooden rocker by the window and sat down, rocking in time with the song.

As I walked out through Dublin city

142

At the hour of twelve at night
Who should I spy but the Spanish Lady,
Washin' her feet by candle light.
First she washed them, then she dried them
Over a fire of amber coals.
In all my life I ne'er did see
A maid so fair about the soles.
Whack for the too rah loo rah laddie
Whack for the too rah loo rah lay
Whack for the too rah loo rah laddie
Whack for the too rah loo rah lay...

When Elias finished, he kept rocking back and forth, Jamie still and quiet in his lap. He'd just nodded off himself when Jamie's sleepy voice broke the silence.

"Elias?"

"Aye?"

"Can I ask you something?"

"Anythin'."

"Could I please have something else for breakfast besides mealie pudding?"

"Aye. No mealie puddin' tomorrow." He chuckled when Jamie relaxed and wriggled closer.

"Jamie?"

"Aye?" Jamie yawned, and then sniffled.

"Can I ask ye somethin'?"

Jamie laid his head against Elias's chest. "Anything."

Elias looked out the window. "The man who would tuck ye in. What was his name?"

Chapter Fifteen

Month Two, Second Season
August

Madoc lay in bed looking at the ceiling. Every time he closed his eyes, so many thoughts would swirl about it felt like mental and emotional vertigo.

After dinner he'd ridden down past the cemetery and into town. It was amazing to see life on the mainland, especially in cities such as Stirling. Just after dark, he saw houses with lights blazing from the windows. Not lanterns. Lights.

Morgan had told him some of the wealthier families actually owned government sanctioned fuel cells. Privileged circumstances could secure the scarcest of resources, it seemed. There were a few contraptions he'd not had the faintest idea what they were for. Kyrie probably would have known, but...

Dear God. What will she say when she finds out Threas is alive? It was all so unbelievable. He'd not really accepted the fact Threas was gone, and now she wasn't. The first night he saw her, he stared as if Christ himself had appeared before him.

"You look as if you're seeing a ghost," Threas said smiling.

"Well, aren't I?" he sputtered.

Threas walked round the end of the loveseat and sat down. She laid her hand on top of his, chuckling at his swift intake of breath. He grabbed her hand and squeezed it hard.

Her eyes glowed, surrounded by the fine lines of a life well-lived. Her long brown curls were pulled back from her face and held with a leather thong. She'd the same countenance, the same build as Kyrie, albeit a bit fuller. Not as hard, but just as beautiful.

Tears filled his eyes. "You're real. I don't believe it. You're really real!"

Threas laughed, touching his cheek. "Yes, I am."

"But, how…" He laid a hand over hers. "You were taken to Edinburgh. We thought…"

"I was hung within hours of my arrival, after which my body summarily burned." She smiled, shrugging her shoulders.

"Damn bureaucracy." Morgan grinned.

Rowan appealed to Morgan as soon as Threas had been taken; time being the factor which allowed Morgan to help Threas when she couldn't Miyanna. Someone with a fair amount of influence, which was to say Morgan, ensured that Threas' transfer was lost. Madoc understood the how, but that left another very important question.

"Why?"

"I suppose to answer that I should start at the beginning." Morgan looked from him to Threas, then sat down across from them and poured herself a drink. "Fifteen years ago. When I first met Nicholas."

She had been asked to attend a political function by her father. The evening had been fairly uneventful, yet not quite dull, until she met a young Minister of Defense by the name of Nicholas Payne. He'd made quite an impression and apparently she had, as well. After a very brief courtship, he proposed.

During the first couple years of their marriage, she began to know a very different Nicholas than the ambitious politician most knew him as. He showed himself to be a kind and loving man.

"The pregnancy went well. Nicolas was the perfect husband and a very expectant father. I went into labor two weeks early and gave birth to a son." Morgan's voice softened, her hand rubbing the ghost of her belly. "Hours after the delivery, I woke up wondering where my baby was."

Her first thought was to go find Nicholas. The world began to melt into a bright light and there was a buzzing in her ears as she walked through the apartments, so she stopped a moment to clear her head. There were voices coming from Nicholas's private study, one of which she didn't recognize.

"It's for the best. You are doing the right thing."

The stranger's voice drew closer to the door. Something inside told her to duck behind a nearby tapestry, peeking out as the tall, dark-haired stranger passed by. At the time she didn't know who he was, but in later years she would learn more about the Senior Administrator of the Cauldron than she'd cared to.

She watched him walk away, a small burlap sack swinging from his hand. She'd no idea how long she stood there, alone, gripping the edge of the tapestry before she finally walked into the study.

Nicholas sat in front of the fire with his head in his hands, crying. She called his name and he just stared a moment, then started explaining how their son had been born with DownSyn and that would not have been a life worth living.

"Everything went black and I woke up in my bed sometime later." Her hands tightened into fists. "I know what he did. What they did."

Madoc shuddered at the intense hatred radiating from her purple gaze, feeling all the drink and food from earlier churn in his stomach. Threas tightened her grip on his hand.

As soon as Morgan was able, she went home to Stirling. Garret worried about Morgan being alone, for obvious reasons, so he hired a personal assistant for her. A few months passed before she returned to Edinburgh. She'd never told Garret why, but when pleading for her to come back, Nicholas began making veiled threats, mostly directed at her father. She returned, but any love she'd had for Nicholas never did.

Thoughts of the babies Madoc and his sister would never know caused hot tears to crawl down his cheeks. He excavated a large pillow from the heap to pull up against his back, hugging another one tightly to his chest. With great effort, he found the way to dreams he would bury deep in his heart and never admit to having.

It was just getting light when Madoc went to the stable to pack his saddlebags. Pink ribbons streaked the sky, the air just cool enough to be comfortable.

"Still an early riser, I see?"

Threas walked over to him and rubbed a hand up and down his back. The long skirt and matching top she wore was a flattering shade of green, making her hair seem a bit darker. She began stroking his horse's nose.

"Should you be...?" He looked around to see if they were alone. The fact she was presumed dead offered a certain amount of freedom, but it still wouldn't do for her to run into someone she used to know.

Threas smiled. "It's fine. No one here knows me, other than Morgan, and Fiona taught her quite a bit about 'discreet' travel, shall we say."

"What about traveling to see your daughter?" In the hours they'd spent talking that first night, he'd told her about Kyrie's blindness.

She smiled and touched the side of his face. "First, Morgan needs my help right now, and I do owe her somewhat of a debt."

He laid his hand over hers, thinking Morgan could bloody well take care of herself, not bothering to hide his thoughts.

"Under normal circumstances, I would agree; however, in a few months..." she rose on her toes to brush his cheek with her lips, "... you are going to be an uncle."

"Dear, God."

The quiet stillness of the dining room made me feel isolated. I took a deep breath and exhaled loudly just to hear the noise.

"How... how are you? My God, how is he?" I heard Elias's chair creak, but could tell he'd not risen. His voice would have sounded calm to anyone that didn't know him well. I, however, did.

"He's got an appointment tae see the psychologist at half nine." He cleared his throat. "Mac, I thought ye might... I wanted tae ask... if you might..."

I held my hand out to him. A tear broke free when I smiled. "Of course, I'll come."

Elias caught the front of his shirt and fanned it out a few times, shifting in his chair. Kyrie sat next to him, her hair swept up off her neck, her face slightly flushed. A small drop of sweat trickled down between her breasts.

Jamie was content to lie on the floor of the psychologist's office and draw shapes in the sand tray, the edges of his blonde hair damp. The windows were open, but not much of a breeze made its way in.

Over the course of the last week, Jamie had been going through various screening processes, some of which had been streamlined or skipped altogether. The parent interview hadn't been much help as Elias didn't know a thing about Jamie's life before they found him.

The curtains whooshed in when the door opened, a gust of air offering a moment's relief. Ms. Hymes stood with the doorknob in her hand a moment before shutting the door.

"I'm sorry." She picked up a file from her desk, then joined them over by the window, crossing well-shaped, brown legs in front her when she sat down, smoothing her skirt with her free hand. "I know it's a bit cooler with the door open, but voices carry down the hall."

She put on a pair of reading glasses, straightening the headband that confined black curls on top of her head, then thumbed through the file.

Elias was impressed at how thoroughly she explained each piece of paper: the scores, the checklists, etc. She was in the process of explaining Cognitive Behavior Therapy when he felt a tug on his sleeve. Jamie's face was flushed, and he grasped the crotch of his pants in one hand.

"Bathroom now."

Elias cocked a brow. "Try that again, please."

Jamie sighed and rolled his eyes, pulling his lips back in the affectation of a smile. "Excuse me. I need to use the bathroom… please."

Ms. Hymes motioned towards the door. "It's just two doors down the hall. Do you think you can find it, or do you need help?"

Jamie shook his head. "It's the door with the picture of the man on top."

"You got it." She smiled.

Elias pointed a finger at Jamie. "Straight there. Straight

back."

Jamie nodded, walking a few steps before bolting for the door, drawing a chuckle from Kyrie when Elias growled.

"It's good that you have expectations for his behavior. That actually goes along with what I wanted to discuss next." She pulled the last piece of paper from the file and handed it to him.

When they'd finished, Ms. Hymes tucked it back into the folder with the rest. "What I would like to do now is explain everything to Jamie… where is Jamie?"

Elias rose, resisting the explicative resting on the tip of his tongue. "Excuse me a moment."

Not a bit surprised, Elias didn't find Jamie in the men's room, only two or three wadded up paper towels and a pool of water on the back of the sink. Well, Elias thought, at least he'd remembered to wash his hands.

From the corner of his eye he noticed the edge of the window screen was pulled back, his mind's eye already seeing a replay of what happened before he even looked out the window.

He spun round, giving in to the phrase that had come to mind before, as well as a few others by the time he'd found the front door.

Rounding the side of the building he drew breath to speak, but was pulled up short when he saw Jamie standing below a beech tree, staring up at about a dozen yellow butterflies perched along the branches. A warm breeze seemed to dance about the tree, but didn't rustle so much as leaf or wing.

A look of intense concentration creased Jamie's brow as

he stood like a statue, watching. Elias wondered if he would have even noticed such a thing himself, much less felt impelled to tear through a window screen to get closer to it. Just when in life do yellow butterflies stop being so important?

Elias walked over to the bathroom window and took his time straightening the screen.

Elias tightened his arm around me as we strolled through the garden, headed nowhere in particular. "Are ye ready to go in?"

"No. Not yet."

I enjoyed our walks together. The conversation was relaxing and easy between us. We talked of everything from weaponry to flower gardens, which is to say I would listen to him talk about flower gardens. This, however, was one of the times we enjoyed not talking at all.

We stopped a moment and he hugged me close. The smoothness of his shirt rubbed against my cheek, the slow, steady thud of his heartbeat ringing in my ear. Scents of peppermint and lemon grass oil, as well as a few others from the insect repellent, made me snuggle even closer to him as his hand traced patterns on my back.

I raised my head to speak, but my words died on his lips.

At first, there was a tender newness that gradually turned into something more. His control was evident and endearing, tempered with the promise of what was mine to take and have taken. He pulled back just a bit, tucking a loose strand of hair behind my ear.

A tear snaked down and hung in the corner of my mouth. My throat felt pinched and my voice squeaked when I was finally able to speak. "*Tha goal agam ort.*"

He pressed his cheek against mine and whispered back, "I know."

Rowan felt a sharp stab under his rib cage. That was the closest he'd come to jogging in a very long time.

He threw the dining room door open to see Jamie sitting in Kyrie's lap. Elias was in the midst of pouring juice into a small glass, spilling a little bit on the table when he started.

They all stared at him, waiting. Rowan drew in deep breaths, holding up the telegram in his hand.

Chapter Sixteen

Madoc sat enjoying his tea, but little else.

The copious haze of smoke was stifling, not to mention the fetor of unwashed bodies. Chairs scuffing against the floor and raucous laughter in no way improved his mood. A late night arrival in Glasgow had caused him to sleep until early afternoon for no other reason than total exhaustion.

"Needin' another cupper, are ya?"

A sensation akin to nails on a chalkboard scraped along his spine. Madoc turned towards the waitress slowly, affecting the semblance of courtesy. Whisker-like hairs trailed along both of her jaws. He did his best to ignore the open invitation in her smile.

"I'm fine, thanks." He raised his cup towards her before taking a drink, shrinking down into his chair a bit.

"Is there anythin' else I can help ya with? I am here to serve."

His ear drums felt as though pierced with needles every time she spoke a word with the letter "s", thanks to the jagged edge of her front teeth.

Adding insult to injury, she leaned close enough for an ample view of her bosom, the reek of her breath crawling up his nose so far he could almost taste it. Evidently her jaws weren't the only area with hair.

He leaned away, catching sight of someone from the bar motioning to him. He shoved his cup into her hand as he rushed over.

The man had a friendly face with dark hair cropped close, his eyes both blue and green, but not quite hazel. More like two jars of spilt paint, with the colors just barely blending.

"Would your name be Monss?"

"Good God, yes." Madoc breathed a sigh of relief. "I mean. Yes. It is."

"My name is Colm O'Mahuna," the man smiled. "Would you care to step outside for some fresh air?"

Madoc nodded hard. In spite of the noise level, he caught the barmaid's comment as they negotiated the throng at the bar waiting to order, willing to forgo reprisal for the sake of escape.

"Och, the pretty ones are always married or up for a bit of back scuttlin'..." she picked up her tray, winking at a fellow barmaid, "... and he weren't wearin' no weddin' ring!"

The streets were jammed, making conversation impossible. Madoc decided not to even try until they got... wherever they were going. The bloke had spoken as if he'd been looking for him and had offered his own name, but that was all. There wasn't time to ponder the point further as they seemed to have arrived at their destination.

156

A small room had been added on to a larger building which appeared to be a brothel, judging by the cup-less leather bras and piercings in the most amazing places of the women milling about outside. One of the ladies in question draped her tongue from her mouth, the tip even with the bottom of her chin. Dead center of it was a wee rubber ball with spikes.

Madoc pretended to look at his shoe whilst his escort rapped a certain rhythm on the broad oak door. After a momentary pause, followed by muffled noise, it creaked open.

Colm turned and motioned for Madoc to go in first, scanning the direction they'd just come from. The door shut out every ounce of light, the only sound the scrape of a lock sliding into place. After a few seconds, his eyes adjusted, allowing him to survey the room.

A large fireplace dominated the far wall, two men in casual dress standing on either side. Colm walked past to stand beside a woman sitting at a heavy wooden table with a lantern on it.

"We weren't followed."

Her long black hair was pulled back, revealing a strong, slightly squared jaw. Piercing green eyes wreathed with thick lashes held his gaze, demanding his full attention with little effort. A smile toyed about full lips as she spoke to Colm in some unfamiliar language before turning to Madoc.

"You've already met Colm. These two gentlemen are Fintan Farleigh and Olen Donohugh. My name is Orla Tomáis." She looked Madoc directly in the eye. "We are with a special branch of the An Garda Siochana. Irish

Madoc sat on the steps of the inn, sipping his tea and enjoying some time alone, the pungent smell of less-than sophisticated living conditions notwithstanding. Morning dew gleamed in the sunshine filtering through smatterings of dark clouds, a stark contrast to the brilliant blue behind them. There'd been a nasty malaria outbreak third season last year; he thanked God his vaccinations were up-to-date.

The evening prior had been interesting to say the least. It wasn't every day a school teacher gets to have a chat with the likes of Orla. She was quite direct and had been forth-coming with most of his questions; however, when he asked why the interest in Alban affairs, all she would say is that Prime Minister Payne had been a "person of interest" for quite some time. If she knew that the prime minister was his brother-in-law, she didn't let on, and he certainly didn't offer the information regardless.

He drained his cup and went inside to see what the oth-ers were doing. Even with the lantern glowing and the sole window thrown back wide, he still had to blink a few times before he could see. Orla sat at the table, holding a map up to the light, then laying it flat to jot notes here and there.

"Good morning," she called not looking up. "Did you sleep well?"

"Well enough." He glanced around the room. "Where are the others?"

"Next door having breakfast." She folded the map and

placed it back in her satchel.

He set his empty cup on the table. "Have you had break-fast yet?"

"No. I was waiting for you, actually." she looked him in the eye and smiled. "Feel like a ride?"

He held her gaze a moment, then smiled, answering be-fore he'd the chance to think too deeply. "I'd love one."

CHAPTER SEVENTEEN

"Jamie?" Elias eased the bedroom door open. Jamie was sitting on the side of the bed, facing the opposite wall, his head hung down.

He crossed over to sit on the foot of the bed, staring at a spot on the floor. "Jamie, I just wanted ye tae know…"

"He's going to kill me." Jamie's voice was so matter-of-fact it was a moment before his words registered.

Elias stared at Jamie's profile. "What?"

Jamie shrugged a shoulder. "When he finds me, he'll kill me."

Elias held out a hand. "Come here."

Jamie slid off the bed, walking around to stand by Elias's knees, much like he had the night of his confession.

"Look at me." Elias placed a finger under Jamie's chin, lifting his face. "No one will ever hurt you again. I will not allow it."

"But you aren't gonna be around." Jamie walked over to stare out the window, shoulders drooping a bit, one single tear resting on a bottom lash.

Elias's insides twisted together. He reached into his pocket, pulling out the pewter badge, rubbing a thumb over the words *Clarior hinc honos*. Hence the brighter honor.

He walked over by Jamie and knelt down. "Anyone who wears this badge is a Buchanan, entitled tae the protection of anyone bearing that name or allegiance." He pinned the badge on Jamie's shirt, then placed his right hand over his heart. "I swear tae you, William Jameson Shaw Buchanan, no harm will come tae you. I swear tae you that I will come back for you."

Without a word, Jamie turned to face the window. Elias looked at Jamie a moment before walking out and shutting the door behind him. All the way down the stairs, he blinked hard at the tears threatening to fall.

Halfway across the yard, he heard a voice from the castle calling his name. Jamie was running full out. Elias knelt down, arms open wide. Jamie threw himself against Elias, crying.

"Is it 'cuz I broke a piece off my flower? I didn't mean to!"

"I'm no angry wi' you, *a bhalaich*. Not even a bit." His hand spanned the entire width of Jamie's back.

"I can be brave while you're gone." Jamie leaned back, the tip of his nose red and running.

Elias held his sleeve up for Jamie to wipe his nose. "I dinna think I could hae left, had ye no told me that."

Jamie's mouth dropped open for a moment, then he sniffled. "Well, if I'd known that, I wouldna have told ya."

Elias laughed, hugging Jamie again. Jared stood a few yards away, his hands in his pockets, discreetly looking down at his shoe. Elias patted Jamie on the back and rose to leave. He'd only taken a few steps when Jamie called out again.

"I love you."

Elias squeezed his eyes shut. It was a moment before he could face Jamie, the image of the small chest thrust out proudly branding itself in his memory.

"I love you, too."

Eros kept chomping at his bit and scraping the ground with his hoof, so I rubbed his neck to soothe him. I had been listening to Rowan speaking with Tarrick when I heard Elias mount up on my right. From the sound of his voice I could tell he was looking at me when he spoke.

"I'll take the lead. You can follow me."

I smiled. "We'll be fine."

The sun burned hot from the sky by the time we'd put any distance behind us, stirring together the scents of road dirt, horseshit, and leather. I could almost hear the grass scorching from the heat. I wiped the sweat from my nose, underneath my sunglasses.

November would be the beginning of the Third Season, of the rains, the floods. Whatever troops we managed to muster were going to have to move and fight in spite of them, but it wouldn't be the first time that had been the case.

The Rising had been in full force. At the time, I was assigned to the 52nd Infantry Brigade out of Jedborough. Intelligence had come in that the Anglanders were going to try and push up to Edinburgh. Glasgow had already been hit.

We moved south and took up position where Anglanders were due to pass through, our wait ending shortly after dawn. The skirmish began, quickly turning the battlefield to a mix of mud and blood. The Anglanders charged, trying their best to hack out victory, lacking formal training for the most part, but making up for it in determination. The steady thump of drums gave the battle rhythm, blades crashed like cymbals in the hellish symphony under the rain of arrows and artillery. Faces blurred into hazy shapes until everyone looked the same, distinguishable only by uniform and civilian clothes, voices drowned out by the constant beating that surrounded me. In battle, conscious thought is replaced with the automation of training, providing a buffer for the actions required of us, the memories of which would haunt us late at night in the years to follow.

When it was over, I looked around, feeling as if my intestines were jammed into my stomach. A sudden urgency pushed up through my esophagus and sprayed what little stomach contents I had out to land at my feet, leaving a thick bulge lodged in my throat.

Everywhere laid the evidence that we'd done our job as soldiers. The rains amplified the smell of feces and urine, bringing forth the unmistakable reek of mortality. I had stepped here and there, my boots squishing in the small streams of copper branching out from bodies as the ground drank the blood of the nameless who paid the price of our victory. The hollow eyes of men and women, old and young, followed my every move.

One of my soldiers appeared before me, lips moving but no sound breaking though the steady tattoo which had just begun to slow. He threw an arm around me, motioning to a deep gash running almost the entire length of my thigh.

Deep, deliberate breaths calmed my pulse, making me realize for the first time that there had been no drums. Only my own heartbeat.

I ran a hand down my thigh. Now that I no longer had my sight, were these to be the things I would see? Was this to be my penance for doing what had been asked of me; visions of things which I now had no escape from?

Eros stopped suddenly and snorted, followed by Elias's low whistle. I felt along my saddle, gripping the hilt of my sword, listening in all directions. Riders were approaching.

"Wait here." Elias rode ahead a bit. I could make out three other voices apart from Elias, but couldn't quite tell what they were saying.

I nudged Eros to my left, closer to Uncle Rowan. "How many are there?"

He sounded a bit worried. "Two speaking with Elias and eight more besides. They keep looking this way."

Seth spoke from behind us. "One of the females is looking through some sheets of paper. It seems… shit!"

Donny, Seamas, and Seth thundered past us. Almost immediately after, I heard the distinct sound of metal clashing, mixed with lots of swearing. The click of a trigger preceded the twang of the bowstring as a bolt broke free from a crossbow. The sound of a horse whinnying was closely followed by a soft thud on the ground.

Rowan exhaled loudly. "Here they come."

Seth rode up beside me, touching my arm. "Are ye alright?"

I realized I was still squeezing the hilt of my sword and let go. "We're fine. Is everyone…?"

"We're good. Donny got a nasty nick on his arm. Elias is

stitching it now."

I sighed, feeling relieved, but a bit annoyed at how use-less I'd felt just then. "What the hell was that all about?"

"Well, they had a wee poster wi' your picture on it," Seth cleared his throat. "Seems ye are wanted for the murder of a Cauldron official and for desertion."

After hearing this bit of news, I said the most intelligent thing I could pull together. "Oh."

CHAPTER EIGHTEEN

Rowan's skin was sticky and the cheeks of his arse felt damp where it rested in the saddle. They'd made quick work of the ride to Glasgow, sacrificing sleep and personal hygiene as a result.

The foul stench of sewage and mud caused a small lump to form in the back of his throat. It was quite obvious which part of town they were in, judging by the smell and the cat-calls of prostitutes as they rode along. He recalled the pub's name and description from Madoc's message, then turned to the others.

"This is the place."

They all dismounted and gathered for a moment. Rowan pulled at the seat of his trousers. "I'll go in and ask after Madoc."

"I'll stay with the horses." Seth offered.

"Shay and I will have a look round." Donny threw over his shoulder as they walked away.

Kyrie took Elias's arm. "Looks like we're with you."

The inside of the pub smelled like armpits and ass. A cloud of smoke fried Rowan's eyes, his throat parched from a lack of breathable air. Mixed voices, cursing and laughing, bombarded from all sides, accompanied by the sound of

167

clinking coins and scraping chairs.

Rowan motioned to Elias, then walked to the bar and ordered a whisky. The barman set down a double Talisker, then turned away without so much as a glance. It burned a trail down his esophagus; he pressed a hand over his mouth to try and smother the coughing fit which followed.

The barman looked Rowan up and down when asked about a woman and four men staying in the adjoining inn. Fortunately, Madoc had left word that they were expecting others, as well as who might be asking questions.

Rowan turned to go join the others when he saw Kyrie smiling at a man with his hand on her arse. Before Rowan could take another step towards them, the man's smile twisted into a grimace. Rowan pushed through the crowd in time to see Kyrie steering the bloke outside by his privates. As soon as they cleared the door, she tightened her hold. The man twisted slightly, closing his eyes. Not the smartest thing to do, Rowan thought, as her free hand doubled into a fist and popped him in the face as she released her grip.

Blood pumped from the bulge of his nose as he staggered back. The jeering laughter of the audience which had followed them out of the pub had the effect of a spark too close to a powder keg. The man charged Kyrie like a wild boar, howling with rage.

With little effort, she sidestepped whilst grabbing him about the shoulders and forcing him to the ground. Showing no mercy, she shoved a knee into his back, grabbed a handful of his hair, and smacked his face against the ground. The crowd uttered a collective 'ooh!' in sympathy, but found it no less amusing.

The man lay under her, groaning, but not moving to get up. Satisfied, Kyrie rose and backed away. For the first time, Rowan noticed Seamas and Donny mixed in the crowd, watching to ensure no one joined in. She'd always been a spitfire, but Rowan had never seen her like this before.

Elias was also in the crowd, casually speaking to a woman wearing nothing more than a garter belt, stockings, and spiked heels. That is, unless one considered the holster strapped to her thigh cradling a short, thick whip apparel of some kind. Rowan lacked the knackers to approach them, instead waiting until the "lady" took her leave, then walked over to stand beside Elias.

Rowan shook his head, watching as Kyrie took Donny's elbow and followed him back into the pub. "Unbelievable."

Something flickered in Elias's eyes. "Aye. For a moment, I thought she was going to lose her temper."

The room was sweltering, so we opened a window, the need for ventilation hedging out the need for clean air.

Elias had brought over food and a bottle of brandy, which he and Rowan were currently sharing. Seth, Seamas, and Donny had taken the horses to a nearby stable before heading back over to the pub, having made a few acquaintances of a certain profession.

Rowan cleared his throat. "You know. The more you drink, the better it tastes."

"'Tis better than a sore cock," Elias answered. "Kyrie, are ye sure ye wouldna like a wee dram?"

My bones throbbed with weariness, and an aching had taken up residence behind my eyes. I curled up in front of the empty fireplace using a bedroll for a pillow.

"No, thanks. I just want to rest my head a bit."

Rowan coughed a bit, his voice sounding husky. "Quick question. How did you handle that fellow so easily?"

I smiled. "I could tell the wanker was about my height when he first spoke. Then, when he charged, he squealed so damn loud I could have heard him from a mile away. The rest was just a rough estimate."

Rowan harrumphed deep in his throat. "Very rough from what I saw."

I chuckled and snuggled deeper into my makeshift bed. Elias and Rowan's voices hummed across the room. My body seemed to melt into the blankets underneath me when I closed my eyes. I had started out thinking how un-real it was I would see Maddy, but soon my mind found its own path.

I saw myself riding Eros through a large field. It went from day to night by the time I'd crossed from one side to the other, winding up at the edge of a lake encircled by trees. The scent of moss and trees and water slapped me in the face. I slid out of the saddle and, for the first time, no-ticed I was naked.

The echo of a splash reverberated all around me. Even though I'd been looking across the moonlit water, I hadn't noticed someone swimming until just then. The water sparkled around his lean body, glistening on his wide shoulders. The lines of his face were blurred together. He held out a hand in invitation and I accepted, the warmth of the water stinging my skin the deeper I got.

From the embankment, a voice boomed across the lake, calling my name. The waterline seemed to have drifted further away, but I could make out the tall dark shape of another man. This one tried to come into the water, but for some reason couldn't step past the edge. His voice sounded desperate, calling to me over and over.

I suddenly felt very afraid and started towards shore, but something caught my leg. When I turned to ask for help, I realized I was now alone. I heard my name again and looked towards the bank, pulling and tugging with all my strength. Whatever it was holding me back seemed to draw me deeper the more I tried to free myself. Something brushed against my cheek.

Then it all just faded away. Slowly I pulled out of the dream enough to realize someone was in fact touching my face.

The atmosphere of the room had changed by the presence surrounding the voice that was comforting me, filling my senses.

"Another dream, Bonnie?"

Chapter Nineteen

Madoc stroked Kyrie's face, feeling as if he were touching a dream.

Tear tracks stained her flushed cheeks, making her seem childlike. Two or three white hairs graced the part running just off center of her shoulder length curls. He much preferred the length of it now; it made her seem younger. For a moment it was as if all her years of soldiering had never happened, as if she'd never been away.

She looked at him, though not quite focusing. So much lay in those eyes, caramel brown from the low light: recognition, tentative joy, uncertainty. God, how he wanted to kiss her.

"We got the key from the barkeep."

Madoc started at the sound of Rowan's voice, feeling a bit sheepish. He'd barely greeted anyone when he caught sight of Kyrie, drawn to her like a moth to the flame.

He answered Rowan, not taking his eyes off Kyrie. "So, you had no trouble then?"

Rowan and Elias cleared their throats, speaking in unison. "No... no trouble... no..."

Madoc touched a curl hanging precariously in front of her ear. "Have you eaten?"

"Yes." Her voice sounded hoarse and raspy.

He took her hand and helped her to her feet, intending to lead her to the table. She let go and walked over unassisted and sat down, the same grace she'd always possessed still powering her limbs.

Rowan crossed the room and hugged him hard. "I've missed you, boy."

Madoc laughed, patting Rowan on the back. "I have missed you, as well."

Rowan pulled back a bit, keeping an arm around Madoc's shoulders. "Things have been going well at Làidir. I know you've been wondering."

What would Rowan think if Madoc were to admit he hadn't been? They joined the others at the table. Madoc took the chair next to Kyrie. He wanted to get the business over with so they could talk privately.

"There are some people you should meet. I thought we might walk next door to the pub and join them."

Kyrie shrugged. "If it's all the same, I think I'll just wait here."

Rowan and Elias looked at one another for a moment, then burst out laughing.

It'd been nearly half an hour since Madoc and Elias walked over to the pub. Rowan had stayed with me, the two of us sitting in a companionable silence, each deep in our own thoughts.

"How do you feel?" Rowan asked.

My throat had felt like a hundred pins had pricked it over and over. I downed the large glass of water he offered without taking a breath. The room was still filled with a dull heat.

My throat stung a bit when I cleared it. "Better. The water helped."

"That's not what I meant." His voice was quiet and tender.

Tiny splinters from some haphazard scratches poked my fingertips as I traced the length of them, picking at them whilst trying to answer to his question. Hearing Madoc's voice had been like finally breathing after realizing I'd been holding my breath. Even so, there was something very different about him.

My senses snapped to attention by the sound of muffled voices just outside the door, preceding a creak when it opened. I could recognize most of them, but there was one in particular I did not. Her voice was deep and husky, with an intimate quality bordering on sensual. She sounded sure of her words, almost to the point of being clipped. It was the voice of someone comfortable with command. I could feel her presence, making it impossible to not know where she was in the room. The perfume she wore was light and bold all at once. As soon as I smelled it, something clicked into place, bringing forth a feeling of relief, but also sadness.

Chairs scrapped against the floor as everyone settled in. Madoc spoke from across the table. "Kyrie, this is Orla Tomáis."

Her tone was polite, but there was a subtle edge. "I trust your journey was not too difficult. We were worried…"

175

"We?" Elias interrupted from behind me, which put him by the fireplace. There was a momentary lull in the room.

Donny spoke from my right in an amused voice. "If you'd been here a bit earlier..." A sharp cough generating from near the fireplace cut him off.

Madoc cleared his throat. "We'd intended to be here when you arrived, but we had our hands full..."

"I'm sure." Elias's voice was as subtle as Orla's had been, but no less direct. I could only imagine the looks passing between the three of them.

It was Orla who answered, filling the silence left by Elias's question. "We were taking care of some last minute arrangements. We're to be heading north."

"How far?" I asked, my curiosity piqued.

"Fort Augustus to meet with the An Ceann-Feadhna of the Gaidhealach," she replied, pausing a moment to let her words soak in. "We're crossing the Wall into the Highlands."

Yet again, Rowan found himself wondering what the bloody hell was going on.

Madoc was cuddled up with some Irishwoman. Elias seemed quite annoyed with said Irishwoman, but now stood with his jaw on the floor alongside his brother's.

Rowan looked at Elias and Seth. "Is there something...?"

"Son of a bitch."

Everyone turned to Kyrie, who was frowning towards the window, her chin tilted slightly in the air.

"Don't you smell that?" she asked, rising at the same time.

Rowan stood. "Smell what?"

Kyrie looked towards the window again, then turned towards where Elias was standing. "Smoke."

Rowan followed Seamas and Donny outside. A rank, scorched smell assaulted them as soon as they walked outside, bits of ash mixed in the high wind sweeping past. The streets were filling with onlookers, staring towards the pall of smoke rising above the rooftops. Men, women, and children, in groups and on their own, poured from the black hole at the end of town, the glow reaching just above the rooftops revealing nothing of what was happening below it.

Voices bounced here and there, asking what was going on. Just as many echoed the answer; Soldiers. Men and women began grabbing the smaller children and shouting to the older ones, jumping into the wave of evacuees, not stopping to look back.

A scruffy-looking man pushed against the current whilst shouting to a woman nearby. "Go home! I'll meet you there!"

Seamas motioned towards the stranger. "Dat's yer man..."

"From the stables." Donny finished.

"Follow her. We'll catch up." Elias shouted as Kyrie took Donny's arm.

Kyrie fell in step behind Donny as he guided her through the crowd, Seamas and the others following close behind. Rowan started after Kyrie, but stopped when Elias caught him by the arm.

"We'll meet them wi' the horses."

Rowan just stared at Elias until Madoc laid a hand on his shoulder. The two of them hurried along after Elias and Seth. A wave of heat slapped Rowan in the face when they rounded the corner of a building, smoke stinging his eyes. Wherever the fire had started, the flames were now playing tag from house to house.

They followed their unacquainted guide through the stable doors. The man rushed over to a stall with a Clydesdale. The roar of a roof collapsing a few buildings down sent the horses into a panic. The Clydesdale burst free, knocking his owner to the ground. White feathered legs clawed the air before it dropped down, ears pinned back, eyes wild and frantic, its halter twisted.

Madoc started over, but Rowan waved him away. "Go help the others!"

Rowan eased up to the horse, crooning in a soft voice, careful not to make eye contact. After a couple of steps, Rowan turned sideways, inching close enough to put a hand out, fingers together, and lay it on the massive neck. The horse raised its ears slightly, but had otherwise quieted down. The air was growing darker and thicker; he knew it would only be content smelling his hand for so long. He straightened the halter and turned to the stranger who was now being helped up by Elias.

"Can ye walk?" At the man's nod, Elias turned to Rowan. "Go. I'll free the rest and be right behind ye."

The man walked along the other side of the horse, hugging his left arm to his body.

Rowan saw Seth and the others standing a few meters

down the street.

It was only moments before Elias followed the mass exodus of horses out of the stable and jogged over to them. They made their way through town quickly, Seth scanning the stragglers for uniforms.

They wound up at a shanty on the east side of town. The woman from the crowd stood out front, wringing her hands. As they drew near, Rowan saw relief wash across her young face.

"Papa!" She started to take a step, then turned to open the door.

Elias had the man sit and lay his arm on the table. He scanned it up and down, touching gingerly here and there.

"Can you move your arm or fingers at all?" When the man shook his head, Elias turned to the girl. "Do ye ha' some cloth and an old broom, perhaps?"

With a nod, she grabbed a sheet from a foot locker and a broom from beside a wood-burning stove. Elias cut three strips from the sheet while Rowan broke a couple of pieces off the broom as Elias had instructed.

When the splint was finished, Elias cut another piece of sheet to loop into a sling. "It's most likely a bad sprain, but best keep it like this until ye can see a doctor."

The man took the whisky his daughter offered and tossed it back. "Yeah, right. If they ain't all gone. Black suits probably scared them away."

Elias nodded. "What brought them here, do ye reckon?"

"Don't know. They did a sweep a few weeks ago. Took off a few pensioners. Some kid in a wheelchair." He nodded for his daughter to refill his glass. "Coulda been the contraband. Unauthorized fuel cells… or so I heard."

179

Elias finished folding the scrap cloth. "We should be on our way. Take care of that arm."

The man raised his glass in salute as his daughter opened the door. "Is yer friend okay? The lady who needed help walkin'?"

"Och, she's fine. Just turned her ankle a bit." Elias smiled.

Elias and the stranger looked at each other for a moment, then the man also smiled, revealing a gap to the right of his front teeth. "Best go see to her, then."

As soon as the door shut, Elias jogged down the steps. Rowan followed him round the side, wanting to stop and stroke the Clydesdale tied to a makeshift hitching post, but didn't get the chance. Kyrie was already mounted on Eros. The others were standing by their horses.

"Everything alright?" Seth asked his brother, frowning.

"Black Suits," Elias answered, throwing his leg over his saddle.

"Who are Black Suits?" Madoc asked, one foot in the stirrup.

Rowan didn't quite understand what the problem was either, but felt a sense of urgency nonetheless. Kyrie answered from beside him.

"ASF. Alban Security Force." She clucked Eros into motion right behind Elias.

Madoc shrugged his shoulders. "Which means?"

Donny jerked his reins to fall in behind Kyrie. "Which means we need ta get the fuck out of Dodge."

PART THREE

TO SHIELD ME IN THE BATTLE TO COME

Chapter Twenty

"I can't do it anymore."

The young mother looked at her hands, twisting the tissue in her lap. "She is in so much pain. I just can't watch…"

She trailed off and buried her head in her husband's shoulder. He kissed the top of her head, and then turned to Lachlan.

It was by far the most severe case of epidermolysis bullosa that Lachlan had ever encountered. At only three years old, their daughter presented with no hair or nails, as well as extensive scarring. She had been unresponsive to any treatment.

"A disabled child means a disabled family." Lachlan set his teacup on his desk. "Perhaps the things we learn now will help us to prevent anyone else from going through what your daughter has."

Lachlan peered over the steeple of his fingertips at the couple as they embraced each other. Some would say ending their child's life was callous and brutal. It had long been his belief that sometimes the cruelest act in life is to allow it to continue.

"As I explained, you will have time with your daughter, even at the end."

They looked at each other as if mentally flipping a coin to see who would go first. Finally, she stood and walked to the door. Lachlan watched Owain escort her out, then made a note to schedule her compulsory sterilization. Normally, he would have notified them during the initial consultation, but they were having a difficult enough time dealing with their daughter's procedure.

"You're doing the right thing." He hoped that sounded encouraging. He sincerely meant it.

"It's just too much to see the pain she's in." The man looked at Lachlan. "What kind of person would enjoy watching someone suffer?"

Lachlan laid his pen down and picked up his tea, blowing gently into his cup. "What kind, indeed?"

Lachlan did a few neck rotations, closing his eyes a moment to ease the strain.

It had been the first chance he'd had to write in his journal since yesterday afternoon, and he had several notes to make regarding the couple and their daughter. They could have just as easily put a pillow over the girl's face to end her suffering. It wouldn't have been the first time he'd seen that happen.

He shuddered hard, staring at his journal to force away the memory forming in his mind. His pen was midway to the paper when there was a discreet knock at his door.

"Come!" Lachlan laid his pen down and sat back in his chair.

Owain shut the door behind him, taking the seat Lachlan motioned him towards. "Sir, I'm sorry to bother you…"

Lachlan waved a hand. "No, no. It's quite alright."

He would never go so far as to say Owain was a friend, nor that he even had any, but they had worked together for many years. Perhaps it was simply the need to be able to relax, even just a bit, in front of someone familiar.

"I thought you would want to see this right away." Owain handed over a small piece of paper.

Lachlan unfolded it and scanned the contents. "When did this come in?"

"This morning, over the Net," Owain answered. "Her presence was first detected about five months ago. She's not been back since."

Lachlan drummed his fingers on his desk. "Have them keep watch. Do nothing until she's seen again."

"And when she surfaces?" Owain asked.

Lachlan picked up his teacup and smiled. "Bring her to me."

Chapter Twenty-One

Madoc yawned, feeling a dull pain in his left ear.

A cloudless sky was muted with the streaks of early morning, holding the promise of another scorcher. Everyone was finishing up breakfast, attending to last minute things, before riding further north. Not wanting to waste daylight meant riding all day and in the heat before stopping to make camp for the night.

He'd noticed Elias's eyes boring into him from time to time. When Madoc would turn the man would practically stare him down to a nub. Elias had been different from the moment they'd met up in Glasgow, Orla's behavior in the room most likely the cause. She saw no reason to hide the fact she was attracted. It was all quite simple to her, really. He was available, and she was interested. What harm could there be in enjoying each other's company? For him, though, it was not so simple.

There was still so much he needed to work out with Kyrie. Also, dealing with the promise he'd made Threas of not telling Kyrie that her mother was alive made his knees weak under the weight of it all. For now he would make do speaking with Elias. Taking a deep breath he walked over to where Elias was busy saddling Kyrie's horse.

After a few moments of awkward silence, Madoc cleared his throat. "I feel we need to clear the air a bit."

Elias finished tightening the straps on the saddle. "Perhaps ye shoulda thought of doin' that before ye saw Kyrie."

Madoc folded his arms across his chest. "What is that supposed to mean?"

"It means that was a lovely perfume you were wearing last night." Elias looked Madoc right in the eye. "Did ye really think she wouldna notice?"

Madoc stared a moment, then brought himself up to his full height. "Look, you and I have never had a problem…"

Elias looked Madoc up and down, then led Eros over to his own horse and swung up in the saddle. He looked huge and forbidding from up so high, but Madoc was not easy to intimidate.

"If ye do anythin' tae hurt Kyrie… more than you already have…" Elias leaned down and looked Madoc right in the eye, "… we most assuredly will have a problem."

Elias clucked the horses into motion, leaving Madoc to stare after him. Not easy to intimidate, he thought, but definitely not impossible.

Night found us making camp after a short pissing contest over whose map was the most accurate. Orla and her men finally conceded theirs was a bit outdated, as it didn't reflect the last change in magnetic north. Elias had managed to keep Donny and Seamas' gloating to a minimum.

My contribution had been to dig a fire pit deep enough

190

to hide the light. Another one, roughly fourteen centimeters in diameter, angled into it for a natural draw.

Seth and Donny were pulling first watch, roving the perimeter. Elias found somewhere to wash up the bowls we'd used for the salt cured pork, bread, and cheese that was our supper. Colm, Olen, and Fintan had already turned in, so they would be ready for their turn on watch. Maddy and Orla had sat with us for a bit before turning in, as well.

Seamas conjured an impressive belch after he drained his canteen cup, inspiring a "well done" from Uncle Rowan. The sleeping bag made scrunching noises as Seamas lay back to unbutton his pants and begin scratching his two most prized possessions, judging from his sigh and the chafing sound.

"Remember the time we tied meat to Elias's cot, and during the night a wild boar..." he spoke between gasps for air, "... drug him ten feet wit' him squealing like a wee girl!"

"So did you before I was done wi' you, ye dodgy bastard." Elias growled.

Seamas cleared his throat in a no-need-to-go-further manner. "I'm going to take a piss and see how things are wit' Seth and Donny."

"I'm right behind ye," Elias called.

Rowan sighed, ending the quiet lull left by Elias and Seamas. "Quite the prankster, were you?"

I grinned. "Seamas and I were the worst."

Rowan's sleeping bag ruffled a bit. "Why did Elias and Seth seem so thrown when they heard we were going up north?"

I shrugged a shoulder. "It's not so much where we are going, rather who we are meeting when we get there."

"You mean the… whatever she said?" He asked.

"*An Ceann-Feadhna*, which means 'High Chieftain', who is currently one Alastair Buchanan," I answered, "… and also their uncle."

Rowan drew in his breath sharply. "Ohhhh."

For a moment, all was quiet except for the pop of the fire, then Rowan finally spoke. "I've not read much about the split after the war."

My foot had fallen asleep and now prickled slightly when I wiggled my toes. There wasn't much to read about that time; however, I had read quite a bit and Elias had told me a lot. Centuries ago, the old countries of England and Scotland were part of what was known as the British Empire, allied with but separate from the former European Union. Sometime following the Second Great War, England began to push further and further into Scotland, due to lack of resources and rising sea levels. Scotland rebelled. Under the command of Brigadier General J. Alexander Fraser, the English were crushed. The two countries eventually merged under Scottish leadership to form the region of Alba.

As time passed, the Lowland ways melded with the English to form a fusion of cultures; however, the Highlanders refused to be anything but fierce, proud, and Scottish.

To avoid civil war, the first Prime Minister of Alba brokered the Highland Home Rule Treaty. Among other things, the HHRT allowed construction of the Wall. After obtaining autonomy, the collective Highland clans formed what was called the *Gaidhealach* and selected a leader known as *An Ceann-Feadhna*, the most recent being Elias and Seth's uncle.

Alastair Buchanan gained guardianship of his nephews after the death of their parents. Since he had no children of his own, Alastair hoped his nephew might one day also serve as *An Ceann-Feadhna*. Elias wanted to study medicine. Alastair wouldn't hear of it. Their last discussion turned into one of the worst thrashings Elias had ever received in his life. That very night a seventeen year old Elias arranged passage across the Wall for himself and his three-year-old baby brother.

"They were taken in by a family in the Lochearnhead area. Shortly after, Elias enlisted in the Forces in order to support them." I swatted at a mosquito. "As far as Elias knew, no one tried to find them."

Rowan was quiet for a moment, long enough I thought the conversation was over. His voice sounded thick when he finally spoke. "I'm glad they are here with you. I know I've not said it before, but I am."

"I know I've not said this either." I held out my hand to him. "I'm really glad you are here with me."

"Well, you might not be after this."

He gripped my hand hard as I tried to jerk it free. His words were punctuated by a thunderous expulsion of gas rivaling that of Odin himself.

I pressed my nose into the crook of my elbow. "Oh, damn."

The wind battered the windows of the Duntreath Inn, accompanied by the sound of debris striking the house. It had been a bit dodgy getting all the way through town, due to the mangled tree limbs and broken glass strewn about.

Elias would have much preferred to camp somewhere after the day's ride and not risk staying in or near town, but the windstorm ended that notion. He and Seth were ushered into the lobby by a gust of wind, leaving the others to tend the horses.

Colored glass panels accented the light woodwork in a pleasing way. Two large figurine planters with Christmas cacti stood on each side of the staircase leading to the upper floor, within reach of the light from a nearby window, but not enough in his opinion.

The reception desk faced out onto a lounge area where five plush settees were situated about the room. Small blankets with a banded design of dark blue, beige, and moss green were neatly folded and draped across the back of each. A large pedestal wood-burning stove with a kettle on top was positioned in the corner.

A petite woman sat perched on a stool behind the desk, going over some papers. Her hair was smoothed into a bun, blonde and silver streaks sparked by the royal blue of her shirt. She looked to be in her mid to late fifties, but even so was quite fetching. She smiled as Elias approached the desk.

"Welcome. My name is May. What can I be doin' for ye?"

He smiled back. "I would like to inquire as to what rooms you have available."

"How many nights will ye be needin', and how many are in your party?" Her voice was quiet and sweet with just enough familiarity to be inviting yet not invasive, making him feel very much at home.

He laid his hands on the desk. "Just one night and eleven altogether."

She flipped open a large book, pursing her lips to one side as she ran her finger down the page. "Aye, but not as many as ye'd probably like. We're a wee stowed."

He tapped the counter. "No problem. I'm sure we'll manage with what ye've got."

"Only one family room which sleeps three, one double, and two singles. That takes care of seven." She looked at him, brows raised. "I can perhaps scrounge up a cot or two extra."

Elias shrugged. "Works for me."

Once the bartering was sorted, Elias walked over to where Seth was standing at the foot of the stairs. Before a word could pass between them, a blood-curdling scream rang out upstairs. They looked at each other for a split second before taking the stairs two at a time.

The door at the end of the hall was slightly ajar. Elias followed Seth into a small bedroom, weapons at the ready. The maid who'd screamed was beginning to hyperventilate. They sheathed their dirks, then Seth rushed over to the maid and began trying to calm her.

In the center of the bed, a young woman leaned against a stack of pillows, not more than nineteen from the looks of her. Bedclothes bunched at the footboard, soaked deep red; splatters and sprays trailed up to the end of a knitting needle protruding from her vagina. Elias had little hope of finding a pulse. Her thin face had gone pale gray, eyes staring straight ahead, dried tear tracks streaking her face and blue-tinged lips. As soon as his fingers touched her neck, her eyes flickered.

"Christ." Seth spoke from the foot of the bed, crossing himself.

"I… I don't feel well." The maid clapped her hand over her mouth. Seth scooped up the small trashcan resting beside the writing desk, guiding her back out into the hall.

Elias knelt down and took the lass's hand, pressing his fingers against her wrist. "I got you, Doll. Can ye tell me your name?"

She'd not moved a muscle, hardly even blinking. When she spoke her voice was as weak as her pulse. "What time is it?"

"Half seven." Elias snatched a blanket from the chest at the foot of the bed. "Can ye tell me your name?"

He tucked the fresh blanket around her body, draping it over her legs, then eased the pillows out from behind her. Once she was as flat as possible, he gently tucked one of the pillows beneath her lower legs.

She was unresponsive to any of his questions. Her symptoms indicated Stage III shock, which meant she was well past what he was able to do for her. Still, he could start her on fluids, maybe even attempt to remove the needle if it came to it.

Seth rushed in, then took the medical kit tucked under his arm and handed it over to Elias. "May sent for a doctor. I got this from your saddlebag…"

"Sherry." Her voice was barely a whisper.

"Are ye thirsty, Doll?" Elias snapped the gloves on, then found a suitable vein. He slid the metal casing from the needle.

"No. That's my name." She stared straight ahead, then closed her eyes as she stopped breathing.

Rowan massaged his lower back, squinting as his eyes adjusted to the low light of the stables. The insect repellent on his arms was dry enough he could pull his sleeves down. At least the sun had set, and the wind had died down a bit.

He'd jumped at the chance to get out of the hotel when Seth asked who might like to have a look round. There was a woeful air about the place, what with the death of that poor girl and all.

The other reason he'd volunteered was to perhaps give Kyrie and Madoc a chance to talk. That idea was shot to hell when Seth asked Madoc to ride along. Donny and Seamas were in town having a pint, finding out if there'd been much local soldier activity recently, so he could understand Seth asking. It wasn't like the Irishmen were offering to help, though Rowan suspected the Irishwoman had something to do with that. Ah well, at least Madoc was out of her...

Rowan pulled up short in front of one of the stalls. The most beautiful Clydesdale he'd ever seen, and had seen before, was lazily munching hay.

"Now then." He reached in to stroke its neck. "I didn't think I'd see you again."

"I'm sure you didn't."

Rowan spun round at the sound of a familiar voice, only to be greeted by a blow to the forehead.

Morgan walked down the corridor of the palace to Nicholas's private study, an uncomfortable churning in the pit of her stomach. Her lunch had already been a casualty of hormones, as well as the case of nerves she'd had since her return to Edinburgh Castle.

Her mind's eye had played out the whole conversation in her head for the millionth time, preparing the words she never dared to say when she faced him. She could never tell Nicholas she was leaving him anymore than she could tell him she was with child.

She opened the massive door slowly. "Nic?"

His leather chair sat empty behind his desk. He'd been invited to a lunchtime concert at St. Giles Cathedral and had probably stayed for the following service put on by the Order of the Thistle.

Morgan released the breath she'd been holding, the only sound in the room a soft thud when she pulled the door shut behind her. The curtains fluffed out in the cross breeze. From the window she looked to the right of the Crown Square at the symbolic sculptures carved in the alcoves of the War Memorial Building, her eye first going to the mailed warrior with sword and shield representing courage, then to the sword and scales of Justice. The Phoenix above the arched doorway caused something inside her to go very still, the anxiety washing away as she thought of what it stood for. Survival of the Spirit. She placed a hand on her belly, the barest hint of life curving out.

As if on cue, a thick lump formed in her throat. She rushed over to Nicholas's chair and sat down, a hand laid on top of a stack of papers, taking slow deep breaths. Something on the page caught her eye. She moved her fingers to the side a bit, blinking hard to clear her vision enough to read what was on the paper.

Morgan rose, straightening the chair exactly as it was before she sat down, and headed for the door to go find Fiona. It was thrown open before she reached it.

Nicholas greeted her with a warm smile. "Looking for me, Pet?"

Chapter Twenty-Two

Elias rubbed the back of his neck with one hand, while cupping his other around the hot mug of coffee May had brewed for him.

The kitchen was closed, but she'd offered to prepare something, as much from the need to keep busy as hospitality. Struck by one of those odd cravings, he'd asked for a traditional Albannachie breakfast, sopping up every bit of egg, beans, and black pudding.

The doctor had arrived within moments of Sherry's passing, officially calling the time of death. Elias stayed until after the lass's body had been removed from the room, but then slipped away before he could be questioned. If May had thought that odd, she didn't say so.

"She was to be married at the weekend." May ran the tip of a finger slowly round the rim of her teacup. "It was good to see her finally get a bit of happiness in life."

Sherry had been orphaned at a young age and forced to live with her uncle, who was horribly abusive to her in almost every way imaginable and some that were not. One night about two years past, she grabbed a cast iron skillet, rapped her uncle in the head, and ran from the house and as far away as she could get.

May wasn't entirely sure of all the details, nor how Sherry had wound up in Duntreath. All May knew was from the moment Sherry turned up on the doorstep looking for work, the lass had been like family. Things had been quite peaceful until a few weeks back when Sherry was walking back to the inn from town and she was attacked by her uncle. She defended herself with the one thing she could get her hands on; a knitting needle from the basket she was carrying. When they were found by a passerby, she was still lying under him, blood all over her face, the knitting needle protruding from his neck.

Sherry seemed to have recovered from the ordeal quite well in the weeks following the attack but then became withdrawn. She would barely eat and when she did, she could hardly keep it down. Looking back, it was clear what had been wrong and that Sherry had chosen to eradicate the problem herself.

May's face changed a bit. "Knowing how her fiancée would react... the position he would be in..." She shook her head.

Elias knew that governmental approval for an abortion would not have been a problem at all, under the circumstances, but there would have been a permanent record. Her mental state might have been called into question if and when she had tried to have children. The Euthanasia & Eugenics Directive had been written loosely enough that it could be interpreted any manner of ways.

His tongue stung a bit as he took a sip of coffee, a few drops dribbling onto his trousers. He set his cup on the table as he reached for his napkin.

May chuckled. "*Bidh curamach.*"

His head snapped up, then he smiled. "*A bheil Gàidhlig agaibh?*"

"*Tha, beagan.* Grandmere used to tell me stories to teach it to me. There was also a song she used to sing. '*Chi Mi na Morbheanna*'."

"I See the Great Mountains," he smiled. "My father would sing that to my brother and me when we'd go out riding."

The last time was about six months before their parents died. The early morning mist lay thick on the ground. The mountains looked as if they'd a huge fountain of pinks and red spurting up into the sky. A two-year-old Seth had refused to share a saddle with anyone other than his big brother. Their father's voice was deep and rich as he sang the words, then he turned to look at them, eyes filling with tears. It was the only time Elias had ever seen his father cry.

He drained his cup, then stood and reached for May's hand. "*Chi mi a-maireach thu.*"

She smiled, her eyes red-rimmed and tired. "And you, as well."

Elias passed through the lounge area, singing to himself about woods, mist, and fertile fields, looking forward to slipping between the sheets. A shadow made him start so hard he nearly bit his tongue.

Kyrie stood on the bottom step, her hand resting on the rail, frowning.

Madoc twisted his wrists in front of him, the ropes chafing his skin, wondering where they were now and feeling quite the idiot.

When Rowan hadn't brought the horses, Madoc went in to see if he'd needed help. It had happened so fast that all he remembered was being shoved to the ground and held there to prevent him from alerting Seth.

Madoc knew they weren't far as they'd traveled on foot. He couldn't really make out any buildings when they pulled the sack from his head, as there was no moon. The only light came from the torches their captors were holding, the blazes tossing about in the wind and casting grotesque shadows on their faces.

Madoc noticed there was one female in the group. Her clothes were as well-worn and ill-fitting as those of her companions, which numbered eight altogether. Madoc didn't place her at first, until she addressed the leader as "Papa". He then recognized the man from Glasgow with the hurt arm. The rest of their party had called him "Tucker". The two of them were facing Rowan. Seth was a couple of meters on the other side of them, on his knees, hands bound behind him.

Tucker lit a cigar, the end firing red as he puffed on it, the shadows of his face making the roundness of it more pronounced. He shot a look towards Rowan, and then turned to face Seth.

"Life is just full of unexpected blessing, ain't it? Here I thought I made out good after tellin' the Black Suits where to find those fuel cells." His jowls jiggled in the wake of his shrug. "Wonder what I'll get for yer little bitch?"

Tucker's daughter glared at Madoc, then Seth, and finally Rowan. "Maybe you should start wi' the geezer."

Her father shook his head, massaging his left arm with his free hand. "I think I need to start wi' the Jock. I don't think he'd be as impressed watching what happens to his mates as they will be to see what happens to him."

Tucker moved to stand in front of Seth. "Yer a big fucker, aren't ya?"

Seth looked up at Tucker, then made a great show of drawing his head back as he inhaled through his nose with a vociferous grumbling deep in his throat. The projectile discharged from Seth's lips like a cannonball, landing dead center of Tucker's chest. Seth surveyed the wad of mucus slugging its way down Tucker's shirt, then grinned.

Tucker backhanded Seth hard, yelping with pain and grabbing his arm. Seth barely moved. Still cradling his injured limb, Tucker nodded at two of his companions standing nearby. They walked over with tins of some sort of pungent liquid, pouring a circle around Seth, splashing some his direction.

When they finished, Tucker smiled. His cigar hung suspended for what seemed an eternity after leaving his fingers. Madoc heard a shout, not sure if it originated from Seth or his own throat. A wall of fire encircled Seth, now a dark shape in the center, no longer visible. Tucker mounted his horse along with half his crew, torches still in hand. He turned to shout another order when a bolt pushed through the throat of the man to his right. Horses reared and shrieked as a barrage of bolts and arrows flew from the darkness.

Tucker's daughter screamed, running towards her father. She slipped in a pool of wet grass, falling down torch and all. The last Madoc saw of her was the shocked look on her face before the flames took her.

Movement beside him caught his attention. He looked over in time to see Rowan throw himself into the conflagration dancing around Seth. Madoc drew air in his lungs, but instead of words, only choking noises issued forth, sweat and tears mingling on his face. He dropped to his knees. In the space of a breath, the dark shape in the center grew in size and looked as if it was wrestling with itself, then rolled from the blaze. Rowan had his arms wrapped tightly around Seth. They fell away from each other when they landed and laid there, coughing from the smoke.

Donny and Seamas appeared from the shadows, bows drawn. Elias ran to his brother, tossing his crossbow to Seamas. In two steps, Madoc was kneeling beside Seth and Rowan, touching the smooth skin of Rowan's face. Rowan and Seth lay side by side, totally unburned.

Elias looked over Rowan and Seth whilst Donny and Seamas took a body count. Madoc hugged his arms around his chest, shivering, fighting the bile rising in his throat at the charred stench thick in the air.

Seamas hooked his bow over his shoulder and pulled out a cigarette. "Six dead and one still smokin'."

"Hang on. Six dead and one still… there were eight altogether," Madoc forced himself to count each of the bodies, then looked at Elias. "Someone's missing."

"Are you sure you wouldn't like me to… ahh fuck," Orla

whispered loudly, accompanied by glasses clinking against the bottle of whisky she was carrying.

"I'm fine, thanks." I ran my hand along the railing, feeling the air on my face cool a bit as we neared the bottom of the stairs. May had opened the flues in the attic as far as they'd go, but the guest rooms on the upper floor still felt stifling.

I felt nowhere near comfortable enough with Orla to let her help me, not that I really needed her to. I'd been up and down the stairs enough to somewhat know them, and it wasn't as if the low light was a bother for me. Still, I was not above being annoyed that I had to use the collapsible cane while with her. I was also not above smiling as her offer to help was punctuated with her stumbling down the last couple of steps.

The lounge area was still and quiet, except for the wind whistling past the windows but nothing compared to the exchange between the vent in the bottom of my door and the window I'd cracked. It was just as well because I had wanted to be up when Elias got back from finding the others, who were most likely deep in their pints and lost track of time. That seemed a bit out-of-character for Maddy, but then again…

A peaty smell with the faint aroma of seaweed made my mouth water before Orla finished pouring my glass. She tucked it into my outstretched hand.

"*Sláinte*." The settee creaked as Orla settled in.

"*Sláinte*."

The whisky tasted strong and fresh, with a slight sweetness that reminded me of lemonade, leaving behind soft warmth as it trailed down my throat.

"This is excellent." I took another sip, letting it sit on my tongue a moment.

There was a faint, rhythmic clink on the side of Orla's glass, perhaps from a ring. My mind's eye pictured her gently twirling it between her hands.

"I didn't ask you down here just to share my whisky," Orla said. Her tone was not quite as blunt as her words, but I found neither to be offensive.

"I figured as much, since the others didn't come down, as well."

"You and Madoc have a history. I respect that," She conceded.

The bottle rubbed the rim of her glass. I tossed back the rest of my whisky and held mine out for more. The bottle made a dull thud on the table when she set it down.

"I'd thought it to be more than friendship, until Glasgow when I saw you with…"

I cut her off. "Maddy is free to do as he chooses."

"I'm not so sure he is." The clinking sound started again, but she said nothing further.

I finished off my whisky, then placed a hand on the table, setting my glass next to it. I folded out my cane as I stood and began moving towards the stairs. "Thank you for the…"

A noise inside the house drew my attention. It could have been a guest moving about upstairs, but something just seemed a bit off.

After a moment, Orla spoke. "What's wrong?"

I shook my head. "I thought I heard…"

My breath caught in my throat. I nearly gagged from the nauseating smell of body odor set in over days, mixed with faint aroma of… burned flesh?

The couch squeaked as Orla stood. "What's that… mmnh…"

I grasped the only weapon I had at the moment with both hands, ready to block… whatever.

"What's wrong, Luv? Ankle still givin' ya fits?"

The voice sounded familiar. Recent. "Dat's yer man… from the stables." Glasgow. What the hell was he doing here?

I'd opened my mouth to speak when I heard the whisky bottle knock against the table, followed by a splash and a curse. My mind pinged several possibilities at once. If Orla hadn't lit a lantern, it was either because there was enough natural light to not need one or perhaps she didn't want to bother, for whatever reason. Surely if there'd been any sort of natural light, he wouldn't be stumbling about the way he was. He'd gone quiet except for the sound of his breathing, which also lent towards the no light in the room theory. I eased back a couple of steps and squatted down, laying the cane on the floor with one hand whilst lifting a pant leg with the other.

Papa's *sgian dhu* didn't make a sound as I slid it from my leg sheath. As high as the wind was outside, I could still make out a faint wheezing when he breathed. I had an idea of where Orla had been knocked out, but didn't want to take any chances. The odds of me cocking this up were high enough as it was.

I took a deep breath, holding the knife in front of me, blade out. "What's wrong, Luv? Can't see in the dark?"

A couple of dull thuds on the floor preceded a meaty hand grabbing my arm, pulling me towards him. I slammed against his torso, feeling the knife bury in his gut all the way to the hilt. I twisted hard, then pulled it free and drove it in again. His breath rushed from his body before he dropped to the floor.

I froze in place. Listening. Feeling everything that was and wasn't going on around me. My hand tightened and I started at the sound of someone stirring, not realizing at first it was Orla. My chest relaxed a bit, allowing me to exhale.

"You alright?" I wiped my forehead with the heel of my hand.

A flint strike preceded the distinct odor of lighter fluid. Orla was right next to me when she spoke. "Christ, what just happened?"

I shrugged a shoulder. "He spilt the whisky. I killed him."

There was a slight pause, then she gave me something to wipe my hands on. "Fair enough, but it wasn't me only bottle."

The wind had died down to a hot breeze, making me shiver during the brief intermissions. While I'd washed up in the kitchen, Rowan popped upstairs and grabbed the first shirt he'd found in my bag, which was sleeveless. I rubbed my hands up and down my upper arms.

"Colm and Olen cleaned up the floor." Orla poured herself another whisky. "Let's hope May doesn't notice the rugs have been moved around until after we've gone."

The others had just arrived when we heard May stirring upstairs. Elias caught her before she came down, telling her we'd had a few drinks and made a bit of a mess, but were in the process of cleaning it up. Taking Elias at his word, she'd gone back to bed. We hated lying to her, but couldn't afford involving the authorities. Were it not for my face plastered about God knows where, one of us could have played the soldier card and no further questions would have been asked.

My chest tightened a bit at the sound of someone approaching, butterflies tangling in my stomach. Madoc stopped at the bottom of the steps.

"Well, they're off."

Elias, Donny, Seth, and Seamas were heading back out to take care of the rest of the bodies, Clydesdale in tow with Tucker slung across its back. Colm and Olen were on patrol whilst Fintan had stayed behind. Rowan's shoulder was giving him fits, so he was already upstairs nursing it with primrose paste and good whisky.

The tops of my shoulders felt drawn up into my neck they were so tight, and there was a twinge in my lower back every time I moved. I placed an elbow on the opposite side of my knee and twisted to each side.

A few moments of little more than breathing passing as any sort of conversation and I was ready to turn in. I was shattered, my skin practically crying out for the feel of the sheets, stuffy room and whistling door not even on my radar.

"I think I'm going up now." I'd reached a hand towards the banister only to have it intercepted by Maddy's.

"Me, too."

Upstairs had cooled off considerably. At my door I felt down the frame to the handle and let us in. I counted my way over to the bed and sat down, the mattress sagging as Maddy joined me. We'd sat there for what seemed like forever before he finally spoke.

"There has been so much to say and no chance to say it for so long..."

I raised my thumb to bite off the hangnail. Maddy pulled my hand away from my mouth and held it in his. He rubbed the back of my hand with his thumb.

"I was so focused on you not letting me be there years ago, that I wasn't there when you needed me now."

The thickness of his voice made my eyes well up, my throat almost too tight to swallow. "If I had it to do again, I can't say I wouldn't make the same decision. I can't say that I would have either." I pressed his hand to my lips. "I can say I'm so sorry..."

"Wee Bonnie, you don't have to." He put his arm around me and pulled me against him. "For so many years all I knew was my island, the school. When your world is so small, it's easy to judge, isn't it?"

Looking back, it was as clear as day to see what had been between us, the tangible evidence having been erased when I had made my choice for both of us. That knowledge made right and wrong cease to exist. The tears we should have shared so long ago surfaced like a great storm, years in the making. When it passed, we just sat holding each other in the calm that followed. I didn't know where we would fit into each other's lives, now or in the future, but if felt good to again know that I would have a place in his. He'd been part of my life, in one way or another, for all my life and I couldn't imagine it any other way.

Maddy cleared his throat and stood to leave. I grabbed his arm, not ready for him to go yet. He took my hand and kissed it.

"I think it best I go now."

I nodded, swallowing hard. "It's okay if you don't want…"

His fingers dug into my shoulders as he pulled me to my feet, his lips tearing into mine with such force that when he finally pulled back, my lips felt swollen.

He rested his forehead against mine. "I will always 'want', Kyrianna Threas Maclaren. Till the day I die."

The door creaked open, and then shut behind him. I stood there a moment, then lay down on my bed and cried myself to sleep.

Chapter Twenty-Three

The sun was just climbing over the horizon when Elias walked into the stable, feeling like his eyes had been turned inside out. Perhaps he'd have time for another cup of coffee before they set off. He heard someone at the door and turned, hoping it was Seth come to help with the horses.

The sight of a tall male in a black uniform pulled Elias up short. The metal plate on the front of the wide stable belt bore the letters "ASF". A small patch with a subdued silver thistle was sewn onto each collar and the front of his beige beret, denoting the rank of Major. Recognition clicked into place as the soldier smiled, his eyes wide.

"Mister Buchanan! I thought that was you!"

Elias smiled and extended a hand. "Lieutenant… well, I suppose that would be Major Bradford, wouldn't it?"

Bradford laughed. "It's been a good, long while since the Fighting 59th. You must be Warrant Officer First Class by now, yeah?"

Elias nodded. "Before I retired. What about you?"

He kept his voice casual, wishing to Christ that Seth would turn up. From what Elias remembered Bradford was an alright fellow, but a loyal soldier nonetheless. Elias preferred to not have another body to bury.

"… so afterwards I was sent to command the Edinburgh branch of the ASF." Bradford pulled off his beret. "I was glad for the promotion, but… well suffice to say, the post came with its own set of challenges."

Elias noticed the lines branching out from Bradford's eyes, the somberness about him. It had been ten years since they'd seen each other, but from the looks of the man, it could have easily been twice that. Elias crossed his arms loosely over his chest, keeping his tone casual.

"What brings ye up this way?"

Bradford nodded, a smile actually reaching his eyes for the first time. "I'm getting married at the weekend."

Before the words had fully sunk in, Elias looked past Bradford to see Rowan and Kyrie walk through the door, arm in arm.

Elias poured another glass of whisky. The cover over the terrace shielded them from the morning sun, which was now high in the sky.

Bradford rested his forehead on the heel of his hand, his uniform top hung over the back of his chair, his t-shirt stark white against the black of his trousers. He lifted his head, taking the whisky Elias offered, eyes red-rimmed and swollen.

"Was she… was she in pain?"

Elias shook his head, thankful it was the truth, as far as he'd seen, anyway.

"Bitch." Bradford slammed his glass on the table, discharging broken shards in all directions. "She just leaves me here to…" He threw his face in his hands, heaving sobs erupting from his very core.

Elias laid a hand on Bradford's shoulder, now understanding what May had meant the night before. The position Bradford would have been in as not only a soldier, but a high ranking officer with the Alban Security Force, would have been precarious to say the least.

If Bradford was not the father, and the child had been born with defects, Bradford would have been not only duty-bound but legally required to have the child euthanized. Bradford spoke, his voice muffled.

"I know why this has happened." He raised his head and wiped the back of his hand across his face. "A few days ago, there was an event at the Edinburgh Cathedral. The Prime Minister himself asked me to attend, so I pushed my leave back."

A group of protesters rushed them as soon as they'd cleared the door. Bradford placed himself in front of the Prime Minister while the security detail addressed the situation. From the corner of his eye, he caught sight of something lunging towards the Prime Minister. In one motion, Bradford drew his sword and turned, driving the blade into the would-be attacker. It was then he saw her face; a woman, seven months pregnant, who had been trying to rush past when she was knocked off balance. Her face was frozen in shock, the hilt of the sword sticking from her round belly, the blade protruding from her back. She stood like that for what seemed an eternity, then collapsed at his feet.

Bradford knelt by her, alternating between pleas for forgiveness and cries for help, drowned out in the surrounding melee. She raised a hand and pressed her fingertips to his lips, blood staining her lips and teeth as she spoke her last words.

"Do you know what it was she said to me? 'It's not your fault.'" His eyes hardened. "Do you know what I got for it? An extra week of leave." He snatched up the whisky bottle. "Seems God was not so forgiving."

Elias had not yet mentioned the attack, and now wondered if he should. It might not ease the pain, but perhaps the guilt Bradford was feeling. Though tragic and senseless, it was an accident. Anyone willing to judge had surely never stared down the length of a blade.

"There's something you should know…" Elias began.

Bradford held up a hand. "I already do."

Elias was confused, then realized what Bradford meant. "Yer talkin' about Mac."

"There aren't many soldiers who don't remember her." Bradford stared down at the table. "Perhaps losing her sight is her penance."

Elias had a good idea of what Bradford was referring to, having served in the same unit during the Rising. Kyrie had never offered the particulars of what had happened, though there had been others more willing to.

"There are soldiers, some ASF, due in sometime this afternoon. A handful I'd invited to the…" Bradford looked hard at Elias. "As long as they don't see you, then I haven't seen you."

Elias stopped at the screen door, holding the handle whilst looking back over his shoulder. "It really wasn't your fault."

Bradford stared down at his hands. A single tear rolled down his already wet cheek. "Does it matter?"

Chapter Twenty-Four

My stomach sounded off with a gurgle so loud it inspired a chuckle from Elias and Rowan.

We'd only stopped once since leaving May's for a quick bite of lunch and to study intelligence Orla had on the Wall, as well as letting the heat of the day pass. The air was still heavy and warm, though the sun had gone down a few hours ago, the only sound that of squeaking saddles and hoof beats.

If there were soldiers as far north as May's place, then it was possible for them to ride even further up. Small intelligence teams, along with an engineer, were periodically sent to survey the Wall, as well as check with local authorities to see if there'd been any unreported activity, such as attempted crossings. I'd accompanied such a team on more than one occasion. The surveys were all classified. As far as anyone outside our chain of command was concerned, we were just on temporary duty at another installation. There had only been one known instance of a leak.

A few years back, a female sergeant confided more than she should have to the love of her night after getting pissed up in a local pub. The man she'd been with tried to use the information in exchange for passage into the north. His dead body was seen hung from the Wall, badly beaten, with a sign across his chest bearing a single name. Her name.

Upon our return, the sergeant was charged with treason. The next morning she was hung by the neck until dead. Between trial and execution she was "aggressively" interrogated by counter intelligence to see if there had been any other breaches in security. Unfortunately for her, the interrogator was hard to satisfy, and the female sergeant had nothing to tell.

Rowan's sharp intake of breath alerted me the Wall must be coming into view, a very intimidating sight, indeed. It had been years, but according to Orla's intel the design had not changed since I'd seen it last.

The Wall followed the north side of the River Tay, stretching entirely from east to west coast. The Iron Curtain was tangible evidence of the centuries-long division that had existed between the Highlands and Alba. The outermost layer was steel mesh with sharp edges, appearing nearly transparent when viewed head-on. Just underneath was a layer of roughly sixty centimeters of high strength concrete. The third and innermost layer, concave steel designed to withstand a blast from hell itself.

A large concrete culvert ran along the length of the top, which served two purposes. First, it made climbing over the top of the Wall damn near impossible; second, it housed shaped charges directed downward. It was an effective way of minimizing damage to the Wall itself, yet inflicting the most damage to would-be aggressors or Alban defectors. In the unlikely event that the harsh terrain and strategically placed ordinance weren't a deterrent enough, the hundred or so guard towers spaced out along the entire length of the barrier were the cherries on top.

Eros slowed, and then stopped altogether. I took the opportunity to pull my canteen from my saddle whilst listening to Orla.

"We're almost to the old Checkpoint. At 0300 sharp we will be granted entrance." She took a drink of water, then continued. "Once in the north, we'll be guided through the *Crioch a' bhàis* and past the second fence line, roughly ninety meters into the Highlands."

She clucked to her horse, the rest of the group nudging into motion behind her. I put my canteen away and flicked the reins lightly. Behind me, I heard Rowan and Maddy speaking to one another.

"I've never read anything about a second barrier?" Rowan asked in a low voice.

"Something tells me it's not widely known about," Maddy answered. "I wonder what the name means."

Maddy and Rowan continued talking quietly between the two of them, not even noticing when Elias answered their question, his voice so low I wasn't sure that he meant for them to. It carried the hint of a memory, years past but never forgotten.

"The Death Strip."

The Checkpoint was the only land-based access to and from the Highlands. When the Wall was first constructed, it was used to grant access to visiting diplomats and the like.

The tension between Alba and the Highlands eventually culminated into a standoff when a high ranking Alban dignitary was denied access into the Highlands. Each side deployed troops near the Wall, prepared for escalation. After a few days of fragile negotiations, each side agreed to stand down and that the Checkpoint would be sealed shut.

In recent years, there were rumors the North used it to send spies into Alba, but nothing had ever been proven. It wasn't as if anyone had the chance to examine the passageway closely.

We stopped to look over Orla's map of the exterior mine field one last time. Things had cooled considerably over the last couple of hours. I rubbed the damp spots of insect repellent on my forearms dry before pulling my sleeves down.

Starting seventy meters out on our side of the Wall, pressure type mats lay just under the ground and were used to activate manual chargers, which would then fire a second set of shaped charges laid another fifty meters in. If I'd had to guess, the wiring of each circuit probably ran along inside some sort of pipe to protect from corrosion. It also made it more difficult to interrupt the circuit.

I would have felt better relying on more than a map, but we didn't have the tools to fashion any sort of detector. Orla had felt it best to carry as little equipment as possible whilst traveling in Alban territory. To me it seemed if Irish counter-intelligence was caught traveling with an Alban fugitive wanted for murder and desertion, what would a little copper wire matter?

Seamas sounded tight-lipped, the faint scent of cigarette smoke wafting round. "Seems straight forward. Who's on…?"

Elias interrupted, the map ruffling a bit. "This is not how I remember it."

"You've crossed the Wall before?" Orla sounded both surprised and annoyed. "When were you planning to tell us?"

"I'm telling you now," Elias snapped back. "Granted, it was a little over twenty years ago."

I pushed my misgivings about her map aside. "How recent is your intel?"

"It was the most recent to come in before I left for Glasgow." She sounded as if she were clenching her jaw when she spoke.

"Unless someone's going to pull a metal detector out of their hole…" I shrugged, "… then this is it. Donny?"

"Right here." He called from my left.

"You, Seamas, and Seth buddy up on the advance. Follow the map, use your blades, and mark anything solid." I wiped my sleeve across my forehead.

"Baby makes four," Fintan added. "I'm not EOD, but I've some time as a grunt myself."

"At least there's a moon tonight," Seamas chuckled. "Shall we then?"

The rest of us waited as patiently as we could manage whilst the four of them navigated the open field at a turtle's pace, poking gently here and there. If the layout had been changed, they'd have no legs to put their heads between and no ass to kiss goodbye.

Beside me, I heard Elias's breathing quicken; his entire presence tensed. I reckoned it was more than just the minefield that had him rattled.

Orla seemed right pissed Elias had not said anything about his previous crossing. In all fairness to her, I could understand why; however, for all the years I'd known Elias it was the one subject he didn't like to speak of and was probably hoping the need wouldn't arise.

The only noise breaking the stillness of night was the wind whipping past the Wall, the occasional low snort of the horses, and, from time to time, my pulse thudding in my ears.

Elias whispered to me they'd made it past the mats and were nearing the last set of charges. As it always happens when things are going well, someone has to cock it up by stating that very fact.

Rowan took a deep breath, then released it, his voice not much louder than Elias's had been. "Well, so far, so…"

Click.

"Hang on, Mac. Almost there." Seth had a death grip on my hands which were resting on either side of his hips. He guided me round in front of him.

"Fintan hit a trip wire just enough tae pull the spring pins loose, but that's no the real problem. Rattled as he was, he compressed one nearby wi' his hand."

Seth placed my hand on Donny's shoulder, who was crouched down in front of me. I knelt down beside him, feeling as if I could think better if I were in closer.

"How are we doing on time?"

Seth answered, "We've little more than an hour. What

about the others?"

I shook my head. "Leave them be. The way these are rigged, it's not worth the risk."

Donny spoke, sounding slightly winded. "Wha' do I do first?"

"You're going to have to cut the wires and reset the pins." I laid a hand on Fintan's back. "You're doing fine."

I turned towards Donny. "What's your status?"

"Wires cut. Pins in place," Donny answered. "Now what?"

I swabbed the back of my hand across my forehead, then wiped it on my jeans. "Dig out all round it to expose the entire device."

The air reeked with the smell of fresh dirt. I waited until Donny was done before going to the next step. "Do you remember what the fuse plugs look like?"

"Yep. Found 'em."

"Good. Unscrew them and take them all the way out."

Donny exhaled sharply. "Done. What now?"

"Now you'll need to tie the trigger down. Do you see it?"

"Yea, but I've nothing to tie it wit'."

I jerked the leather thong from my hair, feeling like someone had laid a blanket over my shoulders.

He took it from my hand. "I'm not questioning ya, but the fuses…"

I nodded. "I know, but the 'jumping' charge is active now. It might be enough to cause the TNT to burn."

"Ah, right." Donny said. "Sussed."

After the trigger was secured, I ran my hand along Fintan's shoulder and cupped his arm. "Alright, ease off it."

His bicep trembled, fatigued from holding pressure on the mine. He straightened up, kneeling in place, exhaling and groaning all at once. "Ah, my Jaysus. I'm gonna kiss ya. Just get yer mouth ready, and yer tongue loosened up."

I exhaled and laughed at the same time. "Hold that thought. We need to make sure the nasty little bugger is sufficiently neutered." I tucked my hair behind my ear.

"The whole device needs to be dug completely up, the jump charge drained, and the trigger removed altogether."

"What can I do to help?" Fintan asked.

"You can be still…" Donny grumbled, then added, "… and, for fucksake, don't touch anythin'!"

I gathered my hair and lifted it off my neck, letting the breeze dry the sheen of sweat on my back whilst I tied another thong around it. My throat was so parched it throbbed.

We'd worked as quickly as we could, Donny following my instructions sharp and to the letter, which meant everyone else standing fast before trying to advance. It had left us with only thirty minutes to move ten people and eleven horses through an active minefield.

The ordinance had been placed to sort of funnel anyone attempting to reach the Checkpoint into a particular position. The path was about a meter wide, which allowed the horses to travel through; however, it put us right where the person who'd laid the mines wanted us, which meant there could be something there that wasn't on the map.

It would have made much more sense to catch a ferry, but the Checkpoint was the only rendezvous point. Traveling over to the coast would have presented its own set of problems, on top of the ones we had already.

My watch vibrated, making me jump so hard I nearly bit my tongue. I eased the crystal up, feeling the Braille on the face. Fifteen minutes left, and by my estimation we weren't even halfway across the field.

Below the ground about a meter from me I felt as much as heard the sound of steel shanks sliding one against the other. I caught the very pungent smell of earth, mixed with the scent of a strong soap. The muted thud of footfalls approached.

All in one motion, I grasped the sheath at my side, pulling the leather strap hanging across my shoulder taut whilst the other hand drew my dirk. A voice spoke to me, first in *Gàidhlig*, then in English.

"*Stad*, lass. My name is Eòin Grant. I am tae be yer escort."

I guided the blade back into the sheath, keeping my hand on the hilt. "My name is Kyrianna Maclaren."

"Well, Kyrianna Maclaren, are those yer people?"

"Yes."

"I kent it best tae come a bit early, but it appears no early enough." He seemed to shift a bit, perhaps raising a hand to wave to the others. My wariness was momentarily forgotten, replaced by confusion.

"Early enough for what?"

"Tae take ye tae tha tunnel."

It took a second for me to sort what he'd just said. "There's a tunnel?"

"Aye," he answered.

"A tunnel," I said, mostly to myself.

"Aye," he repeated. "Much safer than comin' through here. This whole field is set wi' mines."

Goosebumps danced along the skin on my arms, caused by the damp chill of being underground. I wiggled my fingers, my hand falling asleep from raising it to grasp Eros' saddle as I walked along beside him.

It'd only taken about half an hour of walking to get to the entrance of the tunnel. Once inside, Eòin offered a bit more explanation, but not much. The intel Orla had received hadn't been so much inaccurate as incomplete. The intention all along had been to get us to the Checkpoint, where an escort would lead us to one of a handful of tunnels for access into the Highlands. Construction on the tunnels had begun around the same time the Wall was built, but he wouldn't say exactly how many tunnels there were or if any were still being excavated. I would've bet a bottle of whisky that ordinance also ran along the tunnels that could cause a cave-in were they ever breeched.

Walking down the center of the passageway, I could easily extend my arm out to the side or straight up and not touch the wall. I imagined it was large enough to pass troops and equipment through.

Eòin's voice echoed off the walls. "I'll be takin' ye tae Glengarry Castle. The others will meet us there within the next day or so."

We followed along for about another half hour before reaching the exit. I inhaled a lung full of fresh air, the nausea from all the musty smells finally abating.

A massive lump began pushing its way up through my throat. I swallowed hard. Elias stepped up beside me, pulling me in next to him.

"Are ye alright?" His voice was low and, for some reason, the sound of it made tears come to my eyes.

I leaned against him, my stomach settling. "I'm fine. Coming out of the tunnel, I just felt sick."

He chuckled and pressed a kiss against my forehead. "You and me both."

Chapter Twenty-Five

Elias tossed his scotch back, feeling the warmth snake down into his chest as he held out his glass for more of the 40 year old Bowmore they'd found in the master suite.

Upon arriving at Glengarry Castle, they were all shown to their rooms for a few hours' sleep. Eòin had roused them all around noon for a bit of lunch, and also to say Alastair wished a private meeting with his nephews upon his arrival later in the afternoon.

Seth poured them each another generous shot, then leaned back into the sofa. Elias massaged his temple, an index finger trailing to the thickened ridge of his nose, the breeze from the window behind them doing little to dry the sheen of sweat coating his brow and face.

Seth cleared his throat, his voice husky from drink. "He did that to you, aye?"

Elias gripped his nose between his thumb and finger. "Aye, although I dinna remember it."

Seth nodded, and then drained his glass. Elias had never told his little brother the details of the event preceding their defection. In part because Seth was just a wee bairn when it happened, but mostly because Elias had no real recollection of it. He remembered the first few blows of his uncle's thrashing, and the next he knew, he woke up in his bed, feeling as if he'd been trampled by a herd of horses. With the exception of losing their parents, that beating was the worst memory of his entire childhood, one that wound up affecting the course of his life in more ways than one. Had that not happened, he most likely wouldn't have left. He would never have met Donny or Seamas. Kyrie. He would never be able to say he was thankful, but he wouldn't trade anything or anyone in his life now as a result of it.

Voices neared the door. He and Seth shared a brief look, then set their glasses on the table and moved over to stand side-by-side at the foot of the bed, shoulders squared. Elias's breath caught in his throat just before the door flung open.

To say Alastair Buchanan entered the room was much like saying Germany entered Poland. He looked younger than his sixty years, albeit a bit tired. Silver gray hair blended well into the remaining blonde. Slight grooves curved from his nose to either side of his mouth, but did little to age him. The terse look on Alastair's face caused a nervous flutter in Elias's stomach. He crossed his arms over his chest, mentally banishing the unease.

Alastair stood a meter or two across the room, looking up at them, not saying a word. Finally he spoke to Seth in *Gàidhlig*. "Ye've grown tall."

Seth glanced at Elias before answering, also in *Gàidhlig*. "Well, it has been twenty-three years."

Alastair grinned. "It has indeed. How was your trip?"

Seth chuckled. "I've got a funny story about an Irishman and a…" he turned to Elias, switching to English, "…

minefield?"

Elias and Alastair answered in unison. "*Mèinneadair-blàr.*"

Alastair stared Elias right in the eye for a long moment, then motioned towards the whisky. "Och, ye've a whole bottle for the telling."

Two empty bottles stood on the table, another lying on the floor like a fallen foe not far from where the three of them were sitting.

Elias reclined back on an elbow, staring through the bottom of his empty glass at his brother, then his uncle. Seth stretched out on his stomach, his chin propped up on the side of his fist.

Alastair sat back against the end of the bed, his legs stretched in front of him, crossed at the ankles. "Did Uilleam ever tell ye about Da' taking us fishing on his birthday?"

Elias and Seth shrugged their shoulders, shaking their heads. Elias thought he remembered their father telling them, but didn't want to say anything, always willing to hear stories about Grandfather Dùghlas.

Alastair smiled, his eyes crinkling even more. "It was your grandfather's fiftieth, and all he wanted was tae spend it fishing wi' his three sons."

It was not far into the First Season, so the lochs were well full from the rains. After a massive breakfast of eggs, black pudding, potato scones and buttery, they decided to go out on Loch Coruisk. The four of them sailed around for hours, not really catching much of anything and not willing to keep what they did. Sometime late in the afternoon, Dùghlas suddenly clutched at his belly, moaning.

"Ahhh, hell."

"What ails ye, Da'?" Alastair asked.

Dùghlas began rocking back and forth. "It's my condition."

The three of them looked at one another. Finally Niall asked. "What condition are ye talkin' about?"

Dùghlas looked more and more agitated. "My stomach condition."

Niall raised an eyebrow. "Yer wha'?"

"Sometimes my, oh…" Dùghlas dropped his rod in the bottom of the boat. "I need tae get tae shore!"

Uilleam reeled in his line and reached for their father's to do the same. "Let me just…"

"Now, goddammit!" Dùghlas shouted.

They reeled their lines in as fast as they could, then began to row as hard as they could towards land. Dùghlas's moans had nearly turned to howls by the time they neared the shore. The very tip of the boat had no sooner touched land when, in one sweeping motion, Dùghlas threw a foot out, sinking to an ankle in the mud, jerked his pants down, and his bowels discharged like a cannon blast. Niall, who'd been seated behind Dùghlas, practically dove over the opposite side of the boat, which rocked it just enough to knock Dùghlas off balance, causing him to fall forward, head in the muck and ass in the air. Facing out onto the loch as he was, passersby had a clear view of Dùghlas's bare backside, now splattered with the ricochet of mud and whatever was mixed with it.

Alastair sounded as if he were straining to get the words out. "Someone... someone... on shore looked over and... applauded!"

Elias felt his stomach spasm from laughing so hard, tears streaming down his face. Seth fared no better, alternating between coughing and gasping for air. Alastair collapsed into a fit of his own, which went on for several moments. In the subsequent lull, they noticed someone knocking at the door, but had no idea for how long.

He wiped a hand across his face and shouted, "Come!"

His personal assistant stuck her head in the door. "Sir, supper will be ready in fifteen minutes."

At his nod, she shut the door behind her. Seth raised himself into a press-up, then stood. "I need tae wash up."

Seth managed to make it to the cludgie, but not before they erupted in a relapse of laughter caused by the still fresh mental picture the story had evoked. As soon as the door shut, Elias reached over and scooped up the discarded bottle. He placed it on the table with the others, trying to remember the last time he'd laughed that hard.

Alastair cleared his throat. "I reckon we hae something tae talk about."

Elias stared at the bottle, his hand still touching it, then looked over his shoulder at his uncle. "Every Sunday brings with it another week."

Alastair nodded. "Another week, then."

When the cludgie door opened, Elias stood and walked towards it. Seth wiped his hands on his jeans, a familiar

237

twinkle lighting his eye as a grin split his face. He hunched over and clutched his stomach with great dramatic flair, eyes opened wide.

"Ahhh, hell!"

Elias followed Alastair into the formal dining room, at once noticing Kyrie and Rowan over by the fireplace. Everyone else was standing about, chatting as they waited for dinner to be served.

Voices died away, all eyes towards Alastair as they entered the room, commanding everyone's attention with ease.

"*Ceud Mìle Fàilte*. I am Alastair Buchanan. Whilst you are here, my home…" he laid a hand against his chest, "… is your home."

Madoc and Orla were standing nearest, so Alastair approached them first, hand extended. Elias walked over to Rowan and Kyrie.

After a short greeting, Rowan excused himself. "I'm going after another drink."

Elias tucked a curl behind Kyrie's ear. She was dressed casually in denim pants and a matching jacket, but the dark blue next to her smooth skin, hair lifted up off her neck, made her look damn sexy. She smiled and leaned in towards him, making the faint spicy scent of her body wash more noticeable.

"Bowmore, eh?"

"What? Nothing," he stammered. "How d'ye…?"

She cocked a brow and grinned. "I know the smell. I thought you liked Talisker?"

More than once she'd surprised him with her memory of the little things. "I do because it's…"

"… made in Skye," she finished. "Just like you."

He cleared his throat, feeling more than his heart swell, and turned discreetly towards the fireplace.

The door from the kitchen opened, and a tallish fellow peered into the room, brows raised in question. At Alastair's nod, the man stepped to the side, allowing servers with trays of food and drink to pass.

Kyrie perked up. "Ooh, is that the food coming out?"

Elias chuckled. "Aye."

She held out a hand for him. "Shall we then?"

Feeling ready to face the world, he took her hand and walked over to two vacant chairs, minding the kitchen staff buzzing about the table. His mouth watered at the sight and smell of the massive fillet of Angus beef smothered in whisky and tarragon sauce stretching across his plate. They each waited until everyone was served, but he wasn't above running a fingertip along the edge of his plate and slipping it in his mouth.

A wee lass circled the table with a pitcher in hand before spotting an empty glass between Seth and Rowan. Just as she reached between them, Seth growled and snapped at her arm as if he were going to tear a chunk of flesh away with his bare teeth. Elias couldn't tell who squealed the loudest; her when she jumped out of her skin, Rowan when he jumped from his chair, or Seth when she splashed a bit of cold water on the back of his neck. There was a momentary lull, then the room went up like a powder keg. Kyrie wiped her eyes, gasping for breath. She enjoyed more than anyone Seth's larking about, and the fact she'd not been able to actually see it made Elias's eyes well-up from more than laughter.

Hilarity passed, allowing conversation to take its place. Kyrie wasn't one to speak much when there was food in front of her, so Elias took the opportunity to massacre his steak, every bite practically melting over his tongue. With the taste still in his mouth, he took a generous sip of red wine, letting them mix together as they crawled down his throat.

Kyrie moaned as she took the last couple of bites, but it wasn't long before she asked after dessert. "So, what sweets do we have?"

"Cherry and almond flan, topped wi' cherry ice cream; Cranachan, which are raspberries, Drambuie, and honey-flavored ice cream, with shortbread biscuits on the side." He smiled and took another sip of wine. "Also, there is a cheese tray wi' caboc and Highland cheddar."

She groaned and leaned towards him, speaking in a low voice. "You think anyone will notice if I unbutton my pants?"

Whisky and wine had stirred in his system enough to loosen his tongue. "Ye can take 'em off for all I care."

Affecting shock, she pinched his arm, her brown eyes firing small yellow sparks in the candlelight. He was glad he was sitting down, his lower body hidden by the table. He took another sip of wine, then cleared his throat.

"Alastair is having a gathering in Inverness in three days. I wondered if ye might want tae leave tomorrow for a bit of sight-seeing on the way up."

She nodded, easing the button of her jeans loose. "Yeah, sure. Who else is going with?"

His idea of them going alone didn't seem such a plan now. "Uh… I reckoned Seth, Donny, and Seamas. Perhaps Rowan." He fumbled with his napkin. "Did ye want Madoc to come, as well?"

Her smile dropped just a click. "He and Orla are going on their own to Fort William tomorrow night."

Elias opened his mouth to speak, but was interrupted when Alastair stood, raising his glass high in the air. "*Ordugh san dùthaich agus sìth san t-saoghal.*"

Everyone followed suit. Kyrie touched Elias's arm. He leaned down, and she whispered in his ear. "What did he say?"

Elias looked at each of them, feeling the presence of change creep about them like a ghost. He whispered back. "Order in the nation. Peace in the world."

Chapter Twenty~Six

The morning sky reminded Rowan of a child's painting with the stark contrast of blue background, white clouds, and greenery surrounding Loch Oich. He closed his eyes a moment, basking in the cool breeze skirting across the water, thinking the temperature could be no more than thirty-two degrees Celsius, at the most.

When they'd arrived at Glengarry, he'd practically collapsed into a coma as soon as he touched the sheets, not waking until well into the next afternoon. It had been the first sound sleep he'd had since they'd left Làidir.

Footsteps descending the path behind him drew his attention. Elias walked down the hill, wiping a hand across his brow. He stopped just short of where the stone deck met the shoreline.

"Everything's loaded and ready tae go."

Rowan gave a short nod. "Shall we then?"

Elias smiled and nodded back. "We shall."

Massive azalea bushes lined the path leading up towards the manor, the gray stone dormers perched atop like crowns, slightly darker than the stones below. Rowan stopped in the middle of the path as if he'd hit a brick wall, his mouth dropping open. The strangest looking carriage was parked in front of the manor. He couldn't tell how many seats it had, unable to make out more than a couple of heads inside the shadowed cabin.

He sputtered a moment, making Elias laugh out loud. "Is that… what is that?"

"The proper name is a Land Rover," Elias grinned. "But, it's more commonly referred to as an automobile."

The sun was high in the sky, but a cool breeze blew in the window of the Land Rover, causing Rowan's eyes to water. He grabbed at the dashboard, his stomach doing summersaults.

Most history books mentioned the use of automobiles, centuries before during the Petroleum Age. It was exciting to see one in person, but he had to admit it felt a bit surreal to actually be in one, the fact Elias was able to pilot one notwithstanding. Elias repositioned the gear stick in some sort of pattern depending on their speed, causing an ever so slight pause each time.

Rowan frowned. "How did you say it works again?"

The Land Rover made a scraping sound, then sort of growled as Elias pulled back on the gear stick. "Petranol is filtered through the engine."

Rowan squinted, trying to visualize what was happening under the motor cover. In Alba there were steam engines, utilized mostly for industrial purposes. The average person couldn't afford passage on the ones used for travel.

"Does it work like a steam engine?"

Elias shook his head. "No, this is a combustion engine. It's also referred to as a four-stroke. When we get tae our first stop, ye can have a keek."

Kyrie spoke from the seat behind Elias, her chin tilted slightly so the wind hit her full in the face. "Yes, and perhaps you can do a better job of describing it than Seth did."

Elias flashed a look at his little brother sitting next to Kyrie, then looked back at her. "So, when ye asked tae see it, and I said 'wait until later', wha' d'ye reckon I meant?"

Seth jabbed a finger towards Kyrie, who without turning from the window backhanded Seth in the ribs. In the seats behind them, Donny and Seamas chuckled and shook their heads, then returned to staring out at the scenery.

Seth leaned over towards Kyrie to look out her window, describing things as they passed. Rowan looked out through the windscreen, soaking in everything from the sound of the engine to the rocky terrain.

After touring all day, Rowan was of the opinion the Highlands more than lived up to the jagged beauty he'd always imagined, but never dreamed he would get to see. They'd driven through a few glens to Eilean Donan Castle, owned by a family named MacCrae. They all got out and walked along the bridge, the water an almost sapphire blue.

By far the most breathtaking were the craggy mountains and mirrored lochs of Glencoe. A series of spectacular waterfalls gathered at what was known as the Meeting of the Rivers, which culminated into the River Coe. On the northern side of Glencoe was a pinnacled ridge known as *Aonach Egach*, which Elias translated to 'notched ridge'. For all its proximate beauty, Glencoe secreted a sad history indeed.

In ancient times, an English king had offered a pardon to all the Highland clans that had fought against him, on the condition that they swore an oath of allegiance. The only alternative to the oath was death. The Clan MacDonald took the oath five days after the established deadline, but naively believed they would be safe. Unknown to the Chieftain, a force had already been assembled to exterminate the entire clan.

Led by Captain Robert Campbell of Glen Lyon, a man with a grudge against the MacDonalds, the troop left for Glencoe. Campbell asked for quarters for his one hundred and thirty soldiers and, for a little over a week, the MacDonalds entertained their guests, unaware of the brutal directive Campbell had been charged with.

In the early hours of a cold winter morning, the soldiers rose from their beds and set about slaughtering the MacDonalds. Although only forty were killed that day, many more escaped to the hills only to die of hunger and exposure.

Hearing that story had caused a hard knot to ball up in Rowan's midsection, thinking of all those who'd been given refuge at Làidir and wondering if that was to be their own fate once this all played out. He took a deep breath and concentrated on the landscape rolling by, until the feeling had subsided.

The sun was nearly hidden by the mountains now, bleeding red and amber across the evening sky. Elias slowed down and steered into the clearing in front of a wee pub offside the road. Rowan opened his door as soon as the motor was shut off and got out, thankful to finally straighten his knees. He hobbled round to the front of the Land Rover

246

and waited for Elias to raise the motor cover. He listened intently as Elias pointed at different parts, explaining what each did.

The engine looked like an aluminum puzzle, each separate part fitting together to form a block. Elias had called it an in-line six, as there were six cylinders lined up in a row. Petranol, a highly concentrated fuel made from either corn or sugar cane, was sieved through a special corrosion filter called a water sorb before being cycled through the motor. After a full cycle, the fuel was then collected and run through a regenerator, which made it possible for it to be cycled through again. Because of the regenerator, one tank of fuel could last several weeks before it broke down too much to power the engine and fresh Petranol had to be mixed in.

Rowan rubbed his hands up and down his denim clad thighs, wishing the motor weren't so hot. Kyrie secured a promise from Elias that before leaving the Highlands, he would take some of the parts off and let her touch them.

Rowan looked around. "Where are Donny and Seamas?"

Seth answered, motioning towards the pub. "They made a beeline for the cludgie."

Rowan nodded. "Ah. Shall we then?"

Elias shut the motor cover. Seth had opened the back for Kyrie, who at the moment was digging through her pack for something. "We'll be right behind ye."

The inside of the pub was smallish, but cozy. The wall behind the bar was lined with various scotches with nary a space between the bottles. There also looked to be a couple of barrels with taps, most likely filled with ale or stout. A handful of tables were arranged about the room, the largest being the only one that could seat the six of them. The bar-maid picked up a tray and walked over. Rowan took a seat, giving her time to light the large, three-wick candle sitting in the middle of the table.

"Yes, I'd like six pints of stout, please."

She shook her head and frowned. He pointed at a poster on the wall, then held up six fingers. She nodded and held out her hand, looking as if she were thinking of what to say. Rowan stared for a moment, then pulled out six of his two piece Highland coins and placed them in her hand. She smiled wide and said something in *Gàidhlig* as she motioned towards the bar.

After she walked away, Rowan pulled another coin out of his pocket and rubbed his thumb over the thistle etched into it. Trading coin for goods rather than bartering for them was a new concept to say the least. He'd felt a bit odd at taking money from Elias and was still trying to figure out a way to repay. So much about the Highlands was a polar opposite to Alba that Rowan wondered if he were even on the same planet. When a person spends their whole life in one place, their world view forms such a static picture that it becomes hard to imagine other colors even exist.

Kyrie, Elias, and Seth walked in at the same moment Donny and Seamas emerged from the hallway next to the bar. Rowan stuck the coin back in his pocket as Kyrie and Elias settled in across from Donny and Seth.

"I didn't t'ink I's gonna make it." Donny leaned forward, resting his elbows on the table.

Seamas sat down at the far end of the table, then lit a cig and took a deep draw. "Jaysus, me either."

Rowan motioned towards the bar. "I already ordered."

Seth smacked his hand hard on the table. "So, this fella goes into a pub, and the barmaid asks what he wants."

"'I want tae bury my face in your cleavage and lick the sweat from between your tits,' the man says.

"'You bastard!' shouts the barmaid. 'Get out before I get my husband!'

"The fella apologizes and promises not to repeat his gaffe. The barmaid accepts this and asks again what he wants. 'I want to pull your pants down, spread yoghurt between the cheeks of your arse and lick it all off,' he says.

"'You dirty, filthy thing!' she storms. 'You're barred! Get out!'

"Again, he apologizes, swearing to never do it again. 'One more chance,' says the barmaid. 'Now - what do you want?'

"The man smiles, 'I want to turn you upside down, open your legs, fill your twat with stout, and then drink every last drop from it.'

"The barmaid is furious and runs upstairs to fetch her husband. 'There's a bloke in the bar who wants to put his head between my tits and lick the sweat off!'

"Her husband is outranged. 'I'll kill him!'

"'Then he said he wanted to pour yoghurt down between my arse cheeks and lick it off!'

"'He's a dead man!' the husband says, reaching for a baseball bat and heading towards the door.

"'Then he said he wanted to turn me upside down, fill my twat with stout, and then drink it all!'

"The husband puts down his bat and returns to his armchair.

"'Aren't you going to do something about it?' she cries hysterically."

Seth's mouth began to quiver. "The husband says, 'Look, Love. I ain't messin' wi' no one who can drink that many pints of stout!'"

Laughter mixed with a few groans and an "Ah, my Jaysus" filled the next few moments. When things settled, Donny looked round the table, then to the bar.

"For fucksake. Did they have to brew da beer first?"

Rowan shrugged. "I ordered the pints as soon as we arrived."

He and Donny stood at the same time, but Rowan motioned for him to sit back down. "No, I'll go."

Rowan walked up to the bar and waited for someone to come out of the back. It had been at least five minutes before a tall fellow Rowan recognized as the barman emerged. Without a word to anyone, he wiped his hands on a towel, pulled some receipts from beneath the till, and sat down on a stool, reading through each small piece of paper with no apparent haste. After a moment or two of being ignored, Rowan approached him.

"Pardon me, mate. I was wondering if I might get those pints I ordered."

The barman didn't even look up. "Bar's closed."

Rowan held up a hand and shook his head. "Oh, no. I've already ordered and paid. The wee girl that was here earlier took my order."

"The wee girl here earlier is awa' home." The barman replied.

"If there's not a receipt, perhaps she wrote it down somewhere." Rowan pointed towards the till.

The barman carried on reading the receipts, making no move to look anywhere for anything.

Rowan was beginning to get annoyed, but tried to keep it from showing. "Well, could I just have my money back then?"

The barman laid the receipts down, took a few steps, and then pulled some sort of small handgun from underneath the bar, laying it out in plain view, glaring down at Rowan with eyes that were just a touch too close together.

"I said the bar is closed. Mate."

Rowan held his hands up in front of him, turning to walk away. "No problem."

Everyone stopped talking and looked at him as he approached the table empty handed. He shrugged, trying to appear nonchalant, his heart still banging against his ribcage.

"Seems the bar's closed."

Kyrie frowned. "But, what about our order?"

Rowan shook his head, afraid to look over his shoulder towards the bar, but feeling a pair of eyes boring into his back. "The one that took my order has already left, and it doesn't seem she wrote it down."

Everyone stood to leave, except for Elias. "Did he gi' yer money back, then?"

Rowan cleared his throat. "Ah, it seems there was some mix-up with the order and the money. I... think it best we just go."

Elias glanced towards the bar. "Why is that?"

Rowan felt a warm pressure gathering in the pit of his stomach. "Nothing, I just... really, it's not important. We can just go."

Elias's eyes narrowed. "Bullshit."

He stood and walked to the bar, Seth and Seamas right behind him.

Rowan reached for Elias's arm. "It's not a big…"

Elias laid both hands on the bar, seemingly oblivious to the weapon lying not far away. "My friend placed an order and has yet tae be served."

The barman was a good five or six centimeters shorter than Elias, but seemed unimpressed by this. "Bar's closed."

Elias shrugged. "It wasna closed when the order was placed and paid for."

"Well, it is now." The barman waved a hand at the barrels behind him. "Besides, I'm no' tapping a brand new keg for just the six of ye."

"Fair enough," Elias nodded, keeping his hands palms down on the bar. "Ye can gi' my mate his money back, and then we'll be on our way."

"I've no way of knowin' he paid for anythin'."

Elias's gaze narrowed further. "He told ye he paid, and now I'm telling ye."

The barman snorted. "Like I would take the word of a…"

The last few words just sort of fell away. Rowan looked from Elias's broad back to the large reflection in the mirror behind the bar; a dangerous gleam shone from under raised brows as Elias stared straight at the barman.

"A what?"

The barman cut his eyes over at Rowan, then pulled himself up to his full height. "Fuckin' Albaniggars, with their mixed blood and nazi 'soldiers'." He nodded towards Seamas. "Not to mention the fuckin' scangers ye drug in

252

here. If this is the company ye keep, dinna be bothered tae ask for service round here."

This was punctuated by a finger thrust towards a sign by the till, which displayed the right to refuse service to any-one, for any reason. The barman gave off a smug look.

"There's been a misunderstanding." Elias leaned in, his smile dropping with the tone of his voice. "I'm not fuckin' asking."

The barman's jawed dropped a bit, then he recovered. "The till's closed..." he leaned into Elias's face, "... and I'm not tapping a keg."

Before the next blink, Elias knocked both the barman's hands out from under him, his large nose smashing against the bar. The barman sank out of sight, a hand clapped over bloody nostrils.

"You don't want tae tap a keg? Okay." Elias snatched up the handgun. "I'll tap a goddamn keg."

What sounded like miniature cannon fire echoed off the walls as Elias shot a hole into each barrel, streams of beer pouring out like tiny waterfalls. Elias handed the pistol to Seth, then snatched up a mug in each hand.

"Looks like the bar's open after all."

Chapter Twenty-Seven

"Hey!"

I made a grab for Elias's hand before snatching up my napkin and wiping bacon grease from my chin. He had pulled my head back with my braid and let it slingshot forward, then shushed me when I cursed, reminding me people were still trying to sleep.

It had been late by the time we left the pub and had gotten back on the road, heading towards his and Seth's family home in Skye. The caretaker in Alastair's employ hadn't seemed bothered a bit to be awakened at nearly four in the morning in order to give us the key to the main house. A few hours and many scotches later, we crawled into bed. It seemed like I'd barely closed my eyes before he was teasing me awake with the scent of bacon and eggs. I could have eaten another plateful, but I didn't think Elias could sit still long enough for a second round.

I raised the last bite of bacon to my lips, dimly aware he'd taken my hand until I felt something wet against my skin. "Eeww!"

He'd raised my hand as if to kiss it and instead plopped his tongue flat against the back of my hand. I affected severe annoyance, scraping it roughly against my jeans. Truth be told, I liked the rare occasion when he acted so silly.

I tossed back my juice and wiped my mouth. "So much for being patient."

Elias all but threw my denim jacket around my shoulders before hustling me out the door. "Ah, you've never been good at being patient."

"I meant... ugh..." I rolled my eyes.

One of the horses snorted loudly as soon as we walked in the barn. Once I'd a hand on the stall door, Elias went to fetch my saddle. The horse moved his head to accommodate me stroking his neck. Elias passed right by me, accompanied by what I could only describe as an odd metallic creaking. The barest hint of Petranol followed in his wake.

I turned towards the door, keeping a hand on the horse's neck. "Where's my...?"

Elias wrapped a hand around my forearm. "I've something I want tae show ye."

A faint breeze hit my face, drying the slight sheen of sweat coating my forehead. Elias placed my hand on a tank of some sort, made of smooth metal and cool to the touch, with a leather covered seat directly behind the tank.

My heart beat faster with every touch. "Is this... is this a motorbike?"

I could almost hear the smile spread across his face when he answered. "Aye. My da and I built it together."

We knelt down side by side, Elias guiding my hand to different parts of the engine, frame, etc., some of which I remembered from working with Papa in his shop. "We designed the engine ourselves. The concept is very similar to the motor in the Land Rover. We can tear it down later so you can check it out."

I pressed a hand against a round chrome cover he'd called the Primary. "Later? Why not now?"

"Because ye canna take it apart and ride it at the same time," he answered.

I threw my arms around his neck, causing him to stumble back a step or two, and kissed him hard on the cheek. He pressed a hand against my back for a moment, then cleared his throat. I heard the compartment on the side open, then felt him place what he called a half-helmet on my head.

I ran my hands along the dome shape, tugged at the chinstrap, then motioned towards the motorbike. "So, those are called saddle bags?"

The clasp on his chinstrap clicked into place. "Aye. It was often referred to as an 'iron horse'. Hence the name."

I placed my hand on the seat. "How do I…?"

He took my hand and placed it on his shoulder. "Lift your leg. Now just… there you are."

The frame sank a bit when Elias mounted in front of me, allowing both my feet to touch the ground.

"Here. I'll show ye where the foot pegs are." He grasped the lower leg of my jeans to show me where to rest my feet, but I still wasn't sure what to do with my hands.

"Where do I…?"

Elias pulled my arms around his midsection. I clasped my hands together, both nervous and excited. I heard a couple of clicks, then the engine roared awake before settling into a low rumble. I held on a bit tighter when I felt the slight lurch forward as we rolled into motion. I'd ridden Eros full out nearly every time I'd been in the saddle. Speed didn't scare me, but then I'd never been this fast before. Every now and again I would feel a sting as something hit my face, which was bothersome, but bearable. What had me nearly in tears was the wind thumping against my ear drums. The stabbing pressure felt like it was piercing my brain. I tapped Elias on the shoulder.

He slowed and pulled offside the road, leaving the engine running. I jabbed a finger toward my ears and shifted in the seat when he reached under me to open the saddle bag. He pressed a small rubber ear plug into my hand, waiting while I twisted it into my ear before handing me the other one. We started off again, with me happy to trade discomfort for the dull, pain-free whooshing sound as we sped off on our way to wherever.

Elias had said during our drive yesterday that the Highlands were much different than Alba in many ways, one of which was the placement of the villages. In Alba, most of the villages cropped up around churches and the like, though never too close to anything other than a small lake. In the Highlands, life more or less followed the roads between the more populated areas.

Their drainage systems were much more advanced than those in Alba, not to mention the elevation served as a natural deterrent to flooding. Owing to dramatic climate change over the last few centuries, the Highlands now had sprawling cane fields, which were harvested to produce Petranol, one of their most profitable exports. Even with the amount exported, resources were still plentiful and available for the average citizen; something the Alban government would never have allowed.

Time felt as if it ceased to exist. I reckoned we'd been riding for hours. The smell of rain was now thick in the air, making me imagine a dark blanket of clouds hanging above us. I tapped Elias's shoulder again. This time he merely slowed down enough I could shout and be heard over the wind noise.

"Rain's coming!"

He patted my leg to let me know he'd heard me, then sped back up. As we rounded a curve, I thought for a moment we were going to lie right down on our side. I clutched him hard, taking deep breaths to suppress a slight flash of panic. When we were upright again, I felt him turn to look over his shoulder and hoped he wasn't looking at me, a bit embarrassed at how scared I'd been. He seemed to drive a bit slower afterwards, which made me think perhaps he had.

After a few minutes and a few more curves, he slowed to a near crawl, the engine sputtering as if it were going to cough, fart, sneeze and die at any moment. When we'd come to a complete stop, I pulled the ear plugs from my ears.

"Ye alright back there?"

Elias's voice sounded slightly muted. I grasped my nose and blew gently until my ears popped. "I'm fine."

"We're in a wee village along the coast called Faery Glen. I've a cousin here that manages a pub. I reckoned we could wait out the rain, even spend the night if we need to."

"I hope the others won't be too worried if we're not back until tomorrow." I didn't like not being able to get in touch with Uncle Rowan.

"No worries. We can send a message to them." Elias dismounted, then helped me off the motorbike. My legs felt a bit stiff from being stationary for so long.

We'd no sooner crossed the threshold when the heavens opened, a bit of rain splattering my back before the door slammed shut behind us. Elias's description of the pub was very emotive, bringing forth a very clear vision from my imagination. A few tables with matching upholstered chairs were arranged between the bar and the fireplace on the other side of the room. There was a door behind the bar leading into an adjoining restaurant. To the right of the bar was a hallway for patrons to pass through to the other side, as well as the loo.

Elias squeezed my elbow. "How about a...?"

He was cut short by a squeal shrill enough to curl the wallpaper, followed by rapid *Gàidhlig* moving our way at a high rate of speed. I was nearly knocked off balance when what seemed to be a sizable woman practically threw herself at Elias.

He said something in *Gàidhlig*, then touched my arm. "This is Kyrianna Maclaren. Kyrie, my cousin, Deirdre."

Her meaty hands were slightly damp as she clasped mine between them. She paused a moment before she spoke, obviously to Elias, as it wasn't in English. "*Math gad fheicinn?*"

"Nice to meet you," Elias translated.

She griped my hands tighter, her voice sincere. "Aye, nice to meet you."

I smiled. "Thank you."

I heard the concussion of a "pat" on Elias's back. "T*ha mi a' smaoitiunn gu bheil an t-acras oirbh.*"

"*Aidh,*" Elias answered. "*Pinntean nauir a tha sin a'*

260

feitheamh."

Deirdre turned and shouted to someone. I rubbed my palm against my thigh, then touched my ear. "She's very... boisterous."

"She's a loud auld bitch, is what she is," Elias chuckled. "Nearly deaf, is why."

I nodded. "Ah."

Deirdre shoved a pint in my hand and ushered us into the dining area, which was empty save for us, since the kitchen had already closed. She then proceeded to stuff us with corned beef and cabbage, and whatever else we might even hint at wanting.

I stifled a belch behind a fist. "I've no room for a proper dessert, but could do with a wee sweet."

Elias made no attempt to stifle his belch as it ripped from his throat. "If I remember right, Deirdre keeps some chocolate in the downstairs bar."

I perked up at the word chocolate. "Ooh, where is that?"

"Most likely... and I'm only guessing..." there was a familiar tone in Elias's voice when he answered, "... downstairs?"

I pressed my lips together and shook my head. "I meant the chocolate, Prick."

Elias chuckled. "Ye want a chocolate prick?"

I held up my index finger, and then my middle finger. He grabbed my hand and led me downstairs. There were only a few patrons, finishing up their pints, as it was near to closing. After ushering out the last of the stragglers, Deidre took a seat across from where Elias and I sat beside each other on a bench lining the wall. The dark chocolate Elias had found was deliciously bitter, and I was content to savor it whilst Elias and Deirdre did their catching up. Some time had passed before Deirdre rose to go refill our pints.

"She was just telling me the weather has been changing over the last few seasons. The winters growing colder. The storms becoming more and more harsh." Elias leaned in close. "She was also asking what brought me back this way, was I staying, so on and so on."

I'd opened my mouth to speak, but was cut-off by Deirdre's return. She asked me about myself, particularly about how I'd lost my sight. I could tell she was getting a bit tired because she wasn't speaking quite as loudly as before.

"Hae ye been tae see Uncle Alastair?" she asked.

"Aye," Elias answered. I gave his leg a gentle squeeze.

"I didna speak tae him for years, after what happened between ye…" Deirdre broke off into a yawn.

Elias took the opportunity to interject, "Ye seem right knackered, Deirdre. We'll be fine on our own."

"Aye, it's been a verra long day," she sniffled, rising to make her way to the stairs. "Stay down here as long as ye like. The guestrooms are up the stairs, above the dining room. Second and third doors on yer right."

The bar fell quiet for a moment in the wake of her leaving. I realized my hand was still on Elias's thigh, but wasn't inclined to move it.

"Did it bother you? When she asked about Alastair?"

He leaned back, resting his arm behind me on the bench. "No… and yes."

I tugged at a loose thread on the inseam of his jeans. "I get the feeling there's more to your leaving than you've told me."

Elias was quiet for a long time. I patted his thigh. "It's

been a long day for us, as well. Whenever you're ready…"

He took my hand in his before I could move it. "I'm ready."

I pulled the sheet tighter against my chin, snuggling back against Elias's chest. He lay spooned against me, reaching around to rub the back of my hand with his thumb, his voice soft as he described the colors of the early morning sky.

My body still felt as if his hands were pressed against my skin, certain places still wet and wonderfully tender. Any guilt or confusion that I might have felt was far over-shadowed by a feeling of extreme and total release.

After Deirdre went to bed, Elias told me things he never had before, or anyone for that matter, as we finished our pints. He walked over to set our glasses on the bar, and then came back over to take my hand. I stood, arching my back to stretch. He stopped talking in mid-sentence. His hands clasped my shoulders, guiding me to sit back down on the bench. Before I could even think to ask what he was doing, he sat next to me and began kissing me, as if he had all the time in the world and nothing else to do with it. His lips were soft; his beard tickled my chin. He finally spoke, his lips still teasing mine.

"One of us has on too many clothes."

First he pulled the sunglasses from my face, then every scrap of clothing I had on peeled away, until I was totally naked, inside and out.

I shuddered, rubbing my hands up and down my arms. "I'm a bit chilled now."

"So I see." His voice held a deep, husky timber. "I can warm you, but first it seems I have on too many clothes."

He guided my hands over to help him undress. I stroked his shoulders and remembered watching cords of well-developed muscle moving back and forth as he washed his face out in the field. I trailed a finger down the line of hair running from his chest, to abdomen, then lower. Small, tight curls tickled my palms.

He grasped my wrist with one hand and used the other to trace a slow path down between my breasts. "I can be gentle if you like."

In answer to that, I pushed him back and straddled him, causing a sharp intake of breath from both of us.

I leaned down and tugged at his earlobe with my teeth, whispering in his ear, "And what if I don't?"

He hugged me against him and stood, pushing even deeper inside me, knocking our table over in the process. We froze in place as if that would somehow camouflage us should Deidre come down to investigate. Not another sound followed. I exhaled the breath I'd been holding, giggling when I realized he'd done the same thing.

After a moment, I locked my legs around him and began to move, slowly at first, then with more urgency, squeezing his shoulders. In one fluid motion, he dropped to a knee, and then pressed my back against the floor, all without breaking contact. A few broken glasses later, with the sun just touching the windows, we went upstairs to bed.

The sound of his rumbling laughter drew my attention back to the present. "Are ye even listening?"

"Yes… no." I smiled. "I'm sorry, Doc."

"I was only sayin' that I never realized how much I missed it here until coming back." He raised my hand to his lips.

His comment brought to mind a question I'd been toying with for some time. I turned over to face him. "When this all plays out, do you think you'll come back to the Highlands?"

He pressed a kiss against my forehead. "Do you want me to?"

Before I could form an answer, his hand drifted beneath the sheet. "Ye know. I can be quite determined once I set my mind tae something."

"So I noticed." I closed my eyes and pressed my head back into my pillow. "Four times over."

Chapter Twenty-Eight

Elias straightened his collar, then flipped the remaining portion of tartan over his shoulder and fiddled with the clasp of his silver brooch, feeling like a boy getting ready for his first dance.

The two days since arriving at Inverness Castle had been spent preparing for a gathering of local clan Chieftains. Rowan accompanied Kyrie to the shops to find a suitable dress for the evening, sabotaging any chance Elias had of being able to talk with her. Ever since the two of them rejoined the others, they'd had to pretend nothing happened at Deidre's, to the point Elias was beginning to wonder if anything had.

He walked to the full-length mirror to survey the finished product. The fitted white linen *léine* his uncle had tailored for him followed the lines of shoulder and chest. He ran his fingers over the silver thread embroidered onto the cuffs and collar, which formed a pictish boar in the center of a knotwork circle, duplicating his brooch. The tartan grazing his knees blazed an unapologetic mix of red, gold, and dark green. His father's *sgian dhu* rested against his calf, the roundness of it even more pronounced by the thick, knee-length wool hose he wore. He straightened his leather sporran, still studying his reflection when he heard a knock at the door.

"Come in!"

"Alastair wants us to..." Seth stopped in mid-sentence.

Elias turned to face Seth. There had been countless occasions Elias had been proud of his brother, both as a man and a soldier. Still, seeing him in Highland dress for the first time, Elias viewed Seth in a way he never had before. As a Scotsman. A Highlander. Elias was quite taken aback when Seth walked over and embraced him hard. They stood that way a moment or two before Seth leaned back, a single tear resting on his bottom lash. Seth wiped a hand across his face and cleared his throat, moving towards the door.

"Alastair wants us to do a song for the afters."

Elias rolled his eyes, falling in behind Seth. "Ahhh, for fuc..."

Seth had been facing Elias, so he'd not noticed Seth's ponytail was gone. "You cut yer hair!"

Seth rubbed a hand against the back of his neck where dark stubble faded into tanned skin. "Och, weel. I'm still prettier."

Elias jerked his head in a failed attempt to miss the tattoo of smacks on the forehead. Seth darted down the hallway, calling over his shoulder in a high, childlike voice.

"Ha! Can't catch me!"

Elias pushed his plate back, then picked up his whisky glass and leaned back in his chair, looking around the Hall as he hummed along with the piper.

Banners and tartans representing each of the clans in attendance adorned the sandstone walls. Tables lined the length of each wall, as well a few long ones filling nearly all the floor space. Alastair sat at the head of the longest table, in the middle of the room, around which over fifty of the local Chieftans sat. A steady stream of servers carrying trays filled with food and whisky buzzed about, all at once quieting when his uncle stood. Alastair picked up his glass, candlelight glinting off his tartan badge.

"Centuries ago, a wall was built for the purpose of preserving and protecting our culture, our spirit. Yet, there are those of us who have never forgotten the vision passed down through the generations, the seeds of which were planted near the end of the last millennium with the Scotland Act of '98, seen to fruition at the Fall of London, under the leadership of General Fraser. Some have lost sight of that vision. I assure you, there are those of us that have not."

Alastair paused, looking from face to face. "We have before us an ordeal of the most grievous kind. We have been charged with ending a monstrous tyranny, one that has been allowed to continue for far too long, dividing brother from brother." He thrust his glass in the air. "I feel sure that our cause will not be suffered to fail. Let us go forward now... together... once again UNITED!"

Before the last word had left his lips, nearly everyone was on their feet, shouting, clapping, toasting. Rowan stood, as well, but seemed more interested in watching everyone else around him. Kyrie sat next to him, her hands together, looking as if she were staring at something in front of her.

Elias leaned to the side to allow one of the servers to take his plate, then sat down and pulled his watch from his pocket. He flipped it shut and looked back down the table at Kyrie, feeling relieved to simply lay eyes on her. She was nodding at something Rowan was saying, both of them smiling. Elias cleared his throat, turning his attention back to those sitting near him.

One of the night's more affluent guests waved a hand about causing the skin folds hanging from her arm to flap like meaty wings. She'd been out of sorts ever since Seth asked her to speak English in consideration of those who had no *Gàidhlig* and was now on a rant about the state of affairs in Alba.

"My point is the Albans made their choice. 'Globalization' indeed. Some people are meant tae be separate," she turned to her unfortunate neighbor, a hand clutching her gaudy gemstone necklace. "If the Wall had never been built, our lives would be much different."

Seth frowned, a glowing shade of red creeping up from his collar. "If the Wall had never been built, then so would theirs."

Elias laid a hand on Seth's arm and shook his head. Completely oblivious, she looked down at her nearly empty plate before catching the eye of one of the servers to wave the young lad over, then jabbed a finger at the remnants of her steak.

"I'm no happy wi' this steak. I'd like the fish, please."

"My apologies, ma'am, but the fish platters had to have been specially ordered, in advance," he replied with all sincerity.

"Hmmmph. We'll see about tha."

In a flourish of obscenely colorful cloth, the woman rose, everyone grabbing at their glasses when she caught the edge of the table with a massive hip. Donny drained the last of his Guinness and wiped his mouth on the back of his hand.

"If fish is brain food, dat aul bitch ought to eat a fuckin' whale!"

The entire table went up like a match in kindling, hoots and hollers echoing off the stone walls, still floating round when the "aul bitch" in question returned to her seat with a platter of fresh, farm-raised cod large enough to feed a family of four.

Elias leaned a bit towards Donny. "Whales are no fish."

Donny nodded towards the other end of the table where she sat with one hand primly in her lap and the other shoveling in consecutive bites with barely room for a breath. He tilted his head a bit, a fresh pint of Guinness poised for tasting.

"Just as well she's not eatin' a whale. She'd be a fuckin' cannibal, she would."

Elias held his glass to his lips a moment, then finished off his scotch when he trusted himself not to spray it everywhere. He stood and straightened his tartan before heading towards the other end of the table. Kyrie had just stuffed the last bite of her second piece of cheesecake into her mouth when he walked up behind her.

"Fancy a cigar?"

She drained her glass, then turned to take his arm.

Rowan patted his coat pocket. "Are you off for a

smoke?"

Elias laid a hand on Rowan's shoulder. "Finish yer brandy. We'll just go pick out some cigars, then come back for ye."

Rowan looked confused for a moment, then waved a hand as if to say no problem, turning as Seth took up a neighboring seat. Elias noticed his little brother had an odd grin on his face, but didn't take time to ponder it further.

Kyrie clutched Elias's bicep. "Where are we going?"

"Alastair's study."

Elias navigated through the congested banquet hall, feeling a bit impatient. Everyone was nearly done with their meal, and it would be time for the song he and Seth had promised their uncle. Kyrie's skin looked smooth as ivory in the glow of the candlelight, a brow cocked.

"Is there some reason I couldn't have waited here for you to bring the cigars?"

Elias grinned, quickening their pace. "What cigars?"

"Elias!"

"Shhh!"

It didn't make me nervous to follow him in such unfamiliar surroundings. It made me nervous that we were sneaking into his uncle's office, like two teenagers off for a snog. He took my arms and guided me around to sit on Alastair's desk, running his hands up my skirt, stroking my thighs with his fingertips.

"That's a lovely skirt."

The rolling 'r' in the way he said 'skirt' tickled my ears. I tugged at his tartan. "I could say the same for you, Sunshine."

Before I could blink, I was jerked from the desk, my skirt shoved up around my waist, and on the receiving end of a resounding smack on a bare cheek.

His laugh turned into a low growl. "What's this?"

I turned and reached for his face, then pulled him towards me. "Do you like it?"

"Blue is my favorite color," he answered.

I tilted my head to give him better access to my neck. "I know."

He looped a finger into the elastic string covering my hip. "Give it here."

"You want to wear it?" He pressed a finger to my lips, so I lowered my voice.

His mouth was right next to my ear, his breath warm, filling me with a charge of excitement. "I can wrap it around my…"

I put my hand over his mouth, giggling when he nipped the side of my hand with his teeth. "No."

"Why not?"

"No."

He shrugged. "Perhaps ye could do somethin' tae take my mind off of it."

I put my arms around his neck. "Like what?"

He turned me around, then pulled my earlobe between his teeth before whispering in my ear.

"Bend over."

My heart beat against my ribs so hard I thought my eardrums would burst. At least not being able to see meant I couldn't tell who might be staring.

Elias saw me to my seat before joining Seth at the front. I heard the strumming of a guitar as Elias said a few words, the laughter that followed, and then he began singing about labeled parts and a pair of brown eyes. I felt as if I was floating, Elias's voice surrounding me, filling me. It wasn't the first time I'd heard him sing, nor was it the first time I had heard him sing that particular song. It was, however, the first time I'd ever felt he was singing it to me. When he'd finished, tears stung my eyes, breath caught in my throat.

The thundering applause died away as Seth began speaking, but I couldn't understand a word. I felt a million miles away. My lips were tender and swollen, along with my...

I ran my hands down my hips, feeling no elastic band between the fabric of my skirt and bare skin. A smile broke my face as I shook my head in disbelief.

"Son of a bitch."

There was no moon, he told me. No stars in the sky. We lay together in perfect darkness.

Elias spooned against my back, the faint scent of whisky, cigar smoke, and sex hung between us. His breathing was deep and even, which meant he was asleep. I placed a kiss on his forearm, then turned into my pillow, letting it catch my tears.

We'd come upstairs together, not speaking to anyone before we left the banquet. It was late, and people were deep enough in drink we knew no one would notice. Words had not passed between us, no conscious thought of what would happen as soon as the door shut. We knew nonetheless.

He cradled my face in his hands, speaking words I could not understand, using his own language to speak uninhibited. He took his time touching with hands and lips. His very soul seemed to crawl inside my body and wrap around mine, taking a piece for himself and filling the void with a piece of his own. But, that wasn't when it happened.

Some point just short of total exhaustion, we lay together, the only movement uncontrolled twitches of muscle. He reached for me and pulled me into the curve of his body, his arm stretched underneath me in the groove of my neck, our fingers interlaced as he gripped my hand. That's when it happened. An internal shift. The click into place. Perhaps it had been our friendship, our closeness that kept me from noticing. Perhaps some part of me always knew, but kept it secret. Now that I knew, now that it had been awakened, I felt as if I would die without it. My heart filled to the point it broke. The very part of me that had always known now mourned what was gone, changed forever.

I drew a deep breath, placed another kiss on his arm, and wished for a word bigger than love.

Chapter Twenty-Nine

Elias felt Kyrie snuggle closer, snaking her arm under his and around his chest. Early morning sun leaked in around the heavy curtains. He should have been relaxed, and yet...

"Thinking about Jamie?" Her voice sounded a bit muffled.

From time to time, Elias wondered how things were going at Làidir, how Jamie was doing. Elias now realized it was more than that.

She began twirling her fingers in his chest hair. "You miss him, don't you?"

He grinned. "Like I would miss a hemorrhoid... ouch!"

The sharp twinge where she'd tugged his chest hair died away almost as soon as it started. For all Jamie's fits of temper, the lad seemed to be searching for approval. Especially from Kyrie. It had been market day in Corrie. Kyrie and Rowan had moved on whilst Elias and Jamie browsed the wares at a booth with beautiful, handmade Celtic jewelry before moving along to an L-shaped table that had mostly toys and trinkets.

Jamie lit up, pulling his hand free and running over to

something down at the end. A moment or two later Jamie reappeared with a pocket turned out, smiling so hard the corners of his mouth nearly touched his ears.

"What have you got there?"

"I took the spices you gave me and traded for a bag of silver coins. Now I can get one of the pretty rings for Kyrie."

Elias placed a hand on Jamie's shoulder. "But they aren't real silver, Cobber. Just metal discs used for games and such."

Jamie looked as if his heart had sunk into his shoes, a large tear clinging to his bottom lashes. Elias stood, held out a hand, and guided them through the crowd, back over to the jewelry booth.

Elias felt the silver Saint Christopher that Kyrie never took off pressed against the skin on his back, remembering how Jamie lit up when Elias traded for it, then placed it in his wee hand.

Kyrie placed a kiss between his shoulder blades. "The three of us could go to my parents' place. You know... if you wanted."

He rolled over, laying a hand against the side of her face, stroking her cheek with his thumb. "Aye?"

"You'll have to earn your keep, of course." She guided his hand lower. "Are you good with your hands?"

He was enjoying the sight of her with her eyes closed, head pressing back into the pillow, face flushed, when a light knock on the door interrupted him. Growling, he crawled over Kyrie, kissing her forehead as he went, and padded over to the door.

Seth peered in through the crack, so Elias opened the door a bit wider. Mistaking that for invitation, Seth took a step forward. Elias threw up a hand dead center of his brother's chest to stop him coming in. Seth put his hands in his pockets, looking fresh and rested despite a night on the piss.

He grinned, speaking in *Gàidhlig*. "Are you... busy?"

Elias answered in kind, knowing full well why Seth chose not to speak in English. "Aye... I mean I was just... what do you want?"

"Alastair needs to see you and Kyrie..." Seth grinned, "... in his study."

Elias guided Kyrie a few steps into the study, then stopped and waited for Seth to shut the door behind them.

Alastair sat in one of the wingback chairs in front of the marble fireplace, speaking to someone seated directly across from him. His uncle looked up, then motioned them over.

"This is my nephew, Elias..."

A familiar voice cut smoothly into the introduction. "Yes, we've met before."

Elias knew who it was before she turned. Morgan smiled, hands resting on her protruding belly. Elias estimated she was easily in or near her third trimester. A dark haired woman seated next to Morgan laid a hand on her arm, asking if she wanted something to drink. Morgan shook her head.

"No, thank you, Fiona. I'm fine."

Elias thought the look on Kyrie's face when she heard Morgan speak must have matched his own. Coming down the stairs, he never expected to find Morgan, much less a pregnant Morgan, sitting in his uncle's study. The particular chair Morgan was sitting in proved quite distracting, in and of itself. His mind couldn't resist the mental picture of Kyrie sitting in that very spot, dress pulled up to her waist, legs thrown over the arms of the chair as he knelt in front of her...

He cleared his throat. "Ah... how long have ye been here?"

Morgan drew a deep breath and exhaled slowly. "We arrived early this morning. The same friend who arranged your passage did so for me shortly after you left Glasgow. I was, however, a bit delayed."

Alastair sat on the edge of his desk, blowing into his cup. "Word is the fires, coupled with the windstorms, took over half the city before they were under control."

Morgan shook her head. "Perhaps if something had been done sooner..." she turned at the sound of the door opening. "Hey, you!"

Madoc walked over and planted a quick kiss on Kyrie's cheek as he brushed past, then knelt down beside Morgan, placing a hand on her abdomen. Elias felt a difference in Kyrie's touch on his arm, a slight color spreading across her cheeks.

"Now then. You look tired." Madoc smiled.

Morgan chuckled, laying a hand over her twin's. "I'm in bits. My back hurts all the time. I'm starved all the time. I have to piss... all the time. Where's Rowan?"

Madoc cut his eyes over to Kyrie. "Waiting for me."

Morgan nodded. "We can catch up later."

He raised her hand to his lips, then walked over to Kyrie and touched her arm. "I need to speak with you, Bonnie."

Elias shifted his weight, fighting the childish urge to trip Madoc, instead settling for a mental picture of the bastard landing flat on his face. Elias's dislike of Madoc had begun with his deserting Kyrie and now, admittedly, stemmed from more personal reasons.

Elias joined the others in front of the fireplace, thinking what a stupid name "Bonnie" was when he caught sight of Morgan staring at him, a single tear sliding down her cheek.

Madoc hadn't said a word as we made our way down the hall. I was as nervous as I was curious about what he might want to talk about. It seemed we'd made peace with things after our conversation at May's. He'd been away with Orla, so he couldn't know about things with Elias yet. Was there something to do with Orla he wanted to tell me?

"How was your trip?"

"Lovely," he answered. "The Highlands are a vision, to be sure."

"So, I'm told." I smiled.

He stopped in mid-stride. "I... I didn't mean..."

I squeezed his arm. "No worries."

He cupped my neck, pulling me closer to press a kiss

against my forehead. "I... maybe we could..."

A door behind him creaked open, cutting off whatever he'd been struggling to say. He sighed and guided me into a room. I wasn't sure where we were, as he'd not told me where we were going. The echo of a clock ticking bounced off stone walls. The woody scent of pipe smoke clinging to someone's clothes indicated Rowan's presence even before he spoke. He must have used a different tobacco because there was something different about it. Yet, still familiar.

"Hello, Petal."

"Uncle Rowan." My curiosity turned to confusion, as I felt as much as heard someone cross the room towards me. Without my sight, I'd noticed how every person sort of had their own aura of presence, for lack of a better term. It was one of the ways I could distinguish a person without hearing a voice. This one was very familiar, very personal, but very impossible.

The next voice I heard caused something to click into place. It wasn't just pipe smoke I had smelled. It was peppermint.

"Hello, Kyrianna."

I made a fist, digging my nails into my palm, fully expecting to wake up. Moments passed, but I was still standing in the same spot. My voice disconnected itself from my brain in order to function, making me feel even more detached from reality. My lips trembled so I could barely form the word.

"Mama?"

I moved closer to Elias, trying to escape the evening chill coming off the water as we crossed the bridge over the River Ness. This time of year the temperatures in Alba were still hot enough to kill all the wee beasties. Instead of shielding themselves from West Nile Virus with insect repellent, Albans were hiding from skin cancer under layers of sun block.

The last few hours had felt like a bizarre dream. As soon as I'd called her name, Mama threw her arms around me, squeezing me so hard I could barely draw breath. We stood locked together for untold moments before Rowan joined us, then Maddy. We'd spent the entire day, in whatever room I still didn't know, laughing, talking, crying. It wasn't until we were summoned to supper that time had begun to pass again. Sitting there with Elias, Madoc, and Mama all together in the same room made me feel as if I didn't know which Kyrie I was supposed to be. Mama and Rowan were the last ones at the table, and I was content to leave them to it when Elias suggested a walk down to the river. With nothing to distract but the steady hum of rushing water, I finally felt I had it sorted.

It had been one thing to find out Mama was still alive, and then another to find out Maddy had known and not told me. Without putting much thought into it, I well understood why he didn't. It had nothing to do with what had happened between us. He was trying to protect me.

Footsteps approached, accompanied by the scent of peppermint. Elias must not have paid much heed to anything outside his own thoughts, judging by his start when I called out to Mama.

"Now then!" I smiled, squeezing Elias's bicep.

"It's nice out tonight," she answered back. "I hope I'm not intruding."

"No, not at all." Elias laid a hand over mine on his arm. "Kyrie, will ye be aw'right gettin' back up tae the castle?"

Mama answered before I could, taking my arm as she spoke. "She and I can walk back together."

Elias kissed the back of my hand. "Good night, then."

His footsteps faded away, leaving behind an awkward silence. It wasn't hard to talk with my mother as long as we spoke of things with no particular importance. The last time I'd shared anything intimate with her was around the age of thirteen, when I had my first cycle. I knew what was coming and now wished I was in any one of a million other elsewheres.

She sighed. "Kyrie, I wanted to explain why I didn't come to you straightaway."

I shook my head, holding a hand in the air. "You really don't have to."

"It's no surprise to hear you say that. You have always been so very independent." She paused a moment, a small catch in her voice when she continued. "I know it wasn't always easy for you when you were growing up."

My guard dropped a bit. I laid my hand on top of hers. It was a moment before she spoke again.

"It was a selfish thing your father did."

I felt like I'd had the wind knocked out of me. "What my... what?"

"When you were born, I talked to your father about leaving military service. He felt it provided a certain security for us that he wasn't willing to give up."

The shock passed as something else took its place. "So,

serving one's country and trying to provide for one's family is selfish?"

She groaned. "I shouldn't have said anything."

I threw my free hand in the air. "Well, you did, so don't shy away now."

"Your father chose a career that kept him from you, from us… constantly… and yet I am the one that…"

"He was a soldier before he even knew you," I interrupted. "It's what he loved. It's who he was."

"He could have bloody well been 'who he was' on the island, with us," she sighed. "You don't know what it's like. To have someone you love so much, love something else more than you."

"Don't I?" My voice was raised enough I wasn't sure who could hear me, but I was sure I didn't care. "What he did, he did for us, but it was more than that. He sacrificed time with the ones he loved most in service of something greater."

"Something greater than the family that needed him?" Her voice was raised to match mine. "He made the choice to serve, and I was the one to suffer for it."

I jerked my hand away and stepped back. My shoulder hit one of the bridge cables hanging down, the other only air. A swell of panic flared, which I quickly stamped back down. I raised my chin a notch.

"Bullshit."

"Excuse me?" She shouted.

I shrugged. "You didn't lose a thing by Papa being a soldier. Hell, having children didn't even slow you down. You made sure of that."

"So, how is that different? I choose to give myself to a

greater good, as you say your father did, yet I'm selfish for it." Her laugh was almost metallic.

So much between us had been left unsaid for so long; I'd rather that it hadn't come out in this way, at this time, but we couldn't unsay the words we'd just spoken. In all honesty, I didn't want to.

"That's not why, and you know it."

She was silent a moment. "What are you talking about?"

"I took care of Miyanna when you were teaching. During the summers it was Uncle Rowan who looked after us while you did your research," I threw my arms out wide. "What, pray tell, was your great sacrifice?"

"Having you in the first place!"

I stood frozen in place, my arms still extended, her words reverberating off my ear drums.

"I never wanted to have children. Your father did," Her voice was hoarse from shouting. "You're shocked, aren't you? To hear me say that."

I lowered my arms back down to my sides. "No. Only that you were too fucking stupid to realize that I already knew."

My eardrums throbbed from the sounds of wind, water, and shouting. Perhaps that was why I didn't hear, or sense her raising a hand. The next thing I knew I felt a hard sting against my check. I turned back towards her, satisfied in some way that I'd managed to piss her off enough to hit me. Things had always been this way between us, and I didn't want to pretend otherwise just because I was blind.

I had been so caught up that I'd not even heard anyone walking towards us. Rowan's voice gave no indication he'd heard any part of our verbal thrashing, though he was bound to have.

"Ah… Kyrie? Alastair asked for us to come to his study. Do you want me to…?"

I shoved my hand out towards him. "Yes, thanks."

He must have waited until we were out of earshot before he spoke because a couple of minutes had passed before I heard him clear his throat.

"You know. There's a song that says to always look on the bright side of life."

"Yeah." I felt him pull his arm back, so I fell in step directly behind him. "It also says life's a piece of shit."

Rowan laid his hand over mine. "When you look at it… so don't look at it."

A bubble of laughter escaped, cracking my already strained composure. "Not a problem."

Tears filled my eyes, and I dammed each one before it fell. Without another word between us, we made our way back to the castle.

Cigar smoked furled from the fiery tip of the corona Elias had found in Alastair's humidor, thinking it would be a good way to pass the time whilst waiting for Kyrie. He didn't want to intrude on her time with her mam, but he had no intention of going to bed without making sure Kyrie was alright.

The door to the study flung back so hard it bounced off the wall. Alastair charged in, Orla hot on his heels.

Elias crossed the room as he spoke. "What's wrong?"

Orla answered, a frown creasing her brow. "A raid is being scheduled for the last remaining facility in Alba. It seems a member of the staff has fallen into the hands of an Alban interrogator."

Elias turned to Alastair. "Which facility?"

Lachlan stepped out into the hall from the examination room, shutting the door behind him.

It had taken days for Hugh La'Tier to expire. Not once did the man give up any information at all regarding the whereabouts of the Prime Minister's wife. Nicholas would be disappointed. Lachlan wasn't. It had been years since his skills as an interrogator had been called upon to such an extent. Out of respect, Lachlan ended the interrogation without further pain; the man had earned it.

The door to the adjoining examination room opened back wide, as if wiping his mind clean so he could concentrate fully on the task at hand. The woman was just beginning to stir. She had been strong, as well, but Lachlan's experience told him she was about to break. Tired, dark eyes pleaded with him as he sat down facing her. Lachlan smiled, speaking in perfect Russian, pressing a hand against her cheek.

"I think it's time we finish our conversation, Angelina."

Chapter Thirty

Alastair had broken the news to everyone about the plans to invade Làidir. Orla was working through her chain of command to have a Quick Reactionary Force deployed to the island as soon as possible. At the moment storms caused by a hurricane forming off the west coast had damaged some of the telegraph lines, so for the time being the Net was down.

Elias looked about the room. Madoc and Threas stood by the fireplace, both still in a state of shock. Rowan and Kyrie sat in the wingback chairs next to the fireplace. Rowan's face was as grim as a stone statue. The puffy redness of Kyrie's eyes seemed to be glowing even brighter. Whatever had been troubling her when she walked in the study, Elias was sure her mind was now following the same path as his. Jamie.

"How soon would your troops arrive?" Madoc asked.

Orla looked up from the papers on Alastair's desk the two of them were poring over. "In a matter of hours, depending on when the Net is operational again."

Rowan shook his head. "The Net might very well be down until after the hurricane. The ASF will already be on the water, headed for Làidir... or what's left of it."

Orla frowned. "Well, short of riding there yourself, what else can you do?"

Madoc walked over by Rowan. "Maybe that's not such a bad idea."

Rowan looked up at Madoc. "What's that?"

"You and I could start riding to Làidir. If the Net doesn't come back up, at least word is on the way to initiate evacuation." Madoc held up both hands, palms up.

Rowan stood. "Even if we don't make it before the hurricane hits, we might get there before the ASF."

Seth had been standing behind Kyrie's chair, arms crossed and resting on the back. He looked from Rowan to Madoc.

"Your friends are still in the Cauldron, aye?" Seth moved around and took Kyrie by the hand. "I've got an idea."

Madoc tightened the cinch on his saddle. Butterscotch snorted and tossed her head at the blinding flash of lightning, trailed by a clap of thunder.

"Easy, girl." He crooned, running a hand down her long neck, pondering what lay ahead. He'd relished his time since leaving Làidir to the point it had been nearly nonexistent the whole time he'd been away. The weight of the guilt he now felt nearly buckled his knees. Please let me make it in time, he prayed.

He felt as much as heard Kyrie walk into the stable, on the arm of Rowan, talking as they walked over. Her hair was pulled into a ponytail, the length of which was curled around and resting on her shoulder. The green long-sleeve shirt she wore was light cotton, the color of it a beautiful compliment to her dark eyes. Madoc couldn't have recounted a word that passed between the two of them if he'd been strapped to the Rack in the Tower of Old London.

"Have you seen Threas?" Rowan asked.

Madoc inhaled sharply, just realizing he'd been holding his breath, and played it off as a cough. "No... no, I've not seen her."

Rowan took Kyrie's hand and pressed it on the mare's neck. "I'll just pop back up to the castle, then."

Kyrie stroked the mare's neck. "I asked Uncle Rowan to bring me down here to... to speak with you before you leave."

"Oh." Madoc nodded, nervous and a bit excited at what Kyrie had to say, even though he'd no idea what it might be.

Kyrie stopped in mid stroke. Madoc didn't say a word, but took a step closer, recognizing her body language. She had something very important to say, and it was going to be difficult for her.

"You know there's a storm headed for the coast." Her voice was subdued.

Madoc laid his hand on top of hers. "Yeah."

"It's..." a single tear slid down her cheek, "... a category seven..."

Madoc stepped up next to her, cradling her against his chest. "I know, Bonnie."

Her entire body trembled so that his heart finally shattered in his chest. Nature seemed to reflect her emotion; just as the wind began to howl in and out of the stable door, cries burst from her until he was nearly supporting all her weight. After a few moments she straightened, clearing her throat.

"If you get close, but aren't sure you can make it to the ferries, don't try to go the rest of the way."

Madoc pulled her ponytail off her shoulder, noticing that it reached nearly to her shoulder blades.

She sniffled. "The Net may come up before the storm hits, so Orla can send for the QRF."

He cupped her ponytail and ran his hand slowly down the length of it. "Sure."

She tilted her chin up as if to look at his face, her voice shaky. "Promise me that you won't try."

He cupped her face, wiping his thumbs across her tear-stained cheeks. "Promise."

Some of the tension in her face seemed to ease, but then she immediately frowned again. "You know that... even though things are different... that I still..."

He pressed his lips to her forehead, her skin still touching his mouth when he answered.

"Always."

The light scent of peppermint and unfallen rain alerted me that Mama was coming, well before I heard her speaking to Rowan. Maddy pressed another kiss on my forehead, a quick kiss against my lips, and then moved away from me as I heard Mama say, "Come here."

I felt Rowan's hand on my shoulder, so I turned towards

him. We hugged hard and for what seemed a long time, until he finally leaned back, kissing my forehead in almost the same spot as Maddy. Just as he pulled away, I felt Mama take my arm and we walked towards the door. I heard the horses shuffle about, then clop past. The two of us stood side by side, with me squinting into the wind, until the hoof beats seemed to fade into the rumbling sky.

Mama squeezed my arm. "I don't want them to go."

I shook my head. "I don't either."

Her grip tightened for a moment and there was a catch in her voice when she finally spoke. "I don't want you to go."

We stood there a moment, not saying a word, and then I answered with all honesty.

"I don't either."

Rain stabbed Madoc in the face. A symphony of thunder and lightning crashed overhead as they rode into Turnberry. He squinted as hard as he could, willing himself to see through the mixture of wind and rain blasting them full-on. Rowan shouted over the raucous howl, his voice still sounding muffled.

"We need to find cover! It's too late for the ferry now!"

Madoc knew Rowan was right, but it was still a moment before he pulled the reins to reverse course and try to find somewhere safe to wait out the storm. The buildings had been sealed up, floodgates locked into place. Most of the villagers would be gone, but perhaps...

Madoc threw up a hand, signaling for Rowan to stop. "Do you hear that?!"

Rowan looked as if he were straining to hear what Madoc was talking about. At first it had sounded like the scared squall of a cat, but then Madoc realized what it was. Madoc jumped from his saddle, shoving the reins into Rowan's hand.

"Here! If I'm not back in five minutes, let her go and take cover!"

Rowan shouted after him. "You may not have five minutes!"

Madoc wiped his face with his sleeve. As wet as it was, it still helped a bit. He ran down the street, pausing at each alleyway until he came to the right one. The louder the cry, the faster he ran until he was damn near at a full sprint.

He caught sight of a stairwell near the end of the alley which led up to a door in the back of the building. He ran over, taking the stairs two at a time. Broken glass from a large picture window crunched under his feet. He'd barely touched the door knob when he caught a slight movement from the corner of his eye. Standing just inside the tiny flat was a wee girl. The translucent skin of her face was red and shiny. Her eyes were filled with tears, and then widened when she saw him looking at her. She pressed a chubby fist to her mouth.

Madoc looked up and saw a thick piece of jagged glass dangling from the top of the window frame. He tried the door knob, feeling a stubborn click in the palm of his hand no matter which way he tried to turn it. The lass didn't even shake her head when he asked if she knew how to unlock the door. Both distance and the teeth-like edge of glass lining the side of the window frame prevented him from reaching round inside.

He cut his eyes up to the top of the window. Leaning in as much as he could, he offered her a hand. She made no move to take it, though she had quieted except for an occasional hiccup.

"There, there, Petal. Let's get you somewhere safe, shall we?"

Her fingertips had barely brushed his when the heavens seemed to exhale. In almost the same instant, a gust of wind hit the side of the building, causing the glass remnant to drop like a guillotine, slicing into his upper arm. He dropped to his knees.

Bile rose thick in his throat, nearly choking him. The little girl wailed long and loud, blood smeared across her pale forehead. Pain shot through Madoc's skull as everything grew dark.

Lachlan rubbed his right hand with a towel, mentally counting the rotations before switching to the other hand. He wouldn't have time to write in his journal before his 1800 appointment and felt quite annoyed by it. It was rare that he wasn't able to complete one task before moving on to another. Very rare indeed. Perhaps the meeting wouldn't take too long, considering Owain had conducted the initial interview while Lachlan cleaned up and changed clothes.

Lachlan left his room and walked down the hallway, rolling his sleeves down and making mental notes about the morning's procedure. He straightened his tie and opened the door to his office.

Even from behind, Lachlan could tell the couple was very young, probably in their late twenties at the oldest. The husband was a rather large fellow with dark auburn hair, his hand totally encompassing that of his wife. Her hair was pulled back into a bun, a few tiny curls lining her hairline just above her neck. As Lachlan walked behind his desk to sit down, he noticed well-shaped calves extending from a conservatively cut skirt. She seemed quite a handsome woman from what he could make out of her features, dark glasses notwithstanding.

"Good afternoon. I am Dr. Lachlan and you would be..." he picked up the intake sheet from his desk, "... Mr. and Mrs. Buchanan, yes?"

Chapter Thirty-One

Lachlan finished his notes on the intake sheet, quickly scanning to ensure he'd not missed anything in the medical history portion.

He'd wished they'd arrived during the week, rather than at the weekend. Still, he could make sure the necessary examinations were performed. An examination would show if there'd been any corneal or nerve damage in order to ensure Mrs. Buchanan was indeed a good candidate. Once it was confirmed, then he could choose a donor. He'd received word from Edinburgh to ready accommodations for a mass intake, but he'd rather not wait for that.

The words on the page blurred together as he tried to wrap his mind around what he was about to attempt. Corneal transplants had not been successfully performed since the Technology age. Satisfied, he screwed the cap on his pen and smiled.

"Everything is in order. I can answer any questions you have on the way to the examination room."

After he'd ushered them into the hall, he paused to lock his office door. He remained outwardly courteous and patient as they made their way down the corridor. Mr. Buchanan seemed to notice every detail, his eyes touching everything whilst listening intently to Lachlan's description of the facility; Mrs. Buchanan followed quietly in tow.

The door to the specimen wing swung open. Owain shut it quietly behind him, his eyes widening for a moment. "Ah, sir. I was just coming to inform you the attending physician is ill. We've only the resident on duty. Would you like me to call someone in?"

Most of the specimens had been disposed of. They had served their purpose and he'd needed the room for the wave coming in soon. For a moment he worried there wouldn't be a donor for the transplant, but brushed it aside.

Lachlan shook his head. "No, that's not necessary."

Owain nodded. "If you don't need me for anything else…"

Lachlan waved a hand. "No, no. We're fine. It's late, even by your standards, and the storm is moving in."

He motioned for the Buchanans to follow him further down the hall to the staff infirmary, then unlocked the door and stepped aside to allow them entrance.

As the two of them settled in, Lachlan pulled an ophthalmoscope from the cabinet by the sink, along with a glass dropper filled with belladonna to dilate the pupils and set them on the tray next to the examination table. He washed and dried his hands thoroughly, then slipped on a pair of sterilized gloves. Mr. Buchanan helped his wife up onto the examination table, then took a seat in the chair beside it. Mrs. Buchanan lay back, turning her cheek towards him so he could press a kiss against it. Her husband lingered a moment, his face hidden by hers. As soon as she nodded slightly, her husband straightened, smiling a bit sheepishly.

"I hate to be a bother, but I'm in bad need of the loo. The ride here was a long one. Could I possibly...?"

Lachlan cut in. "No problem." He took a step towards the door, then looked at his gloved hands.

Mr. Buchanan opened the door and motioned down the hallway. "If you just point me in the right direction, I'm sure I can manage."

Lachlan gave directions to the closest toilet, then took a seat on a stool, the wheels squeaking as he pulled himself up beside the examination table. He took the ophthalmoscope off the tray and shook it to charge the battery, then clicked the light on and off. He looked at his patient, who was currently picking at the side of her thumbnail and chewing her bottom lip.

"Would you like to wait until your husband returns?" he asked.

She nodded. "Yes, I'd rather wait."

Lachlan laid the instrument back on the tray. "Have you been married long?"

"No." She ran a hand down her skirt. "Not long at all, actually."

Lachlan rested an elbow on the table, careful not to touch his glove to anything. "Your husband seems very supportive of you coming here."

She smiled. "Not at first, but he came around."

Lachlan returned her smile, even though he knew she wouldn't see it. She tilted her head slightly, and before he could inquire further he noticed the faint echo of footsteps approaching the door.

"Right then. I just need you to remove your sun shades," the door opened and shut behind him as he took the belladonna off the tray. "There, now. Are you ready to… begin?"

There had been something familiar about her that he couldn't quite place. Now that he had full view of her countenance, he recognized exactly who she was.

Lachlan heard a strange clicking sound and turned towards the door, looking from the metal barrel pointing straight at his chest, then up at Mr. Buchanan, then to the even larger fellow with dark hair standing next to him. From the resemblance between the two, Lachlan sussed they were brothers.

Mr. Buchanan answered in a deep, even tone. "Aye. We're ready."

Lachlan set the belladonna down slowly. He'd only seen a hand weapon once in his life whilst traveling abroad, but he knew full well the brutal power the stranger held in his hand; it was the very reason the Alban government outlawed them. The dark-haired one offered a hand to Mrs. Buchanan, if that indeed was her name, to help her off the table.

"The others are waiting for you."

When the door shut behind them, Mr. Buchanan hooked his foot around the leg of the chair next to the door and pulled it towards him, then sat down. No expression moved the man's features.

"Listen to me very carefully. I'm going to ask you one question, one time."

Lachlan pulled his gloves off and laid them neatly on the tray, then looked at the weapon pointed at his chest. He was many things, but a coward wasn't one of them. Nor was he a hero.

"What did you want to know?"

Elias met Seth coming down the hall towards the examination room. "Was that cannon fire?"

"Aye, I think so. The Irishmen have Kyrie. Donny and Seamus checked all the cells, but they're empty," Seth frowned. "Where's the…?"

"I took care of him." Elias answered.

Seth's eyes narrowed. He opened his mouth to speak, but was cut off by Donny and Seamus tearing around the corner. Seamus remained at the end of the hall to keep a look-out while Donny filled them in.

"Well, the doctor wouldn't say if anyone was being housed outside, no matter how politely I asked." Donny wiped the blade of his *sgian dhu*, then tossed the bloody rag on the floor.

"Did ye finish him?" Seth asked.

Donny nodded. "Done and dusted."

"The staff's already cleared out." At their puzzled looks, Elias continued. "Apparently there was another passage besides the one we used."

They each checked their magazines, then looked from one to the other. Not a word passed between them as the muffled boom of cannon fire shook the ground beneath their feet.

Seth racked the slide on his weapon to chamber a round, grinning. "Shall we then?"

They fell in behind Seamus as they left the hall. The

sound of thunder hitting the ground grew louder as they neared the front of the facility. Lantern light illuminated the large window panes with an ethereal glow, shadowed slightly by the dust and debris hanging in the air.

Seamus darted over to the window and cracked one open, kneeling just offside with his pistol at the ready. The rest dropped to a knee a few paces behind and waited for him survey the situation.

"Looks like da gate's about ta come down. If we're goin' ta make it to da barracks, we'd better go sharpish."

Seth moved over and grabbed the door knob. "Ready?"

At their nod, he flung the door back so hard it smacked the wall behind it. Halfway across the yard, the gate fell. Elias could make out flashes of red and white uniforms flooding the mouth of the surrounding wall, firing off rounds as they charged in. From the corner of his eye, he caught sight of three to four Alban soldiers rushing towards the gate before turning to charge back at them. Donny and Seth turned and fired their weapons, taking out each one of the soldiers.

Elias saw Seamus make it to the door of the barracks, and then saw a flash to his left, just as he heard a weapon discharge. Seth tripped and landed on a knee. Elias raised his pistol and started firing to give Seth and Donny time to get inside the barracks. Seamus laid down cover fire as they ran for the door, slamming it shut behind them once they were all four inside.

Donny and Seamus each took up position by a window, alternating between firing and ducking down to reload. Elias knelt down next to a window on the other side of the door in order to reload. From the corner of his eye, he saw

Seth slide down the wall to the floor, face pale and blood pooling in his lap.

In one motion, Elias was beside Seth, pulling his brother's shirt back to assess the wound. A constant flow of blood drained from a tiny hole in the midline of Seth's abdomen, just above the navel. Elias pressed his palm hard against the wound. Seth laid a hand on top of his, their skin sticking together with a mix of fresh and dried blood.

"*Mo bhrathar.*"

After a moment Elias looked up, a familiar, albeit faint gleam in Seth's eyes. "John and Mary on their wedding night. Mary was a wee virgin and had ne'er seen a naked man in all her life. John tells her, 'I'll go outside the door and just put a bit 'o me cock in at a time, so as to not scare ye.'"

"Mary sits waiting on the bed. One inch of John's cock sticks in past the door. He asks her, 'Are ye scared, Mary?' She giggles and says, 'Jaysus, John. No, I'm not!'

"He puts in another inch and again asks, 'Are ye scared now, Mary?' She giggles again, 'Oh, Jaysus, John. No, I'm not!'

"He puts in one more inch and says, 'Are ye scared now, Mary?' She giggles, 'Oh, Jaysus, John. No, I'm not!'

"John shouts to her, 'Then sod it, Mary! I'm comin' up the stairs!'"

Their laughter mingled together. Seth's was short-lived as his breathing became more labored. Elias's eyes locked again with his brother's, this time not looking away. In the eternity that passed, visions of their childhood flashed before Elias: Seth's first steps, his first horse ride, helplessly watching as his little brother fell from a tree they weren't allowed to climb and cutting his thigh on a branch. Their father forced him watch as the gash in Seth's leg was stitched, hoping it would make an impact. It did. Watching the skilled hands of the doctor was when Elias realized he wanted to go into the medical profession.

Elias pressed his free hand against Seth's cheek. "Are ye scared, Seth?"

The corner of Seth's mouth lifted a bit as he whispered. "Jaysus, Elias. No, I'm not."

Seth's head rolled to the side, his eyes staring into nothing. For a moment there was only the sound of gunfire and breaking glass. Elias ran his hand down Seth's face to close his eyes. He pressed a kiss on his baby brother's forehead, then picked up a pistol in each hand, shattered the window and started firing.

CHAPTER THIRTY-TWO

The door creaked as Rowan opened it back wide, stepping aside to allow the nurse to pass, a tray of used bandages occupying her hands.

It had been five days since the hurricane. They never made it to Làidir, but it was just as well. The island had been evacuated just before the storm hit. The Net had come up long enough for Orla to call in the QRF to get everyone off the island. The ships made it back to *Éire* just before the worst unleashed. By the time the ASF arrived, not much was left; some parts of the island had been swept clean to the ground.

When the five minutes had gone by, Rowan waited another five and another, until he had no choice but to let the horses loose and take cover. As soon as the worst had past, he searched for Madoc. By the time Rowan had found him, Madoc had managed to crawl in through the window of a building. He was unconscious, a small child crying beside him. Before Rowan could even check for a pulse, he heard the voices of a small group of townsfolk making their way through the streets to assess the damage. They showed the way to a makeshift hospital which had been set up a few kilometers from town.

This was the first time Rowan had been allowed in Madoc's room. The doctor was trying to keep the risk of infection as low as possible. Rowan's mind still refused the words the doctor had spoken to him just hours after they'd arrived. He had to see for himself in order to make them real.

Madoc lay propped up on pillows sleeping, blankets pulled up to his chin. Whether six or thirty-six, his face always looked the same when he slept. Always the same slight frown between the brows. The corners of his mouth drooped down just a hair.

Madoc stirred, his eyes immediately searching, smiling as soon as he saw Rowan. He eased down to sit beside Madoc, not saying a word, tasting the salt from his tears before they dripped from his chin. Madoc reached up with his right hand and pulled the blanket back, exposing the bandaged stump of what had been his left arm.

"There it is, or there it isn't."

Rowan swallowed hard. "Does it... does it... hurt?"

"Not so much," Madoc laid the covers back down. "The doctor called it a 'long amputation' or something like that. The cut caused irreparable damage to the blood vessels and connective tissue."

Tears dried on Rowan's face from the heat of his anger. Why, he thought. Why did this have to happen? Why did any of it have to happen? Madoc held out his right hand. Rowan raised it to his lips, then cradled it as if it were a precious stone. Madoc's voice was soft when he spoke.

"There is no chance, no destiny, no fate, that can hinder or control the firm resolve of a determined soul."

Still holding Rowan's hand, Madoc rested his head back

on his pillows and closed his eyes.

PART FOUR

BLESS MY RISING IN THE EARLY MORNING

Chapter Thirty-Three

Morgan's back felt like it was ripping apart. She turned on her side to give Elias better access to her back. His big hands smoothed away as much of her pain as her body would allow. In the rests between the pains, which were getting closer together, he was crooning and humming to try and soothe her. He was almost annoyingly calm for someone who had never experienced this before.

The door softly thudded behind Fiona as she entered the room. She'd gone to get more towels. "It's time to check her again."

She walked over to the opposite side of the bed from Elias. She lifted the sheet and reached down between Morgan's legs. "The head has crowned. Time to start pushing."

Morgan was instantly put at ease by the softness of her friend's voice. There was no one else she would rather have here with her.

311

Fiona sat down at the end of the bed. "Scoot a little farther down. Elias, sit by her and support her back. Now, pull your knees up and hold them with your hands." She pushed the sheet back up over Morgan's knees. "When the next pain comes, take a deep breath and push."

It was only a moment before another contraction. Morgan breathed deep and bore down as hard as she could. An intense pressure grew stronger between her legs, making her hope this would be over soon. The pain passed and Fiona patted Morgan's knee, then reached over to the tray beside her and picked up the small scalpel.

"I'm afraid you are going to tear, so I'm going to make a small incision."

Morgan felt a momentary burning, which was overpowered by another contraction twisting her lower back.

Fiona laid the scalpel back on the tray. "Sit her up and let her push."

Morgan couldn't see exactly what Fiona was doing because of the sheet draped over her knees. Nor did she care at the moment. This pain was more intense than the others had been. She felt dizzy and nauseous, but continued to push with all her might. The pain subsided, though not by much.

"That was good. I think one more push should do it." Fiona offered encouragingly.

Elias smoothed Morgan's hair back from her face. She had just laid her head back against him when she felt the familiar twinge in the small of her back. She sat up, determined this would be the one.

Fiona's voice became more urgent than it had been. "Don't stop! Keep pushing! Keep... there you are!"

As if by magic, Fiona held up the wrinkled source of aggravation. A loud squeal pierced the air in protest. Tiny hands shook as if to hold each cry even longer. Morgan leaned back against Elias in sweaty relief and disbelief. This little life had been inside her for the last nine months and yet, it still amazed her to see a living, breathing baby.

Fiona clamped the cord, then placed the baby in a small cradle at the foot of the bed. Morgan watched Fiona make the necessary checks. Fiona's head snapped round to look at Elias. She had a strange look in her eyes as she nodded for him to come there. He eased Morgan down onto her pillow and walked over to stand next to Fiona. Morgan closed her eyes and prayed, Please let everything be alright.

She felt the bed sag beside her; a small warm lump pressed against her chest. With a firm grip on her fears, she opened her eyes and looked. The wailing stopped as soon as their eyes met. Dark blue eyes gazed at her, almost squinting, then widened with what Morgan could only describe as recognition. After a moment or two, Elias pulled the blanket back from the wrinkled little face, freeing unruly sprigs of dark curls.

"He has black hair," he grinned, his eyes filled with tears. "What will you name him?"

"I'll name him after his father." She cupped her hand around her son's head and smiled into the blue eyes still staring at her. "Hello, Seth. It's nice to meet you."

Chapter Thirty-Four

Rowan pulled himself deeper into his Macintosh, wiping his nose on the cuff of his sleeve, then put his arm around Kyrie's shoulders. She and Elias had only just returned from Skye the day before where the two of them, along with Donny and Seamas, had scattered Seth's ashes.

Loch Oich was quiet and still, almost as if it were showing respect for what was about to take place. Elias and Morgan had spoken in depth about what they wanted to do in order to honor the blending of faiths; he had to admit they couldn't have done so more beautifully.

Jamie stood between Jared and Kyrie, holding each of their hands. Donny, Seamas, and Alastair were on the other side of where Morgan stood in-between Elias and Madoc. She held baby Seth close to her chest, rubbing his small head and giving him kisses on his forehead and cheeks.

315

Threas was next to Madoc, her arm linked in his as the four of them watched Fiona bless a string of lapis beads she'd called "birthing beads". Once finished, Fiona handed the beads to Elias, then walked over to stand next to Rowan. Elias placed the beads around Morgan's neck. She looked up at him and smiled.

"We gather today to bless a child, a new life that has become part of our world. We gather today to name this child." She looked down into her son's face. "To call a thing by a name is to give it power."

Morgan and Elias took a step forward. She looked at each one of those standing around them.

"To be a parent is to love and nurture, to lead a child to be a good person." She faced Madoc and Threas. "You stand beside us for the love of this child. Will you tell God who you are?"

Madoc held up his right hand to Threas, then smiled at Morgan. "We are Madoc and Threas, chosen to be Guardians for this child."

"Do you know what it means to be a Guardian?" Morgan asked.

"It is to love and nurture. To give guidance and counsel. It is to be a second mother and father, and to be there when called upon," Threas answered.

Morgan and Elias walked over to Seth's marker placed under the tree he'd fallen from as a child. Madoc stood next to Elias; Threas next to Morgan. Each person filed over to form a full circle around the four of them. Elias reached into his pocket and pulled out a small vile of oil wrapped in a piece of Seth's tartan, then dabbed some on his finger. He drew a small cross on his nephew's forehead. Morgan kissed baby Seth's cheek for a long moment. She turned towards the stone which bore his father's name before looking at her son again.

"You are known to God and to us as Seth Uilleam Dùghlas Buchanan. This is your name, and it is powerful. Bear your name with honor, and may God bless you on this and every other day."

Jared was standing closest to a small table with a decanter of wine and matching pewter *Quaich* that had been placed next to the marker. Elias and Morgan walked over to stand in front of Jared as he poured wine into the *Quaich*, then took a drink and passed the cup towards Kyrie. Rowan smiled as Jamie reached up to help guide Kyrie's hands.

Morgan and Elias stepped over to stand in front of Kyrie. Elias laid his hand on the side of Kyrie's face and brushed her cheek with his thumb. She closed her eyes a moment, then raised the *Quaich* to her lips. She took a sip, and then passed it over to Rowan. When it was their turn, Madoc and Threas each said a few words. Elias took baby Seth from Morgan and held him up towards the sky. He first spoke in *Gàidhlig*, then in English.

"*Gum bi thu, a naoinein bhig, fallain, ionraic, sona air feadh do bheatha gu léir*," Elias held his nephew out in front of him and looked into the small, smiling face. "May you be healthy, upright, and happy all throughout your life."

A tear crawled down Elias's cheek as he began to sing in *Gàidhlig*. Rowan didn't understand a single word, but felt each one nonetheless. He looked at Madoc, Morgan, Threas, Kyrie, and then finally back at Elias and the baby. Rowan's own eyes filled with tears and when they finally broke free, he did nothing to stop them.

Rowan wiped his nose, and then stuffed his handkerchief back into the pocket of his Macintosh. He massaged his lower back, exhaustion filling every muscle fiber he owned.

After the ceremony, they'd all gone back up to the manor for a late lunch before heading to the ferry. Orla stood next to the entry point, a gentle hand on Madoc's elbow, nonplussed at the way Madoc was staring back at Kyrie. Even though Làidir had been destroyed, it still seemed somehow wrong that Madoc wasn't returning there, but the lad had made his decision.

A look passed across Madoc's face, as if something had just occurred to him. He stepped forward about a half-step, then lifted his right hand in a wave. Rowan had returned Madoc's wave, still Madoc stood with his hand raised. Rowan turned to Kyrie. Before he could utter a word, she raised a hand in the air to wave at Madoc. After a moment, they both lowered their hands. Madoc turned to Orla, and the two of them boarded the ferry, her men in tow.

The ferry horn wailed to announce its departure as it pulled away from the dock. The sound still hanging in the air, Kyrie wrapped her arm around Rowan's midsection and laid her head on his shoulder. Rowan rested his head against hers for a moment, then drew a deep breath.

"Petal, there's something I've wanted to ask you for ages now."

She sniffled. "What is it?"

He raised up to look at her, then pressed a kiss against her hair. "The night of your accident, how did you find your way back?"

Chapter Thirty-Five

Elias reined up in front of the small house, the sweet mixture of rain and sap prominent in the cold March air. He stayed in the saddle, hand on the butt of Seth's pistol, waiting. The door opened. Lachlan stepped out on the porch and waved. Elias dismounted and tied his horse to the hitching post.

"Is he in there?"

"As agreed."

Lachlan walked down the steps to the hitching post on the opposite side of where Elias's own horse was tied. Elias watched Lachlan check the saddle, then place a boot in the stirrup to mount up.

"Does the name Miyanna Maclaren mean anything tae you?"

Lachlan paused a moment, his foot stuck in the stirrup. He looked down at Elias, then threw his leg over the saddle. Elias watched as Lachlan rode away.

"I'll be seeing you."

He walked inside, giving his eyes a moment to adjust. Owain was tied spread eagle to the heavy wooden table in the middle of the main room; a small sheet draped across his lower body down to his knees.

Elias pulled on the apron that was folded neatly on top of a nearby surgical tray and tied the strings securely in front of him, speaking as he pulled on a pair of gloves.

"Just so you know, this is going tae hurt you a lot more than it does me."

He walked over beside the table. Owain squealed in terror, throat muscles straining, eyes rolling around wildly. Elias smiled and laid a hand on Owain's forehead.

"Trust me."

About the Author

M. H. Mayfield enjoys smoking good cigars, drinking Guinness by the pint, and swearing in Irish or German. She spends her time writing, practicing Bikram yoga and running with her dog, Niko. She's a member of the American Homebrewers Association, as well as a lifetime member of Sigma Tau Delta and The Mile High Club. She once drank 11 pints of Guinness without throwing up. The Rains of War is her first novel.